I was COMPELLED

A Novel by

Ken Gorman

ISBN: 978-1-969865-83-1 (sc)
ISBN: 978-1-969865-84-8 (e)

Rev. date: 01/19/2026

*To my wife, Betty,
forever beautiful*

PROLOGUE

"**B**axter!"

The sergeant's scratchy voice cruelly roused me out of my makeshift bunk. Following a hazardous morning patrol, my fatigued bones begged to be left alone. Nevertheless, I stood with my buddies, at ease, awaiting the newest ball-breaking order.

"They found the bodies under the bridge in the Euphrates River," Lieutenant Rip Munson announced to the assembled squad.

His pained look was all too familiar, and the uninhibited emotion in his voice made me cringe.

"Their heads were covered with hoods, and they had been bound and gagged, execution style," the lieutenant added, presumably to provoke outrage.

"Whoa, I was on patrol there yesterday," the new recruit said.

I looked around at blank faces staring at the lieutenant. We all knew that two guys from our platoon had been captured. Both just nineteen years old. Hell, they were not the first killed since nine-eleven and they wouldn't be the last.

Ripley Munson's body language made a statement; hands on his hips, resembling the stance of General Patton. No pearl handle revolvers though. He maintained his West Point bearing from morning to night. Led by the manual and the military code of conduct, and was proud of it. Ambitious? Why he'd spit-shine his blond crew cut to get a promotion.

If the drama of Munson's revelation was to motivate me to kick ass, he was mistaken. I knew why I was in this godforsaken place, and I had no regrets. We had to respond to nine-eleven is the way I looked at things. I sure can't imagine another disaster like that in the US, so I'll do my part for my country. As far as I was concerned, it was a no-brainer to get involved in this fight whether driven by patriotism or that annoying angst in my gut. That's why the other guys are here as well, I assumed. We're all in this thing together.

"Get some rest," Munson commanded. "New orders for tonight will be coming down from HQ."

It didn't take long for us to get the word. The Unit was scheduled to go out on a night mission in four hours. A Shiite informant had identified to Headquarters the location of a Sunni safe-house. Bomb makers were high priority targets for good reason. It would be dangerous, but everything we did was risky.

There's nobody for me to write home to, thanks to that slut Lauren, so I decided to sack out until zero hour. After one month in Fallujah, there was not a lot to say anyway. Nothing but eyesores. After all, I'm not an ecstatic tourist who takes pictures and can't wait to tell everyone back home about the sights. But I'm unable to sleep and there's nothing enjoyable to read either. Besides, there was a pungent smell in the tent, like a locker room full of sneakers and sweat clothes, and no showers.

Damn, I can picture in my mind those tortured, dead young soldiers. And what about their poor parents?

Funny how we all deal with our anxiety before a mission. One guy is munching on a Hershey bar. I can never eat before a raid, but I'm sure famished when we get back to the base. Even MRE entrees taste good. Look at "Scarecrow", the hillbilly.

Treats his weapon as if it were human. Over in the corner there's the guy we called half-wit, staring into space. Snores erupted from opposite sides of the tent in irritating harmony. I wished my mind were that uncluttered.

Regardless of the peculiarities of my buddies, I'd thought and acted like a tough kid from the Bronx until I met these guys. Sure burst my balloon.

A cup of hot coffee might help me unwind. I got up and sat next to Sergeant Racek. He'd been through it all, but his grim face and deathly silence made me uneasy. He seemed to be in a daze.

"Look, Baxter, just don't wander ahead of us. Keep your eyes open," he warned. "You've been too damn nice to the Iraqis, but you gotta treat everyone as your freaking enemy."

What's that? Is he smoking a joint? Christ, I don't wanna be next to him out there tonight. Most guys took anti-anxiety pills or Prozac to cope with the stress, but not him, or me for that matter.

Was this my fifth or ... no, it's my seventh time out on night patrols. Scared shitless every single time. After those rocket firings today and searching the area for our missing buddies, I was tired as hell and feeling on edge. *Man, I wish I could go on R & R.*

I stretched out on top of my sleeping bag on my side this time, resting on my elbow. Glancing at my gear, I had an odd reminder of the *GI Joe* equipment my friends and I played with as kids. Jeez, I wondered what Mario, Johnny and Big Frank were doing back home after their graduations. Selfish creeps didn't want to join up with me.

* * *

"Come on, you guys. Where the hell is your patriotism?" I had chastised them, reminiscent of when we were teenagers.

"Up yours, turncoat college boy," Mario responded,

speaking for the others. "Don't be so freaking gung-ho. You always think you havta be the one to get involved."

"Let's all stick together and get the murders that did this on our soil," I pleaded. "We can't let them get away with it."

"Like you stuck with us in school? Bullshit. Why don't you join the stupid Peace Corps instead?" Big Frank gave me the finger as they waved goodbye.

* * *

"Maybe they were the smarter ones," I whispered into my pillow. I knew how disappointed and upset they were when I enrolled at Rutgers University in New Brunswick, New Jersey. I saw it as a personal growth opportunity, and my poor mom agreed one-hundred percent.

What the hell good was a college education doing me here anyway? Sure, I had enjoyed certain class work, and the partying. On the other hand, bitter experiences could not be overlooked. *Actually, obliterate them from my mind forever.* Then September 11, 2001 convulsed my insides. Forget for now being a policeman dealing with the dregs of society. Forget the John Jay College of Criminal Justice. I had another, higher priority, as I continued to reflect on that fateful day.

At the start of senior year, I sat on my bed paralyzed at the sight of the second WTC building crumble to the ground, smoke and dust everywhere, as people scampered away from an unfathomable vision. I fell to the floor on my knees in a prayerful trance. "The maniacs that did this," I cried out, "are going to pay." I pounded the bed with my fists. A TV reporter announced that, *employees on the top floors called their wives.* "Christ, they all knew they were going to die. Good God almighty."

The roar of tanks rudely disrupted my wanderings. They were only back-up firepower for this early morning mission.

x

I continued to lie on my back, hands clasped behind my neck. Except for heavy breathing, an unnatural silence filled the tent. Life in the States seemed a million miles away from this decrepit setting. What the hell, I was here lending a hand to unfortunate people. It kept me going.

Too bad my parents, God rest their souls, didn't have any other kids. At least I could have bonded with a brother. "Or even a sister would have been nice."

"What ya say?" the new guy asked.

"Nothing," I replied. "Just thinking out loud."

"I hope it's not too muggy out there tonight," he said.

"Hey, get used to it. Hell of a lot better than bivouacking in the snow at Fort Drum in upstate New York in the middle of January." The Mountain Division wasn't for me, but now I was having second thoughts.

I could tell by the new guy's accent he was from the South. Couldn't let myself get too friendly with him ...or anyone else for good reason. Shaking my head, not at the weather, but at the thought of other guys who never made it back from these patrols, I got a bad feeling about this duty assignment.

"Let's get moving, Corporal," Lieutenant Munson yelled at me.

I must have dozed, so his order startled me. The squad was dressed and arranging their gear. It only took a minute for me to catch up and join them in formation outside the tent. Racek distributed night goggles to each team leader. It was my turn to be lead dog and the new guy was assigned to me. I noticed him shiver and heard him whisper a prayer. *Hope he includes me in his appeal to the Almighty.*

Three Humvees transported us to the vicinity on the outskirts of town. The first time I rode in Army vehicles during basic training was real cool. I couldn't wait to go on leave and show off to Lauren in my uniform. What a jerk I was!

As we drove the short distance to our objective, the utter

silence among my buddies gave me a strange tingling sensation. Like when my father died. Just recalling that incident made me melancholy. *Guilty too.*

Someone farted, but no one laughed, as the truck bumped along on cratered roads. Concern about IED's was our silent preoccupation.

Sergeant Racek broke the peculiar peace. "You've all been briefed, so just stay behind the leaders as we approach the house. Watch for civilians and round them up away from the main target."

The Humvee came to a gradual stop. "Oh, shit, here we go again," I whispered to myself. Climbing out of the truck, it struck me that I didn't recognize the guys in front and back of me. Sculptured faces with deep-set eyes. Black guys, white guys, made no difference. Maybe it's because of the helmets. The imbedded reporter and his photographer looked petrified.

Forget it. There's work to be done.

The new guy didn't get his wish. It was sticky, and dusty to boot. We had to walk about two hundred yards to the house, far enough to feel clammy. Weapons at the ready. The half-moon was the only light.

"Follow me," I whispered to him, "and stay low."

We crept along the wall in front of the house. Racek signaled to me to move ahead. I pointed at the gate, and the new guy brushed by me and opened it. Thank God it didn't creak, like the rusty gate at my apartment building entrance when I was a kid. I took the lead again into the small courtyard followed by the new guy, two other teams and an Iraqi interpreter. Another team moved around back.

The house appeared to be deserted. Dismal place like all the others, I thought, as I surveyed the entranceway. Maybe it's another false alarm. My heart began to race at the possibility this may be a trap. The new recruit was hyperventilating as he peered at me for direction ...and courage.

I tossed a grenade at the front door. We hid behind a garden wall and shielded our ears and faces as the grenade exploded. Dust swirled around us. The door simply disappeared.

"Go!" I had to push the new guy.

He entered and positioned left while I scanned the right side of a vacant large room. With my night vision, I spotted a picture of Saddam Hussein on the far wall. There was stuff on the floor right below the picture—*bomb making paraphernalia.*

A candlelight flickered through the open door in an adjoining room.

There's somebody in there.

We dropped to the floor as bullets ricocheted over our heads. The noise was wild, like hundreds of pinball machines clanging at the same time.

"Throw the grenade!" I yelled at him.

He had pulled the pin when something came rolling at us from the other room looking like a baby's toy.

God help us.

That's all I remember.

CHAPTER 1

Three years later...
"I don't like my job."

Spewing out the bile of my past to my psychiatrist was my responsibility, complete with exaggerations. His job was to ferret out my brand of reality, classify it and prescribe treatment.

Dr. Timothy Burkett continued writing in that damn notepad of his. His eyebrows arched as he flipped back several pages.

"Let's see," he said. "You started the job only four months ago. What's the problem, Drew?"

"My supervisor harasses me. He questions me constantly and expects my paperwork to be completed faster than anyone else's in the office."

"Uh-huh. What's his name?"

"George Parker. He treats me like I'm dumb just because I take my time. One old lady snickers whenever I stammer."

"Are you sure you're not just imagining it?"

"Oh sure. They all laughed out loud when I tried to aid a guy delivering office supplies and slipped on a rug, knocking over boxes and a tall metal shelving of file folders, you know what I mean."

"Oh no!" he chuckled. "I know it must have been humiliating, but you have to admit it sounds comical. What did your boss say?"

"He surveyed the mess and gave me a disgusted look. Then

he growled, 'I don't know what the hell I'm going to do with you, Baxter. You are one of a kind.'"

It's hard for me to explain what it's like confined in a Branch Office of a large company, Outsource Data Corporation, where you can't belch without the whole world knowing it. If I knew it would be like this, I never would have accepted this job. But I needed the money.

"A VP in the Philadelphia home office is a great guy," I explained to Burkett. "He's a former Colonel in my Unit in Iraq, who learned I had been in the Trenton VA Hospital. He tracked me down to my home in Lavallette and recommended me for a job, despite Parker's objection. He's aware it might take time for me to adjust to working in an office after so many years." Actually, it was my first position since college, not counting the military or bumming around in Vegas.

"Perhaps, they're being overly-attentive to make it easier for you to get your feet on the ground, learn all the procedures and fit in with them."

"No way, Doc. I tell you they consider me an outsider." I shook my head and added, "They don't want me in their section. It's really pissing me off, and Parker better lay off me."

He shook his head at me, checking the time. Shifting position in the armchair—his "quasi laboratory"—Burkett's broad six-foot frame seemed poised to conduct a new experiment ...on me.

"When we met last month, you began to tell me you lost interest in sports after your teenage years. Had to do with losing your temper."

"Oh, yeah, I remember."

"Can you tell me more about that?"

I wondered what was the point of telling him about experiences when I was a kid. Doc's a nice guy and he's been sincere with me ever since the VA sent me to him. But what was all his time and effort going to do for me? *I feel fine now.*

"Come on, Drew, you know I'm interested in you and hearing about it."

"Okay. You knew I grew up in the South Bronx. Believe me, it was a tough neighborhood. Well, sports were our main interest and activity. We played all kinds of street games to fit the season of the year. We formed teams, although some residents and the cops called us gangs."

"Different games sound like fun."

"Yeah, right. So sometimes we would play guys from other neighborhoods. I was always the captain and—"

"Yes, you had told me that."

"Well, the captain makes the line-up and assigns positions, and all that crap. I guess I was a loudmouth during the games, you know, bitching when someone made an error or shouting at the other teams, because I wanted to win. They sure didn't like it. So, one time after the game, these shanty Irish guys grabbed me and held me by the collar. They were gonna beat the hell out of me. I was scared, but I kicked the guy holding me in the shin and ran like hell. They never caught me."

He wrote more notes on his pad as I wet my lips. Is he so smart he can understand me better from a simple old story?

"Is that all?" he asked.

"Whether it was stickball, baseball or touch football, I took charge. My actions always got the other teams mad at me."

"Typical teenage bluster," he commented.

"My friends grumbled that I was a bossy troublemaker and acted like a bully, which upset the hell out of me. So as I got older, I just gave up on sports."

"You felt you took the blame for taking charge as captain?"

"Yeah, why not?" I hesitated and, with my eyes closed, blurted out, "My poor mother never knew I was a pain in the butt."

Doc wrote more notes and turned back pages of his pad for the next few minutes. I leaned back in the leather armchair and questioned in my mind how he could possibly make sense from analyzing my statements.

I can't and won't spill my guts out to him about everything.

"Did you always want to join the military?"

I hesitated. "Actually, never gave it a thought. As a kid, I visualized becoming one of New York City's Finest. Track down the bad guys and become like the detectives on *NYPD BLUE*. My father even encouraged it. That all changed because of nine-eleven."

"I see. You didn't want to become an officer with your college degree?"

"No way. I wanted to get into the action right away and serve my four years. My obsession with a girl delayed my enlisting until after graduation." I grinned and added, "So it never was a career path for me ...too much chicken-shit, if you know what I mean."

Burkett jotted some notes in his pad. "Your sense of duty is commendable."

Is he trying to hypnotize me with that pendulum clock? He never goes one second over the allotted time for these sessions.

"At our very first meeting, Drew, you mentioned recurring nightmares. Could you tell—?"

"Wait a second, Doc. That's when my hearing was real bad. You asked about dreams, didn't you? Sure, I fantasized. Sports, girls. No big deal. When I was a kid, I envisioned the worst possible dream, or actual calamity, would be to be wedged in the entrance to a cave without use of my arms." I shuttered thinking about.

"All right," he whispered, closing the notepad. "Perhaps we'll talk about that some other time, too."

He gave me a puzzled look, as if he didn't believe me.

"Let me backtrack on something you said a few meetings ago. When your father fell down the stairs in your house, were you at home?"

I stared at the floor. "Yes. I was in the kitchen helping my mother with the dishes."

"Had there been any conversation with him or plans for the following day?" He opened his notepad again, prepared for my response.

I wish he didn't dwell on that accident. What the hell does it have to do with anything?

"Look, Doc, I don't wanna talk about it. He was coming downstairs in his pajamas and had an accident. That's it."

"Fine." He turned off the timer. "Try and give your new job more time and be patient with your co-workers, especially with Mr. Parker. Okay?"

"I'll try. Believe it or not, Parker takes delight in declining customer rebate requests because of paperwork technicalities."

"There may be more to it than you know. In any case, how about same time next month? Oh, and continue on the medication for now."

"Sure, but do something for me more than just prescribe medication, okay?"

He bit his lower lip and stared at me. Several quiet seconds went by.

"I want to get your feelings about the war next time, if that's okay with you. I notice you only have a slight limp now, so the therapy has healed the atrophy. Also, your stammer is barely detectable."

I felt my stomach muscle tighten. My lower jaw crooked to one side. Here it comes, I bet. Hell, I'll play along to make him feel like he's making progress.

"We'll see." I shook his hand and said, "See you in a month."

"Before you go, let me say one more thing." He folded his arms across his chest. "I've said from the beginning that your recovery might take an extended period of time. You'll be able to assimilate into society instinctively, and we'll both know when there's been improvements. But, ultimately, it's up to you. Don't view me as an adversary. Together, we'll get to the bottom of the distress caused by your injury."

"I hope so."

How does he really know what my life is like? One day, cheerful for no good reason; the next, worrying about everything and everybody. I even forget how to tie my goddamn shoelaces some days or how to get messages off my cell phone. Just having the guts to get out of bed some days has been a struggle.

The sign for Lavallette jolted my senses. "Already." I had traveled south on the Garden State Parkway, exited onto Route 35, and passed through Point Pleasant, Bay Head and Mantoloking. Just names on a map. Too rich for my taste ...and pocketbook. The session with Dr. Burkett in his Red Bank office preoccupied my memory as I drove home by rote.

After spending too many months in Trenton Veterans Administration Hospital as an inpatient and released under Dr. Burkett's care, I had decided to remain in New Jersey rather than go back to the Bronx. The most convenient and least expensive location would be somewhere on the Jersey shore. Besides, it's an attractive vacationer's life. My childhood presented the answer. Lavallette was my choice, a borough rated as one of the top places to live in the state. After settling in my new place, I drove into town for the first time as an adult and registered to vote at Borough Hall. At the entrance, a five-foot tall signpost supported a 4x4 foot plaque, which read:

Welcome to our Town, named in honor of Admiral Elie La Vallette, a French nobleman and Commander of the USS Constitution (Old Ironsides) during the Civil War.

The session today with Dr. Burkett was not much different than other visits with him over the past eight months. The good news was he got me thinking about the past and my memory seems to be improving, even though flashbacks were detached. I still had doubts about the ultimate benefit of all his questions and my tedious responses. As long as he didn't bring up that specific experience in Iraq, I'd go along with pinpricking my brain. I know I'm not crazy. What the hell, a lot of us came back with battle fatigue or shell shock, or whatever they call it. In any case, I hoped the medical doctors were right that my physical condition would be back to at least ninety percent in a few months. Just getting my decrepit body into the Suburban hurt like hell.

"Lousy job," I scowled at the thought. "If Parker continues to give me a hard time, I'll just pack it in. I'm not going to take any more nonsense from that nitpicking dictator."

I passed a billboard of the new Yankee Stadium and smiled. What's happened to my old pals? Either they don't want to see me now that I live in Jersey or married life has changed them. That's not for me, for sure. A few beers with them for old time sake would be fun. We could reminisce about the times we sat in the bleachers at Yankee Stadium just bullshitting about everything and rooting for Jeter and Mariano Rivera.

"Who am I kidding?" I said, looking in the rear view mirror. "It's been years since we've seen each other." *Out of sight, out of mind. That's life.*

I held the wheel tighter. "Lemme get home and get this day over."

Dripping wet from the shower, I stared at my naked body in the bathroom mirror, muttering to myself, "Those army docs did one helluva job."

I knew I'd never get used to the odd-looking skin pigmentation on my right inside thigh near my groin. Scars go down my leg looking like a road map with lots of detours. I flinched as I rotated my right shoulder, which had healed without surgery.

And I'm supposed to be a lucky guy!

Later in bed, as I rested comfortably with my head on the raised pillow, the taste of the chicken potpie meal I ate for supper remained. Vanilla ice cream would do the trick. Despite feeling tired, my usual analysis of the session with Doc Burkett occupied my brain, as it leap-frogged from one issue to another. I don't know how the term *shrink* came about, but he had condensed my life, as shitty as it was, into specific events and relationships. "I guess that's the way he operates," I mumbled, as I turned on my stomach.

Sleep came easy for a change.

"Catch it," I shouted, leaping up in bed. The subconscious scene surrounded me. Fear gripped my body, as if an intruder had entered my home and was outside the bedroom door.

The digital clock read 2:30.

In a cold sweat, I cried about the nightmare. Always the same. Over and over again. I never could reach the soccer ball-shaped object, which appeared to float in front of me like planet Earth in a display of the universe hanging from the ceiling. The bed sheets became an oversized handkerchief as I shielded my face in my hands.

"No more!" I screamed. "I've got to tell Burkett the truth as soon as possible."

Sitting in bed I felt weak and my throat was dry. On the way to the kitchen to get a soft drink, I turned on the TV for a late movie. "Oh great! I love *High Noon.*" I popped open a can of diet Pepsi, grabbed a bag of pretzels, and nestled on the living room couch with a cozy smooth blanket.

"Good for you, Coop," I hooted at the TV screen.

The scene showed Gary Cooper turning back to face the bad guys, disregarding his new wife's objection. Marshal Will Kane is my favorite movie character of all time for his courage to take upon himself what he knew was the lawful and honorable thing to do.

I love this part when the judge packs up to leave town. I mouthed his words, "Don't you remember, Will, sitting right in that chair, he swore he'd come back and kill you?"

The soda and pretzels were almost finished.

"That's it, Coop, tell the cowards to go to hell. Stomp on that badge and…"

Where did I put my Purple Heart?

From under several sweaters in the bureau drawer, I located the leather case with United States of America stenciled in small gold letters on top. Opening the case, I rubbed the frayed edges of the ribbon and the distinguished face of George Washington.

The award opened the floodgates of my mind. I stretched out on the couch, warmed by the blanket.

"On behalf of the President of the United States and a grateful nation, I award you, Corporal Drew Baxter, the Purple Heart for your bravery in the face of the enemy and wounds suffered in battle." Standing at my hospital bedside, a Brigadier General had spoken those words and saluted me.

The excitement of the recollection awakened my senses. My parents would have been proud. No longer tired, I allowed my mind to wander. *Think, man, think.*

* * *

The sign read *Heroes Way*. They were carrying me on a stretcher. As we bounced along a short distance, I heard them speaking, but the words didn't sink in at first.

"You're at an army hospital in Landstuhl, Germany, son. You're safe now."

Does the priest expect me to smile back at him?

"Take him to ICU," another voice ordered.

Only bits of their conversation made sense … *fractured femur and shoulder … superficial …hematoma …concussion … something about amnesia.*

Carefully they lifted me from the gurney to a bed. The odor of disinfectant was pervasive. My leg. It hurt real bad. And the headache wouldn't go away.

"Oh God, please help me!" I gritted my teeth to withstand the pains. *Is this the end?*

There was shuffling around my bed and annoying murmurs. Darkness came suddenly as I seemed to be swirling in space among the stars.

Three days later.

"How are you feeling today?" a nurse asked.

"Okay," I answered with a hoarse voice. "May I have some water?" I cranked my neck to each side to see where I was.

"Of course," she said with a smile. As she held the cup and straw to my lips, she said, "You've slept on and off for three days."

"Where am I?"

"You're in Landstuhl Medical Center in Germany."

"Three days?"

"That's right. You arrived here about forty-eight hours after you were wounded in Iraq." She shook her head. "A medic applied a tourniquet to your leg before you were medivaced to an aid station for surgery. Then you flew from Bagram Air Base outside of Baghdad to Ramstein, only a few miles from here."

I stared at her plump face, fearful to ask about my buddies. But I had to know. "There were two teams that followed me in and—"

"Corporal Baxter, I'm sorry to tell you this, but the others in the raid didn't make it out."

All killed. It's my fault. I began to cry.

"It's okay," she said. She held my hand and kissed my cheek.

After a long second, she said, "I have to do therapy on your leg. It will only take a few minutes."

She was gentle, but it hurt. My stomach growled. "I'm pretty hungry now."

"Great. When I'm done, I'll tell the doctor you're lucid and then bring you some soup, bread and tea. How's that?"

"I don't have a headache any more."

As she was about to leave, she whispered, "Colonel Sloan will be with you in two days to discuss your case. You can expect to go home then."

"Home?"

"Well, back to the States. To Walter Reed Army Medical Center in Washington, D.C."

What's going to happen to me? Will I lose my leg?

"Drew Baxter, Hello, I'm Colonel Sloan."

"Yes, sir."

Nuts, he's too serious. It must be bad news.

"The nurses and attending physicians tell me you're coming along fine. Is that how you feel?"

"I dunno. I haven't walked yet, and they're giving me a lot of pills."

"Yes, you need medication for the pain after surgery."

"My mind's a blank about things here. I can't even tell what time it is."

"Soldier, based on what you went through, it's expected you would be disoriented. In fact, it's normal you'll feel despondent until your health improves. Just like many of the men here in this wing of the hospital."

I looked around the ward, but couldn't relate to any one person or thing. After licking my lips several times, I said, "I guess I'm just afraid."

"That's what I want to talk to you about. Believe me when I say you are going to get better. You were fortunate to get to surgeons in Iraq so quickly, but you lost a considerable amount of blood. They operated on your wounds and stabilized you until you could be transported here."

I shifted my position in bed, anxious to hear what he would say about my injuries.

"The laceration on your left cheek is healing nicely and there shouldn't be any noticeable scar. Your shoulder will remain strapped another week or two and then, after a few months of rehab, you'll have ordinary use of your arm." He grinned and added, "Unless you're a weight lifter."

Cute. "What about my leg?"

"One more thing first. Although you lost some hearing in both ears, fortunately, you'll recover normal hearing in time."

"Great. And my leg?" *Answer the damn question!*

"Yes, well, you have suffered massive vascular damage. Grenade fragments ripped into tendon and muscle in your upper right thigh. We performed skin transplants here, but further repair may be necessary back in the States."

"So, I won't lose my leg?"

"Absolutely not! There was a strong pulse in your leg when you were brought into surgery. I expect you will regain your ability to walk and move about, even play a round or two of golf. However, it will take time and rehabilitation. Do you understand that?"

"I can put up with it." My heartbeat was back to normal at the thought of a full recovery from my injuries.

"Last, you did receive severe blows to your head. I know you've had recurring headaches and—"

"I got this bump on the side of my head. I guess it'll go away."

"Yes, but you did go through a traumatic experience. Besides periodic migraines, your eyes are often out of focus. Right?" He checked my chart.

"The light bothers me sometimes. Maybe I just need glasses."

"You have a temporary stress injury, so I intend to recommend neurological tests when you get to Walter Reed."

"Whatever you say, Colonel."

"You'll be released in a few days and be back in the States in no time. Good luck to you. By the way, a Brigadier General will visit you later today to honor your service."

"Thank you, sir."

* * *

"Goddamn doctors."

I threw the blanket on the floor and kicked it out of my way. The last three years since I returned from Iraq had been pure hell. A drunkard. Miserable rehabbing at Walter Reed. That distressing Vegas folly. Panic attacks. Lonely. Always running away from one thing or another.

What do I have to do to get a real life? At least I don't have those awful migraines like the ones acted out by Jimmy Cagney in the movie *White Heat.*

The stigma of a mental problem will probably be with me the rest of my stinking life. *So damn unfair. An outcast warmonger, that's what I am.*

"Why didn't I just die like all the others?" I prayed to the ceiling, as if it would open up to the gates of heaven.

Back in bed, I pulled the sheets over my head, hoping to block out the memories. Loneliness was the hardest to swallow.

"I ...can't ...take it ...any ...more."

Sleep didn't come easy.

CHAPTER 2

From his warm reception, it was obvious that Dr. Burkett was pleased I had called for an earlier appointment.

"You seem tense today, Drew," he said, eyeing me closely. "How about telling me what's on your mind."

I recounted my vision in detail to him, even labeling it a nightmare. All he did was shake his head and take notes.

He put his pen down. "I'm glad you came forward with this information at last. Any upsetting, repetitive episodes like that add to our understanding and you have to—"

"Doc, it's really bad sometimes. Will I ever get over it?"

"That's what we want to get a handle on. I understand how you feel, but you must open up with me on your experiences and emotions."

"Okay, I'm trying."

"First, I'll tell you that flashbacks after a near-death experience are not uncommon. Medically, you have shown no signs of insomnia, sleepwalking or epileptic seizures. While the analysis of your condition can be complex, positive results are achievable in time. Each revelation becomes a fit in solving the dilemma."

"I understand. Just hope you're right."

"Everyone dreams. In medical school, the subject of dreams fascinated me and I decided to focus part of my practice on analysis of their meaning rather than research. REMs, rapid eye movements, reveal the time and duration of images. The most common dreaming has to do with anxiety or, in your case, a terrifying scene."

"To think that all I worried about as a kid was avoiding tackles and zigzagging eighty yards for a touchdown. How things change."

"Can you tell me what else you see in your dream? Describe the place or the environment. Is there any light? Is it a war zone? Any people?"

I closed my eyes and tried to make sense of the scene. "It's a twilight zone, Doc. Alternating between fuzzy darkness and revolving figures in bright lights."

"What are you doing to 'catch it' as you say?"

"I feel myself reaching out, but grabbing at air. Like I'm watching a 3-D movie with those weird glasses. I can't ..." Tears clouded my gaze at Burkett. I felt humiliated and weary.

"Drew, you're doing fine. Something will jog your mind, so don't torment yourself to see the picture in your dream. It will become clearer as time goes on."

His soothing tone relieved my angst. Grinning, I said, "You've got yourself a number one nut case."

"Nonsense," he said, raising his voice. He dropped his notepad on the floor and shifted forward toward me, looking straight in my eyes. "Listen, you remember I told you there's various ways to treat returning vets who have been through what you have."

"Yeah."

"I think it's time you should participate in group therapy. I have patients in Monmouth County Medical Hospital, but I prefer that you associate with military people in the same situation as you. It's an effective way to desensitize you to the trauma."

Oh hell! What's he talking about?

"Haven't I been coming along okay under your care?"

"Yes, but you can improve further with a broader treatment

of your illness." He removed the *Newark Star Ledger* from the shelf and said, "Did you know about twenty percent of veterans returning from Iraq and Afghanistan are suspected of a stress disorder? There is a report in today's paper that Congress has appropriated a substantial sum to address the problem."

"That's good news."

"I'm going to arrange for you to attend two sessions a month as an outpatient at Trenton VA hospital. Doctor Robert Masters is the group leader. He has experience with cases of Post-Traumatic Stress Disorder and excellent results in this work. You can trust him, believe me."

"I don't know, Doc. I'm not sure I can listen to other guys' problems and speak about my own." My palms felt moist.

"Drew, you'll be alright. You've got to address your lack of confidence and depression one step at a time. Group psychotherapy has a proven record of accomplishment. Give it a try! You go to the Trenton VA anyway for periodic physical checkups."

I slumped down in my seat. He wasn't asking me, he was telling me. Suppose I come across as a dummy or neurotic to guys I don't even know. Burkett even thought I was suicidal at the outset of our meetings because of my Vegas disaster. But he was right; I had to beat this thing.

I sat up straight, and gave in. "If you think it will improve my condition, I'll do it for awhile. Maybe it'll even make things better at work, too. You know, how well I'm doing socializing with everybody."

"Of course."

Burkett didn't laugh often, and his professional training has made him come across as stoic. But when his face lit up, it made me feel good, like I could have a normal life.

"One more thing. Do you have a girlfriend yet, or are you

comfortable with any woman socially at work or where you live?"

Why is he doing this to me? He knows how frustrating this subject is.

"Naw, Doc. I can't seem to get into any deep conversation with any female. I mean, there's this one woman at work, Carolyn, who smiles at me every morning and asks if I want coffee, but I don't think we have anything in common and—"

"How do you know unless you talk to her? She's not married, is she?"

"I don't think so. She's not wearing a ring, and they call her Miss, so—"

"So why not ask for a date or meet somewhere out of the office?"

"I don't think I can do that."

"Come on," he said, clasping both hands under his chin. "Look, you're a handsome guy. I'm sure women are attracted to you."

"Let's face facts, Doc, and get to the real issue." I caught him off guard by my sharp retort. "If one thing leads to another and there's talk of sex, it won't work."

"Why?"

"You saw my medical records. Even I'm repulsed at the sight of my thigh. It's a turn-off."

"Do it in the dark."

"You gotta be kidding me," I snickered. "So what happens if I get lucky with some babe? Turning off all the lights makes it alright?"

"Sure, why not?" he said indifferently.

"Damn, you have an odd answer for everything." I eyed him closely wondering if he was for real.

He turned the timer off, knocking it off the stand. He massaged his beard, or is it a goatee, and gave me an adamant stare. This was Burkett at his fastidious best, which differed from an otherwise tolerant approach to my condition and me. His empathy had obliged me to accept him as a considerate person.

"Don't you understand I'm making a point? You can't go through the rest of your life feeling sorry for yourself." He pointed a finger at me. "And you're not going to be a recluse. Is that clear?"

The firm warning and his stern look surprised the hell out of me. He sounded like my father, who was always forceful, but instructive and open with me.

"When I see you next month, you can tell me about your group therapy sessions, and I want you to promise me you'll ask Carolyn for a date. Why not bring up dating in the group sessions and find out how the other guys are managing with the women in their lives." He stopped to write on his prescription pad. "Take this. I'm going to increase the Ambien sleep medication for a short time."

It's not as if I don't want to become friendly with Carolyn, for chrissake. My sexual problem isn't the same as others.

"If you think I'm ready, I'll give it a shot."

"Great. With good news coming out of Iraq, I want to get your thoughts on the war next time, as I suggested at our last session."

"Well, I'll say my piece, but believe me, the coverage in the media is bogus. Anyway, I don't see how my opinions are relevant."

"I'll be the judge of that." He put his hand on my shoulder as I stood to leave and said, "I must tell you that I believe we're making gradual but steady progress from the first months we were together when we met once a week. After what you went through at Walter Reed, returning to the Bronx for a short time, and then Las Vegas, it's important to acknowledge positive developments."

My face lit up as he referred to his notes.

"Your cognitive skill and grasp of information have improved. The stammer in your voice is not as evident, and you're no longer lethargic. While I'm sure you're not the life of the party, you are not as introverted as you were when I first met you. Therapy is necessary to work on sporadic clumsiness in your movements. Finally, you can't be afraid to become emotionally involved. It's a wholesome thing."

"Can you believe I was a social livewire in college?" I said, biting my lower lip. "And my SAT's were better than average, I think. Gave me bragging rights among my friends, too. Anyway, thanks for the status report, Doc. I appreciate it."

As I drove home, the usual reflection on the day's session controlled my thoughts. Carolyn was a pretty girl, probably five years younger than me, and she had gone out of her way to be pleasant and get to know me. Not like the other creeps in the office. Maybe when she's in the coffee lounge next time, I'll ask her if we could meet for lunch or after work for a drink. Hell, the worst she can say is she's busy or has a boy friend.

"Introverted." I repeated Burkett's opinion. *Like my mother? What does he expect after what I've been through?*

There's that Yankee Stadium billboard again. Bet my old pals have a better life than I do. In spite of our differences and no contact, I really do wish them well. When they think of me, I'm sure the feeling is mutual.

I wondered how specific they got in group therapy discussions. A bunch of nut cases. Did I have to hear what other guys had gone through, and bring back my own memories of those night patrols? They'd probably brag about being macho and act like it. The Group Leader had better not badger me or I'd walk out. If all they did was tell war stories and complain, I'll tell Burkett it was not for me.

Home at last. Maybe I'll take a walk on the beach again to pass the evening faster. That's one thing I never get tired of. The blackness disturbed only by the moon and countless stars, faithfully permitting souls to enter heaven.

I hate doing laundry.

Hope there's a good movie on TV to put me to sleep.

CHAPTER 3

"Today's the day I'll speak to Carolyn," I whispered as I exited my car in the parking lot of the Outsource Data Corporation, situated on the outskirts of Toms River.

Approaching the main entrance, it occurred to me I had never been on the second floor of the two-story modern building. The scenic setting, with large Maples lining the wide entrance, was in a prime location easily accommodating employee parking and access to highways from local road Route 751. I knew the department that occupied the entire top floor processed credit card charges for numerous Fortune 500 companies. This operation was the newest branch, opened early this year, which reported to the Philadelphia Eastern Division office.

It was common knowledge that my department, which shared the first floor with the employee cafeteria, was an afterthought. The management needed a location to handle product rebate programs for a few select clients. Those programs had fixed expiration dates.

I'd rather work in the larger function upstairs, which was a boom to employment in several contiguous counties. As far as I was concerned, the work in my section was as boring as my co-workers. My initial assignment had been filing batches of rebate documents by customer name. Then I learned on a PC how to verify the original purchase had been paid and that the products, mostly personal computers and appliances, had not been returned. Switching assignments throughout the day reduced the boredom. Mr. Parker told me I would be taught the data entry of confirmed rebate amounts to the Home Office, where checks were drawn. "He's trying to appease me for his past bitching about my productivity," I said to myself after leaving his office.

"Good morning, Mr. Baxter."

"Da, da, da, good morning." I gave Carolyn a sideways glance as she passed my desk. *Jeez, I feel like a school kid.*

As soon as she goes on break in an hour, I'll follow her to the cafeteria. Where should we go or meet? I bet she'll have a suggestion.

"These documents have to be checked to this list right away, Baxter," Parker said, virtually dumping them on my desk.

"Yes, sir," I said, quickly shutting off further fantasizing.

For the next half hour my attention focused on the work in front of me, requiring total concentration. *Only a few more documents left before I—*

"That's not the way it's done, Miss Hoover! I told you that yesterday."

The loud voice startled everyone. Parker was berating Carolyn for all to hear and see.

"Sorry, Mr. Parker," she mumbled, her voice quivering.

"The Home Office expects the results and my report this afternoon. Give it all back to me!"

Carolyn stood, now tearing up, and headed to the ladies room.

As Parker crossed in front of my desk, I said, "Take it easy, Mr. Parker. She's only a kid you know, so give her a break."

He stopped and glanced at me with disdain. "Look you! Mind your own business. I'll deal with you and your work later."

"Fine. Just go easy on the girl!" I pushed away from my desk and said, "And I'm getting my work done correctly and on time, so don't threaten me."

"Really?" he said sarcastically. "Well, I've put up with your inefficiency long enough." He took several steps toward his office and added, "Just stay out of how I manage the staff."

I thought for a second, but couldn't hold my tongue. *I've got to say it, point-blank to the bully.*

"You embarrass her like that again and I don't care who you are, I'll knock your freaking head off."

The employees were in a panic. The other man in the office stood and yelled, "Take it easy, Drew!" Other noises were indistinct.

There was a momentary stand-off. I thought of Will Kane.

I stood, knocking over a swivel chair, and advanced slowly toward him as he held his ground. *If he makes one move, I'll deck the bastard.*

"That's the last straw, Baxter," he proclaimed, face red as a lobster. "You're fired. Please leave the premises immediately or I'll call security."

I searched the faces of my co-workers. They were beyond shock. I'd seen the same apprehension in Iraq. Fearful of disaster.

What the hell do I do now?

No reason for me to make any more trouble. For me or for them.

I scooped up my car keys from the desk and walked swiftly to the door. Now I felt foolish, so I avoided their faces. Nobody said anything, but I knew all eyes were on me. I had lost my cool, but for a damn good reason.

As I reached my car, a high-pitched shout of my name spun me around. I saw Carolyn running to me.

"Mr. Baxter ... Drew. I'm so sorry this happened to you."

As she hesitated to catch her breath, I pondered my next move, taking advantage of a private meeting.

"You were special to stick up for me and—"

"He had no right to treat you like that."

"Yes, but you risked your job for me. I'm going to write a letter to the boss in Philadelphia so you can get your job back."

"Listen, Carolyn, I appreciate it, but don't bother. It was only a question of time before I'd quit anyway. This kind of office work isn't for me." *Maybe now I should apply to become a cop again.*

She reached out and held my hand. "Isn't there anything I can do?"

I wondered if this was the right time. Should I ask if I could see her again for cocktails or a movie?

"Well, Carolyn ..."

"I want you to know that what you did was the nicest thing anyone has ever done for me," she sighed. "I'm gonna tell my boy friend when I see him tonight."

"Boy friend?"

She kissed me on the cheek and said, "I'll never forget you." Then she ran off, waved to me as she entered the building, and disappeared out of my life forever.

I sat numb in my car, mindless to where I was and what tomorrow had in store for me without a job. I didn't want to live on unemployment benefits. My dad taught me that. I sure let down my army friend in the home office of ODC.

To hell with you, Dr. Burkett.

Rather than go home or to the bar/restaurant, *Sail Inn,* in Lavallette where I might be recognized by some of the locals, I drove past my place and parked on a side street in the next town, Seaside Heights, only five minutes away. At one time, I was a regular at the *Crab Bar and Grill* on the boardwalk. I wanted to be alone. After wandering up and down the boardwalk for several hours, and fighting a stiff breeze off the ocean as if it were the enemy, I detoured into the *Crab Bar.*

"Bartender, give me a Bourbon and water, and keep them coming!"

"Yes sir. Someum to celebrate?"

"Naw, just thirsty."

Within the hour the bar became jammed. Customers were two deep at the waitresses' station, checking out their skimpy outfits.

"Hey pal, stop shoving!" I moved my half-empty glass away from the intruder in my space.

"Sorry, buddy, I gotta squeeze in to get my drink."

As his long reach backed away from the mahogany bar, his hip banged against my bar stool, which caused me to knock over my glass.

"You jerk," I screamed. "Watch what ya doing?"

"Hey, calm down! Who the hell do you think you're talking to?"

I gingerly moved off the bar stool and faced the guy. "I'm talking to you, asshole. Who the hell doya think?" I staggered backwards and grabbed for the bar.

"Go screw yourself," he snickered, "you sloppy drunk."

As he turned away from me, I lunged at him and swung an overhand right that glanced off his neck. I fell into his chest and held on. He looked shocked.

"You nut case." He shoved me away with his left hand and punched me in the face with his right.

My legs couldn't hold me up. I crashed to the floor and felt shooting pains in my shoulder and jaw. The crowd noise level was urging me to get up by the count of nine.

What am I doing here? Jesus, I can't move.

"Get him out of here before I call the cops! Does anyone know him?"

Why is the bartender bending over me? He and another guy held me under the arms and virtually carried me out the door.

"Lemme alone," I mumbled as the cool night air hit me. I thought my head would explode.

"Do you know where your car is or where you live?"

"Why not? I want, *hic*, my change from the bar."

"We put it in your pocket."

I looked around, but couldn't place where I was. "Which way is Laval ...?"

They pointed me down the street past back entrances to honky-tonk stores and bars. "This street runs into 35. Just go straight and you can't miss Lavallette. Okay, fella?"

"Yeah, I'll make it."

As I weaved down Route 35, familiar sights of walking the same route with my father years ago flashed before me. *Try and catch me, Dad.* Cars whizzed by me, and their headlights made me lose my balance, like I was riding the high seas. I flopped down on a sandy spot off the side of the road until the pain in my leg subsided.

Where am I?

"Good riddance to Carolyn, and that fink Parker, and the lousy job," I yelled into the darkness. "Screw em all."

Each time I lay down, dizziness threw off my whereabouts.

"I'm getting close," I slurred, maybe an hour later, when I saw the sign for Tierce's Seaside Delights candy and ice cream store across the street.

"This is it. At last."

There were a dozen bungalows on Osprey Street, mostly unoccupied this time of year. Finally, I reached my front door. After fumbling with house keys for a minute, I entered and didn't bother to turn on the lights. I tripped over the coffee table and collapsed onto the couch.

I dreamt of a Rutgers basketball game. The players were swirling around the court, but their oversized sneakers weren't touching the floor. I saw myself in the middle of the game and felt like I was on a merry-go-round, shouting, *Throw me the ball.*

I bounded up on the couch with a start and staggered to the bathroom.

That dream is bizarre! Or is it the same as the vision about the round ball I'm trying to reach?

CHAPTER 4

"**R**eal calm compared to yesterday at this time," I told myself at first sight of the Atlantic from atop the sand dunes on a cloudless morning. And what wonders would the ocean divulge today? A beached whale by chance, like a lasting memory when I was a kid? Shark teeth? Debris from a shipwreck? Beautiful shades of blue or aqua, or a murky brown? Dolphins leaping out of the water in ballet formation?

This was the third day I've strolled or jogged on the beach since I was terminated. The long stretches of tall grass on sand dunes to protect the beach from storm waves and winds offered a picturesque sight of nature.

A hangover no longer slowed my movements. After being on the wagon for I don't know how long, the lingering effect of one night's drinking had made me sick as a dog, another low point in my life. Worse still, the mysterious dream, more like a nightmare, stuck in my mind.

Never again, dammit! I'm on the wagon for good this time.

I'll be here most of the day again. My house, actually a bungalow, is only a few minutes walk from the beach. I rent the place on an annual lease that costs slightly more than a summer rental.

My parents vacationed on the Jersey shore when I was a kid, and the Lavallette beach was their favorite. I had mostly pleasant memories of those times, including the boardwalk and amusement park in nearby Seaside Heights. Unfortunately, my parents' relationship became strained for a few years about that time.

* * *

"Throw the ball higher this time, Dad."

"Son, you've worn me out. Let me rest for a while so we can go to the boardwalk tonight. I promise I'll ride the rollercoaster with you, and there's a Longboard surfing contest we can watch. Why don't you have a swim and cool off?"

"Okay, Dad." Bobbing in the ocean up to my neck, I looked south to the Seaside Heights skyline, easily identifying the rollercoaster ride.

I watched my dad go and sit in his beach chair next to my mother. She hadn't looked my way, and I wondered if she was mad at me.

Riding the waves in to shore on my belly, with or without a boogie board, was real cool. What fun, mixing with other kids.

After thirty minutes or so, I high-stepped out of the surf and dried myself in a large beach towel with the design of a New York Giants helmet.

"Oh, oh." I heard my parents arguing. Again. My grandmother's name was mentioned twice. *Do they hate each other*?

"Come on, Mom and Dad, can we get ice cream now? Please?"

* * *

It's sure great here on weekdays. No "Bennies" visiting this time of year, wearing casual shoes and dark socks up to their calf. There was no one within a couple of hundred yards of me on the beach, except the girl jogging this way. Maybe I'll take up fishing from the shore. Sorry I never tried my hand at surfboarding. Any hobby at this point would be a reprieve from boredom. How peaceful it would be to strum a guitar on the beach all day.

The girl, a teenager, waved as she passed, while I gazed longingly at her.

Females? After Lauren and Carolyn, no romance and no more disappointments for me. *Wait a minute! What am I thinking?* I needed companionship bad, even if it was platonic.

Maybe I should get a dog. We could run on the beach every day. Good exercise for me, too. A small dog would be a great companion and—

"Who am I kidding?" *Who would train him or take care of him when I'm away? Naw, it's a bad idea. The poor dog would go stir crazy in my small place just like me.*

I tossed shells to the water's edge. Sandpipers danced across the wet sand avoiding the incoming tide, eating crustaceans before they migrated to wherever. Chances are I was with my parents in this exact same spot on the beach building sand castles many moons ago. How many generations of families enjoyed their favorite locations on Jersey shore beaches?

"Footprints in the sand!" I blurted out.

Oh, there's that song back again. During my time in Trenton VA hospital, I became obsessed with it, singing, humming or whistling it day and night. The doctors observed my conduct with concern. Following a showing of the old movie, *The Thomas Crown Affair,* the song and its disconnected and irrelevant words haunted me. Burkett was told all the details, but never questioned why the lyrics stuck with me. One verse was:

> *Keys that jingle in your pocket,*
> *Words that jangle in your head,*
> *Why did summer go so quickly?*
> *Was it something that I said?*
> *Lovers walking along the shore,*
> *Leave their footprints in the sand.*

The lyrics of *Windmills of Your Mind* seemed to symbolize my musings and confused state since Iraq. What was the songwriter getting at with the diverse and baffling lyrics?

The words and melody finally exhausted their stay with me in the hospital ...until today. Thankfully, the song no longer had the same mysterious hold on me as before.

What's happened to my life? How is it judged that someone is going crazy? Am I?

As the sun rose in the sky, I peered out to the infinite horizon like a sea captain. The panoramic sight boggled my mind as always. From one day to the next the ocean acted according to a grand plan. A successful voyage for some; a tragedy for others. I once read a poem that described the unending ocean cascade. How did it go?

> *Fiercely, furious, shattering waves,*
> *tearing at the coastal core.*
> *Peaceful, balmy, tranquil waves, gently soothing every pore.*
> *Snaking, whispering, tumbling waves,*
> *coming ever on the shore.*
> *Sweeping, rolling, lapping waves, through*
> *the sands of time and yore.*

After walking about a mile to the south and back, I found a comfortable spot of fluffy sand to sit and rest. Beads of perspiration itched the small of my back. A helicopter flew by fifty yards offshore on the lookout for sharks. Staring at white caps caused by a distant tanker, I wondered how different things might have been if I had enlisted in the Navy. Imagine! Seaman Baxter. "Baloney, I can't even swim," I murmured.

I stretched out on the sand lying on my stomach.

What better place than this for reflection about the past?

I got lost in the shuffle at Cardinal Hayes High School. Senior class too large. It upset me when I failed to make the baseball team, but Dad consoled me and pointed out many opportunities ahead. I loved reading about Julius Caesar in Latin class. In senior year I discovered a fascination for an extra-curricular activity—the Hospital Volunteer Program. The interaction with patients, old and young, was a moving and exciting experience for me; also, general assistance to the nursing staff was much appreciated. Unfortunately, the cost of a medical school education was prohibitive, but the pleasure of contributing to a patient's well-being has lingered with me.

My four years at Rutgers opened my eyes to life west of the Hudson River. Forget my old pals. It didn't take long for me to learn I wasn't as smart as I thought or acted. Fortunately, political science and American history courses came easy. Those subjects intrigued me. I figured a job in the State Department was in my future, rather than a policeman. Even took two years of Spanish and, for extra credit, studied the lives of presidents, the constitution and all twenty-seven amendments. The professors thought I had a strong voice suited for a politician or a radio announcer. The idea of a career in medicine was forgotten.

Schoolwork was going great until Lauren came along in my senior year. She was gorgeous, but what a two-timer. After that night in her dorm, I thought we'd be together once we left Rutgers. I should've known better.

"Guess what, Lauren. I'm joining the Army the day after graduation."

"Why would you do that?" she snickered. "You'll get yourself killed."

"We can't let those Arabs get away with what they did. I thought you'd be proud of me and—"

"You're kidding. With a college education, I think you're ridiculous." She turned her back on me and stormed out of the cafeteria.

In basic training at Fort Dix, I heard through the grapevine that she ended up with every Tom, Dick and Harry in town. No big surprise to me.

My mother had died of a stroke during my sophomore year at Rutgers. As I matured, I realized her kindly demeanor during my childhood contrasted with emotional outbursts as she aged that convinced me she had health problems. Her introverted nature did not foster closeness between us, which I sincerely regretted, but I knew she loved me.

"That Dr. Masters was too suave, and sneaky, to suit me," I whispered into a towel as my recollections shifted to the group therapy sessions.

Those visits were a waste from my perspective. Some of those guys have big problems. In fact, one sat in a corner with his back to the wall grumbling to himself about people disliking him. Everyone ignored him. A few sat quietly in a catatonic state, wearing army fatigues. Soldiers have snapped with PTSD in a variety of ways, so I was not the worst. The bare grey walls of the square room eliminated any distractions, but heightened my paranoia.

I could tell that the Leader, Dr. Masters, paid special attention to my demeanor, as if he expected I might cause a disruption. I joined in with the others easily, discussing sports and jobs, including sweet Carolyn. I stayed out of family talk. They all laughed when I told them about my first time on guard duty in the boondocks of Fort Dix where I was left for two extra hours from midnight to four am ...without a watch. Everyone turned somber when the subject of our units in Iraq or Afghanistan crept into the conversation. Some guys cried.

"That's alright to let out your emotions," Masters said. "We can share in the memories and suffering we endured by talking it out together. Let's have a moment of silence."

Not me. I didn't cry, but I was off-base to think these guys saw themselves as heroes. Neither were they simpletons, at least not pre-Iraq. Just regular men like me with invisible scars that could fester out of control. Despite the leader's clever hints, I didn't get into any details about Fallujah and the raid that killed my buddies. Hell, I couldn't even recall the new recruit's face or name. In a failed attempt to ease our concerns, Masters disclosed, "The most decorated soldier in World War II, budding actor Audie Murphy, suffered a severe case of Post-Traumatic Stress Disorder."

We all looked at one another when Masters informed us of the VA's National Suicide Hotline. Our eyes communicated, "Not me, sir," but he knew better. "You have to face your fears," he emphasized repeatedly. "Accept our help and trust us to support you."

In hindsight, whether I admitted it or not, the therapy was beneficial. He was believable.

I felt the sun burning my back. *Where am I? How long have I been lying here*? Sitting up, it only took a second for my head to clear. The beach looked even more beautiful, and the blueness of the sky was extraordinary.

"Not a care in the world," I mouthed facetiously.

The ding-a-ling-ling sound of the ice cream truck distracted me. "Do I wanna get some ...?"

This is ludicrous! I can't go on being a beachcomber the rest of my life.

Doc is going to give me hell when I see him next week. "No girl, no job, no more group therapy," I mumbled. "At least George Parker is out of my life, but I'm so mixed up. Just not fair."

What the hell is Dr. Masters going to say to him about me?

After college, I expected a better life. Even my application to be a Jersey State Trooper a year ago was rejected "for psychiatric reasons." Ain't that a kick in the ass!

I pitched a large pebble into the ocean and watched it skip twice before it sank. A sudden anguish slowed my breathing. I gasped for air, trembling from a self-imposed chill.

"What am I going to do?" I whispered in desperation. "There's no one I can turn to."

How far do I have to walk in before I ...

Two jets from Maguire Air Force base soared overhead. I watched them climb higher as the contrails disappeared to the south. I wondered where and what their mission was.

God, there are guys still over there in harm's way. Who knows their fate when they come home ...if they make it?

"I hope the war ..." The words stuck in my throat. Memories of a ravaged place were too vivid. The hot sun and sand made the remembrances more real and frightening. I could see Lieutenant Munson's profile coming toward me out of the mirage.

I stood and gritted my teeth, digging into the biting sand with my feet. Suddenly, I thought of my parents and their expectations for me. *They didn't want a loser, and I'm not going to be one.*

"Stop it! This is not right. I'm going to fight this thing." My body stiffened. Fists clenched. "With Doc believing in me, I can have a normal life. I know I can. I'm a survivor and—"

"Is everything alright, mister?"

I looked around into the face of a young boy who came out of nowhere. *He looks like I did at that age.*

A novel tranquil feeling came over me as all motion had stopped.

I smiled at the boy. "I'm fine, son. Thanks."

My life is worthwhile. It can't end up like this. I just won't let it!

I raced back to the house to telephone Dr. Burkett.

CHAPTER 5

Entering Dr. Burkett's office, I was upbeat, but took care to conceal my apprehension. Even forgot my watch. *Will he think I sounded either irrational or overly elated on the phone? Oh, what's the difference? He's the only person who can facilitate my recovery.* "We're making progress," he had told me the last time.

"Thanks for rearranging your schedule, Doctor. I really wanted to see you as soon as possible."

"No problem at all. As a matter of fact, I intended to give you a call today."

"Oh?" *What can that be about?*

"I sensed your determination on the phone," he said, eyebrows raised at my undisguised enthusiasm.

"Doc, things didn't work out with the job as I told you on the phone, but believe me, I feel more optimistic than ever that I can lick my problems. With you, of course."

"Drew, you've advanced over the last few months from dejection to hopefulness. Regaining self-confidence is a major step forward. I've seen positive signs in your behavior." He picked up his notepad. "You have a more ambitious outlook for the first time since we met. We've built up a lot of trust over these past months. I want you to feel free to open up with me and—"

"I promise. I'm not holding anything back." In my heart, I wanted to tell him the whole truth, but could not ...or would not.

"Good. Let's start with what happened at your job."

"Sure. I may have been out of line, but I couldn't allow that lousy supervisor to put down Carolyn in front of—"

"Pardon my interruption," he stopped me. "What I want to know is why did you react the way you did?"

I allowed his question to swirl around in my head. "I just knew if I didn't distract Parker, Carolyn would hurt real bad so ..."

Burkett mumbled a few words I didn't catch at first.

"What was that you said?"

"Nothing," he said, looking at the ceiling. "Just listening."

I could swear he said, *Damsel in distress.*

"So you would have felt guilty if you did nothing," he added before I continued my answer.

"You bet," I exclaimed, "although the confrontation with Parker didn't make me feel very good either."

"Okay. Your reaction was understandable given that Parker over-stepped his bounds, but you know violence isn't the answer."

"I realized that right away, Doc. Just got carried away like I used to. Even cursed myself for the lack of control and stupidity."

"Let me say I'm pleased by your newfound assertiveness, whatever the reason," he said in a serious tone. "As I've told you from the start, however, there will be ups and downs in everyday situations, a natural emotional pattern following the trauma you experienced. You understand what I'm saying, Drew?"

"I do." *Burkett seems dubious about my resolve.*

"I'm obliged to confirm you haven't had any alcohol, right?" He pointed his finger at me to emphasize the seriousness of his question.

"Not a drop in two years ...except for the other night. I screwed up real bad."

"Are you still going to AA?"

"Naw, that local group were a bunch of holy rollers or hypocrites more interested in socializing. To be honest though, they express their feelings better than people who have been sober their entire lives."

"Please give them another chance."

"Believe me, I'll be okay. The whole episode at work just got under my skin. Like the universe was caving in around me. It was a one time thing."

His closed left eye had suspicion written all over it. Nevertheless, my commitment to sobriety was steadfast.

"I'll take you at your word, but—"

"Doc, I promise you. Please trust me."

"We'll see. Here's a temporary change in your medication. I'm reducing the dosage for depression, but increasing the *Klonopin,* which controls panic attacks. I want you to be honest with me about any drinking in the future."

After taking a call on his personal line and writing out a new prescription, his facial expression changed to a coy smile.

Surprises and the unexpected make me jumpy. I sure can't explain why, other than due to my experience in Iraq.

"Let's move on. I've got some good news for you about another position. My roommate at Rider College, now Rider University, was Hank Jorgenson. He's the mayor in that new community, Barnegat Junction, down near you. He informed me he needed another employee in the Town Hall now and more in the future. I've recommended you to him."

Oh my God. My pulse beat faster than my brain could absorb the news. *Is my luck changing?*

"You have basic computer skills, right?"

"Yeah."

"Mayor Jorgenson scheduled an interview for you next Monday. What do you say?"

"Do you really think I can handle it? I mean it sounds great and all, but ..."

"Look, Drew, this is a wonderful opportunity. It's a stimulating workplace." He stopped to reach into his briefcase and remove a folder. The title on the cover was in plain sight. *Veterans Administration Hospital, Trenton, New Jersey.*

"Your enthusiasm on the phone and coming to see me today indicate you're ready to start fresh and accept responsibility, other than that one incident at work. As you've said often, you need employment—"

"You got that right."

"This position fits your educational profile and the work will be interesting, for sure. Here's the business card of the person in charge. Call first to let them know you're coming."

I leaned forward on the couch and inspected the card. "Doc, I appreciate this very much. I won't let you down."

"As for meeting a young woman, I'm sure there will be occasions for you to establish a rapport. Perhaps at church or the fitness center or wherever. And don't feel let down by Carolyn. It's not as if you were jilted."

I nodded in agreement. *But when will I meet someone? Church? I haven't been to one since my parents took me as a kid.*

Burkett opened the VA hospital folder and glanced over two or three pages.

I crossed my fingers. The last thing I wanted to hear was a recommendation that I should be committed to a place like Walter Reed.

I'd kill myself before I let that happen again.

"This is the other matter I intended to call you about. How did you feel about the two group therapy sessions?" He closed the folder and held one page in his hand.

"Overall they were okay. Things got a little tense when a few guys recounted specific combat experiences."

"How did you get along with the group?"

"Great, for the most part. One guy, I think he's kinda senile, got me mad and—"

"Why?"

"He had a chip on his shoulder about everything and everybody. Always acting tough and complaining. So I called him a mean-ass grinning baboon."

"Oh-oh."

"Yeah. He said the only job I'm capable of is boring assholes in hobby horses. All the other guys laughed, except me." I flipped my hands in the air and added, "Masters stepped in before we came to blows."

He tried to hide a snicker. "Tell me about the incident at Home Depot!"

"That's in the report?"

"Very relevant to your condition, don't you think?"

"I felt like a fool. Several air conditioning units fell off a pallet. The noise jolted me and I dropped to the floor on my knees, shaking, and hid my face." *Fallujah.* "Customers avoided me until a young man helped me stand."

"Drew, don't you think the program was helpful for you?"

"Not really, although I sympathized with one guy who lost a leg. Almost everyone had nightmares somewhat like mine. Half of them were divorced." I shook my head.

"Go on."

"Well, they described their nightmares in detail. Frankly, it seemed to alleviate their sadness when they opened up to the group. Some guys became less inhibited; others more hostile. I guess it would be good for me also if I could only give a clearer picture of ..." I hesitated, staring at the floor as the memories I'd been unable to shut away flowed back to me.

"Easy, Drew. You may not see the benefit yet, but those sessions are contributing to our understanding of what drives your behavior. You're not alone in this and shouldn't become frustrated over it. It will get better. Just takes time for people to come to grips with distressing events."

"Uh-huh."

"I've noticed, by the way, you haven't mentioned your dream recently."

I stood and walked back and forth in the office crammed with books on shelves and magazines on the floor. "Doctor Burkett, you know best that it'll take time. And you're right about my nightmare. It's been a couple of weeks since the last one."

"Would you like to hear what Dr. Masters thought of you?"

"Sure." I figured I'd take his view with a grain of salt at best.

"First, he and I talked on the phone about your return home from Iraq and your overall political views on the government and society. We wanted to learn if you exhibited negative feelings or resentments."

"Listen, Doc, I told you my opinion once before."

"I know, Drew, but I wanted to get Doctor Master's impression of your exchanges with other veterans. It's part of our evaluation of your head injury."

"Wait a minute!" I jumped up, heading for the door. "What the hell do the two of you think I'm going to do? March on D.C.? Cause a riot?"

"Calm yourself right now and please sit back down! We're not accusing you of anything, so no more shouting and hear me out."

I hadn't seen him so ruffled before, but he upset me first with the insinuation about my loyalty. I sat and glared at him.

"As a matter of fact, Masters said you showed no extreme views one way or another. Nothing radical like a Timothy McVeigh, for example."

"Or Jane Fonda," I interjected sarcastically. "Look Doc, I love my country too much to get implicated with any extremist agenda. I'm not for violence, so can we stop all this—"

"Fine." He raised his hand for me to stop, while forcing a cough. "Let me read to you this note he sent me with the file. You'll find it quite revealing:

'Dear Tim, The attached contains the usual boilerplate report on the group sessions attended by Drew Baxter. The favorable evaluation reflects his willingness to participate and his well-balanced decorum, even a sense of humor. I should add my impression (nothing more than that) he seemed detached from the common problems the others had experienced. He was the only one who raised his hand indicating a readiness to return to Iraq if called. To some he's an enigma. Docile and considerate of others, yet combative for a cause. He wants (or needs) to be liked. While he may exhibit self-pity, infrequently to be sure, I agree with your referral note to me that narcissistic behavior or tendencies are of no concern.

The discussion of family life triggered an obvious withdrawal. The periods of depression and guilt you described to me about him may be rooted in his childhood and exasperated by a moderate case of PTSD. Suggest you explore his nightmares more closely. I hope this provides added insight to the case. Bob' "

I sat motionless, waiting for Burkett to explain the unexpected positive report on my role in the therapy sessions and to interpret Masters' conclusion, or personal observation. The last part of what he said disturbed me. *Doesn't everyone want to be liked?*

"Does his opinion surprise you?"

"First of all, I didn't like him. I'm not sure what the hell he's referring to, but I'm happy about his view of my sharing at the meetings."

"He's saying your original symptoms of trouble getting along in civilian life, and complaining at Walter Reed followed by the dehumanization circumstances in Las Vegas, are not necessarily from the shock in Iraq that has left invisible scars.

He suggests your recovery period from the ordeal has been relatively short, even a quicker healing than many who were at ground zero on nine-eleven."

I don't get it. Is this good news?

Burkett leaned forward toward me as if he needed to verify he had my attention.

"Periods of insecurity and guilt may pre-date your military service. The usual warning signs of battle stress are diminishing in your case. Recently, I attended a mental health forum in New York City, specifically to explore all facets of your specific case with colleagues who specialize in trauma recovery and behavioral peculiarities. Even natural disasters, like Hurricane Katrina, leave an impact. That's what I want you and I to address in the future."

"If that's what you think, okay with me." I paused, and then owned up to past misdeeds. "Look, Doctor, once I joined the army I did get wild on occasion. Weekend leaves became cruising time for drinking or fighting or partying with girls. I'm not proud of myself for any of it. And it was all before my injury."

"It does sound out of character. Let me finish about the forum. An army colonel submitted a paper about a study to predict soldiers who may be disposed toward post-traumatic stress disorder and—"

"What a waste! I don't believe it's possible."

Burkett's furrowed brow revealed his reaction to my inappropriate comment. "I also heard of a program in Jacksonville, Florida called APEX that has had success with injured soldiers to regain concentration and confidence. They use computer simulations to help the men thrive in pressure situations."

Is this another blind alley? Oh heck, Master's assessment could have been a lot worse.

"I highlighted Dr. Master's comment about family—"

"Come on, Doc, all that talk by Masters was not relevant to our problems."

"Nevertheless, Drew, I'd like to delve into your past once again and your relationship with your parents. Try searching your earliest memories before our next session. Okay?"

His request was reasonable as always. I nodded my head slowly up and down. "Sorry for my outburst, Doctor," I said meekly.

"Apology accepted. Next time we'll talk about whether you should attend the group therapy session again and further treatment, including anger management. However, the fact that you're taking an interest in and enjoying activities, despite everything, is an encouraging sign we can work on going forward."

"That's fine. At the same time I'll fill you in on my first days in the mayor's office."

We shook hands. I felt a bond had been established between us.

"I don't care what Dr. Masters thinks, that house in Fallujah still has me on edge," I whispered as I drove south on Route 35.

How about Doc Burkett looking out for my welfare? He was as excited about the new job as I was. The position sounded too good to be true.

Am I qualified to perform in a service function and interact with people? I gotta control my behavior.

I'm going to take advantage of this opportunity. Money has always been a major problem for me. Money! How I wasted my military severance pay! Another sad chapter in my life.

A billboard sign for Atlantic City reminded me of Las Vegas. Why the hell did I have to see that sign and think about that stinking place again? It's like a jinx following me around. I had told Burkett all the gory details about what happened in Vegas once I finally started to open up to him, probably in our second or third session together many months ago. I admitted to him I became totally unhinged after my discharge. That discussion became the key icebreaker in our association.

* * *

"I read in the file you went to Las Vegas when you were released from Walter Reed Hospital," Dr. Burkett had said to start the session. "Can you tell me about it?"

Is he trying to trick me? This doctor's a pretty smooth talker, but not condescending like the others at Walter Reed.

"May I call you Drew?"

"Sure." *Nice friendly gesture.* "Frankly, I hate to think of my time in Vegas. Come to think of it, Doc, my early release from the hospital is a story in itself."

"First things first, Drew. It's important I know what happened in Las Vegas."

I drew a deep breath, figuring maybe it was time I got it out of my system. I'd take a chance and confide in him

"Look, Doctor Burkett, I had a lot of cash when I got my discharge papers. Living in the Bronx again without my parents was the absolute pits, to be honest. I finally ended up in the North Bronx with Irish guys who could be rowdy, but basically an okay bunch. I saw my life was going nowhere fast. So I wanted to get away from everything. Have some fun, you know. I heard guys talking trash about the gambling and girls in Vegas, so I figured why shouldn't I get some action." *At least, that's part of the story.*

"How long did you plan to stay?"

"I'm not going to tell you I planned to leave when my dough ran out, because I was always lucky at gambling. I thought it would be easy to get a job in the casinos and stay a few years at least. Caesar's Palace was my favorite haunt. I expected to make a bundle. Maybe even get married to one of those showgirls."

"So what made you decide to leave?"

I paused and recalled that no-good liar of a roomie, Scotty.

"The first five or six months were great. I shared an apartment with Scotty and two other Iraqi vets. Some wild things went on at times, you know, orgies." He shook his head, lips tightened. "Hey, I'm not proud of it. I was drunk half the time."

"Please continue."

"I had odd jobs making a few bucks and tips. I lost a small amount gambling but knew my luck would change. Blackjack was my game and I was learning to count cards like a pro."

"Sounds rather naïve, Drew. Don't you think?"

"Hell no. I practiced in our room and the guys marveled at how good I was." I sat up straight flaunting the news of my skill.

"If you were losing, why didn't you leave then?" Burkett eyed me like I was just a kid.

"I was down a few thousand bucks, but we got a great tip on a sport bet, a pro basketball game. I financed it all for the group. We expected to make a killing, like it would put us all on easy street. My roommate, that louse Scotty, took off with the dough and—"

"Why did you trust him?"

"At first he came across as an okay guy, you know, no family, down on his luck, but we treated him as a buddy. We were known as the four amigos." I threw my arms in the air in defeat. "So I was wrong. The liar didn't place the bet, and I lost all my savings. Lousy hustler."

"You never saw him again?"

"What do you think?" I growled. "I ended up on the streets begging for coffee money. What the hell, money was everywhere, and people were there to spend it for God's sake. After awhile, I suspected some creeps were following me to steal my things. Then I got into a fight with a policeman who was harassing the hell out of me." *What a sorrowful experience that was.*

Cheap wine had become a sorbet to cleanse the taste in my mouth of my own body odor.

I walked around his office like I were circling a crazed animal ...or my prey.

"Do you know what it's like to grovel?" I squinted hard at Burkett as if he were the cause of my despair.

Burkett slouched down in his chair. His perfect white teeth covered his lower lip until he sighed, "I can only imagine it."

A claustrophobic feeling gripped me in the small office, creating an *Alice in Wonderland* scene in my mind.

"All the more reason why you can hold your head up high for the resolve you have to reclaim your life," he added firmly, abruptly sitting upright to catch my attention.

"Yeah, that's the good news. Thank you." I needed his response to regain my sense of place and self-control.

"Tell me what happened next!"

"The judge said I was incoherent and held me in jail overnight. I tell you, Doc, spending the night in that holding cell was absolute hell. It's not what I wanted my life to be."

"Understood," he said in a weak voice.

"So, after checking with the military, the judge sent me back to the VA hospital in Trenton rather than keep me in a Nevada mental institution." Simply thinking about Vegas and hitting rock bottom was difficult for me. "As you know, they kept me there for five months until I became an outpatient."

"I'm glad you told me the whole story."

Dr. Burkett came across to me as truly sympathetic. How refreshing after my experiences with those demanding head doctors at Walter Reed. I swear some of them in the psych ward were off the wall themselves. That being said, the deranged major who shot up soldiers in Fort Hood, Texas is an unspeakable exception in the extreme. Whatever possessed him?

Thankfully, I have faith in Burkett. He understands the suffering I've been through and that I want to get better.

"What were you going to tell me about your early departure from the hospital?"

"It's kinda unbelievable. On the one hand, the therapy at Walter Reed was excellent, except for the first week when they placed me in a ward that was worse than the cuckoo's nest; on the other hand, living conditions were demoralizing." I scratched the back of my head recalling the contradiction. "I decided to scribble a note to the Commanding General, real polite of course, about the shabby quarters."

"Who advised you to do that?"

"I did it on my own."

"Really!"

"Next thing I know, they tell me I'm okay and will be dismissed with an Honorable Discharge."

"Well your letter certainly worked." He looked at me in amazement. "You have read about the mismanagement there, haven't you?"

"Sure. No surprise to me."

"You do have a tendency to put matters on your shoulders, Drew. Very noteworthy."

After writing notes for a minute or two, he stated, "Let me say this about your new job at Outsource Data Corporation. It's not a simple thing to manage financial affairs and live within a budget. If you need advice with take home pay, deductions, benefits and living expenses, please keep me informed and I'll suggest an advisor who can assist you. It sounds like a wonderful position."

"I appreciate that, Doc. I believe I've learned my lesson from that Vegas fiasco."

* * *

My confession to Burkett as well as the Las Vegas experience seemed like ages ago, but how I lost my money still left a bad taste in my mouth, like day-old flounder. Our relationship was on solid ground from then on, at least from my perspective.

Instead of going directly home from Burkett's office, I decided to stop at Kohl's in the Toms River Mall and pick up a blue blazer, a couple of button-down dress shirts, and two striped ties. I wanted to make a good impression and get off on the right foot in Barnegat Junction. I can't botch this chance up like I did at Outsource Data Corporation.

Too tired to even watch TV, I went straight to bed.

3:10 a.m.

"Look out!" I jerked up in bed, shaking from the same terrifying scenes as before. I saw the face of someone who looked like the new recruit in my unit.

Not again. I was sure I had undergone the last of those bad dreams.

"God, let me get rid of these demons."

Please.

CHAPTER 6

I spent Monday morning with the personnel service firm that had conducted my initial interview the previous week. Evaluated as satisfactory on my background, and based on the recommendation from Dr. Burkett, I was hired subject to the formality of a physical, which I passed at Toms River Medical Center, although those damn questions about my injuries bugged the hell out of me.

I waited in a conference room in the Town Hall of Barnegat Junction that afternoon for the mayor's right-hand man, Billy Wilcox, to finally greet me and see how I was coming along. I had to complete a stack of Civil Service and employment forms. He promised to return in thirty minutes.

The openness and high-ceiling atrium was not unexpected, given the building originally had been a book supply warehouse. A long, tile counter-top ran from left to right across the entranceway, with a cashier's cage on one end and a security sign-in at a controlled entry on the other. The left side of the atrium had ample space for expected additional staff and an emergency exit door, while four desks were placed one behind the other along the right side wall. At the rear, there were offices for the mayor, for his assistant, Mr. Wilcox, a conference room, and an unoccupied office. The mayor's secretary sat at a desk outside his office.

"Sorry I couldn't get back to you sooner," Wilcox said two hours later. "A lot going on around here today."

"I'm sure." The wall clock read 4:50.

"I'll turn over all this paperwork stuff to Miss Carswell, the mayor's secretary. Let me welcome you aboard and wish you all the best." A big smile disclosed crooked teeth, as he extended his right hand and held mine tightly. "First thing in the morning, I'll introduce you around and go over your duties."

"Great. Thank you very much, Mr. Wilcox. Goodnight."

The dawn couldn't come soon enough on Tuesday. I took extra time in the shower and noted a quiver in my hand as I shaved. My clothes had been laid out the night before, so I left the house right on time and, coincidently, ran into Wilcox entering the building ready for work.

"This is Angie Carswell," Wilcox said as he balanced a cup of coffee between report files in each hand. "She's indispensable here, so you can find out just about everything from her."

"How do you do?" *She's real pretty.*

"Nice to meet you, Drew. We go by first names here, if you don't mind. Good luck to you." Sitting at her desk, she reached up and gave my hand a gentle shake.

"Okay with me, Angie. My pleasure meeting you."

Wilcox repeated the introductions with three female clerks, each more matronly than the other. "When they're not at their desk, they work on Property Tax records, Licensing and Permits, and at the Tax Collector/Cashier window for fines and checks sent to Town Hall. The Public Works Department is located next to the Police Station and Courthouse down the street."

While the three women were equal in rank, one in particular, Lena Losonsky, was the clear extrovert and leader of the group.

Everyone seemed friendly and cooperative, well, except for Wilcox, who made me uneasy for some reason. I felt comfortable I'd fit right in. *But what about my assignment?*

"Come on in to my office," Wilcox ordered, "and we'll discuss your role."

"Yes, sir." I noticed the mayor's empty office one door down from Wilcox.

"We want you to be a jack of all trades, you know what I mean. You'll handle campaign pledge records on your PC and serve as back-up during lunch breaks and the like. Gotta treat all the taxpayers with respect." He folded his arms across his chest, clearly enjoying his influence. "Also, we may have you handle certain correspondence to relieve Angie's workload."

"Of course," I nodded. *What the heck do I do with pledge records?*

"Across the street is the law firm of Cohen & Mahoney. They're the town's legal counsel." He pointed in the direction of a storefront with a prominent shingle. "There are numerous official documents going back and forth that you will be on call to pick up and deliver."

"So I'm the runner," I said as a joke.

He stared at me, then lowered his voice for emphasis and said, "We have very important legal transactions that require safe handling. You'll be responsible for keeping them in proper order for the Mayor and Council Executive Committee meetings as well as monthly public meetings."

I nodded again, realizing the office staff must fill in the details for me to learn my jobs. Wilcox sure wasn't going to teach me much.

"Oh, Mayor Jorgenson won't be in 'til Monday. Lucky guy is attending a Mayors' Convention in Atlantic City. So Angie has the time to handle your orientation on the workings of the office." He grinned and said, "By the way, your accent is a dead give-away where you're from."

No kidding. And I'm damn proud of it.

It took the rest of the day for me to supply my desk, become familiar with the floor plan and telephone system, read office procedures related to my duties, and engage in small talk with each of the four women. Angie apologized for overloading me with manuals and the like. "Take your time, Drew. I'm happy you're here with us."

Wilcox left a memo for me stating he'd scheduled a meeting for me to meet Frederick Cohen at his office at ten on Wednesday morning.

At home that night it occurred to me I was putting on a good front about everything. In truth, I was nervous and wondered if the women detected my anxiety.

The décor and furniture of Cohen & Mahoney's entrance foyer were unimpressive; not what I expected. The half-open door to his office revealed the trappings of an attorney's workplace—a bookcase with thick legal books wall to wall up to the ceiling.

"My name is Drew Baxter. I have an appointment with Mr. Cohen."

"He's expecting you, Mr. Baxter. Go right in."

"Hello, Baxter. Turns out I have another meeting, so I'll get right to the point if you don't mind."

"Yes, sir." *I bet he was a football player.*

He looked at me from head to toe, as if I were under consideration for a male model TV commercial. "All the sealed packets you will pick up or deliver are official town documents. They're confidential between the mayor's office and my firm, as town counsel."

"Understood."

"You are not to talk to anyone about this work, including the four At-Large Councilmen. Is that clear?"

I began to stutter. "Anything you say, sir. No problem for me."

He shook my hand and led me to the door.

I waited for a line of cars to pass before crossing the street to Town Hall. Was this how lawyers conducted town business all the time? That guy wanted me to be afraid of him. What the hell was the big mystery anyway? Oh well, lemme get back for my meeting with Angie.

"That's all there is to it," Angie said, sitting next to me at my computer after explaining the donor pledge system. "You can also process mailing labels and second request letters for donations directly from the system. Wilcox needs updated donor listings periodically to review with the mayor."

"It's quite a list. I had no idea how well organized it is for a small town."

"Well, Mayor Jorgenson has won two four-year terms, so maintaining a list of contributors and friends to his campaigns has been critical to his elections, even more so now."

"How come?"

"With only two years left in this term, rumor has it he may be asked to run for state senator for Ocean County. Since the town was incorporated ten years ago, he's been the only mayor we've had. Did you know that, and that he was named in *Forbes* and *Crain's* as one of the top young entrepreneurs in the country before his interest turned to politics?"

"Impressive. No, I didn't know any of that. I can't wait to meet him and—"

"You'll get your chance first thing Monday morning. Oh, I should mention you must get the donor listings to Wilcox on time." She peeked around the office. "He can be quite demanding," she whispered.

As Angie stood to return to her desk, I said, "I appreciate your kindness. This is all new to me, of course, and all of you have definitely made me feel welcomed."

"That's great. Ask questions anytime, okay? Don't feel as if you have to become a whiz at all this over night." She smiled and touched my hand.

"Thanks, Angie."

The remainder of the day was uneventful, as I learned the

job procedures of the "three matrons", my secret codename for them.

On Thursday morning, a note on my desk from Angie asked me to take phone calls until she arrived. I listened to several recorded messages.

"Mr. Mayor, thank you for getting Sanitation to clean up the mess in the empty lot next to my house." Beep.

"Mayor Jorgenson, I'm calling to let you know my son got the part-time job we spoke of. Really appreciate it." Beep.

"Hank, the Chamber of Commerce wants to honor you for the rapid business growth in our town at the annual awards dinner. Please let us know as soon as possible." Beep.

"This is Harold Trotter. I still have a problem, Mayor, with the sale of my farm. Please call me. You have my number. This is my third try over the last two months to speak with you." Beep.

Based on his faltering voice, Trotter sounded like an old-timer. I'd make sure Angie brought this message to the attention of the mayor as soon as possible.

Next message. "Mayor Jorgenson, the traffic through town is becoming horrendous. What are you gonna do about it?" Beep.

For the next hour or so I took numerous calls, all in a similar vein conveying gratitude to the mayor or asking personal favors. It struck me how active Hank Jorgenson has been in the affairs of the residents. I felt pleased to be a new member of the mayor's staff.

Angie was due in shortly.

The phone rang. "Lemme speak to the mayor right away."

"Sorry, sir, he's not in the office today. May I—"

"Look, I need information right away about the zoning off Bay Street," said the gruff voice.

"Hold on, please." *Wilcox isn't here. What the hell do I do?*

I checked the town directory and committee assignments.

"Since this is a zoning matter, sir, you might call Councilman David Pitman. I believe he—"

The caller had hung up, evidently in a big hurry. Not a happy camper. I recalled a few complaint letters dealing with local ordinances and zoning issues. "Not all joy in Barnegat Junction," I speculated.

Angie thanked me for handling the calls.

"Wilcox holds a staff meeting every Friday morning," she informed me as I was leaving for the day. "Have a good night, Drew."

As the new guy on the block I sat in the back of Wilcox's glass-walled office as he conducted his weekly meeting. I observed his presentation style closely and judged him as unsophisticated. *I guess that's what the boss expects in his right-hand man.*

During a coffee break earlier in the week, Angie had filled me in on Wilcox's background. After graduating from Trenton State, he became a real estate agent in Princeton. Notwithstanding a rugged look and stocky build in a five-foot-four-inch frame, his success in sales of residential and commercial properties was outstanding. Angie hinted his mannerism, unlike the mayor, could be "intimidating".

"They're so dissimilar," she had said, "and he's ten years younger than the mayor. I have no idea how Jorgenson ever became associated with a person like Wilcox."

"You'll all be pleased to know the mayor's approval rating is at an all-time high," Wilcox announced with a smile. He had removed his sport jacket and rolled his shirtsleeve one turn above his wrist. "There are several hot-button items you should be alert to. First, with the population increase we're experiencing, Mayor Jorgenson will propose to the State Transportation Department a widening of 751 similar to Route 9. Next, the new Grammar School building on Pine Street will officially open next September."

There was polite clapping.

"The mayor has a meeting scheduled with a developer for new upscale homes on the west side of town."

The staff let out "oohs" and "aahs" at this information, recognizing the implication for further growth and lower tax ratables.

"The town attorney is working on several ordinances concerning smoking in public places and parking restrictions. Following this meeting I'll be with attorney Cohen and Police Chief Campbell to wrap up the details. With regard to the fiscal budget ..."

He continued to discuss subjects that went over my head, as he leaned back in his chair, hands behind his head. *I used to understand all that accounting stuff in college.* I lost track of his points and almost dozed, until I heard Wilcox address Angie.

"The mayor has informed me he is promoting you to administrative assistant," he said in a booming voice.

There were cries of approval for Angie, who seemed genuinely surprised by the news. Wilcox congratulated her and ended the meeting. Angie left surrounded by the delighted staff.

"Baxter, would you remain a minute?"

I hoped he wouldn't ask me about the issues covered in the meeting, especially the budget. *Is he going to test me?*

"Yesterday, you took a call from someone about the zoning at Bay Street. Do you know who it was?"

I thought for a second. "He didn't give me his name and—"

"And you forgot to ask. Not very smart of you."

"I'm sorry. There were so many calls and I was trying to input data to the donor file ...just didn't get a chance to ask."

"Well I know who it was," he announced in an arrogant tone. "You referred the caller to Pitman, right?"

"Yeah, but—"

"Hey, didn't you understand from Mr. Cohen that you were not to have anything to do with the councilmen?"

"Yes, but I was only trying to assist the caller speak to the right person."

"Let's get something straight right now."

He walked toward me and bent down, his face in mine. My nose twitched at the smell of coffee and cigarettes.

"This is politics, man. The mayor has political enemies and there are people who are trying to take advantage of the growth opportunities in our town. Mayor Jorgenson works like hell to keep business on the up and up."

Of course, so what's his point?

He backed away, staring at me the entire time. "You've gotta learn to do your job and keep your nose clean. Don't volunteer anything and check with the others if you're not sure who or what you're dealing with."

"Mr. Wilcox, I'm sure it won't happen again. Believe me, I do want to do a good job for the mayor."

"Okay then. That's it for now." With a casual wave, he dismissed me.

"TGIF," I whispered, driving home to Lavallette from Barnegat Junction. I'm exhausted. The work in the mayor's office was incredibly busy and admittedly confusing to me. The phones never stopped ringing.

"I've got a lot to learn," I said to myself, "but it's all manageable, except if I have to get occupied with Cohen." I hoped my screw-up on that curious phone call didn't jeopardize my job. *I sure like working in Town Hall.*

"I've gotta stop mumbling to myself. They'll think I'm crazy."

A picture of Angie scurrying about the atrium crossed my mind and refused to allow another thought in. While she wasn't a raving beauty, there was a special allure about her delicate good looks complemented by a firm, well-proportioned figure. Her green eyes virtually demanded to be noticed, like matching emeralds in a jewelry store window. She was like the girl next-door type, with class and personality. *I've got to know more about her.*

After eating at nearby Red Lobster, I was ready to hit the sack. No TV for me. As I turned on my stomach and dug my head into the soft pillow, the clock on the nightstand glared at me like a cat, and blinked 10:15 ...10:16 ...10:17.

Despite being weary from my arduous first week in a new work environment, I was restless in bed. Maybe the lobster didn't agree with me. I turned over on my back and opened my eyes. The cursed clock now read 11:52.

What was it with Wilcox? I had better stop picturing him as "Shorty" before I kid about it publically and get in trouble.

I overslept Saturday morning and felt energized to have two days off.

Rather than spend the weekend on the beach, I went to a high school football game in the afternoon between the Toms River North Mariners and the Toms River South Indians, and to the Sail Inn on 35 for fish and chips. As I chatted and listened to the local regulars, the past never entered my mind. The baseball pennant races incited a heated discussion, which reminded me of the good old days at Yankee Stadium. I slept late again on Sunday, read the *Asbury Park Press*, and took in a James Bond movie, *Casino Royale*.

The two-day interval went by quickly and I looked forward to meeting the mayor on Monday, albeit with an understandable degree of anxiety.

CHAPTER 7

Trepidation was the order of the day as I drove on rain-slick roads to Barnegat Junction on Monday morning. A restful night took the pressure off any extreme worry of my scheduled meeting with the mayor.

Shortly after 9:00 a.m., Angie motioned to me that I could go in the mayor's office.

"It's a pleasure to finally meet you, Drew," Mayor Jorgenson said after I waited for him to end a telephone conversation. "Sorry I wasn't here to welcome you last Monday."

"Thank you, sir. I'm very happy to meet you."

I was taken aback by Hank Jorgenson's lean six-foot-two frame and handsome, even rugged look. Flowing, blondish hair, large blue eyes and ruddy complexion, with a captivating smile; Brooks Brothers suit, designer tie, Ferragamo shoes fit the mold. His commanding presence reminded me of Lieutenant Munson.

"Dr. Burkett told me quite a bit about you. War hero and all you've been going through the last couple of years. You sure look like you're holding up well despite everything."

"I feel good. Thank you." *How much did Doc Burkett tell him about my background?*

"Tim is a terrific guy."

"Yes, he is. He's very professional."

"That's great." We sat at the two chairs in front of his desk. "I understand you excelled in Political Science at Rutgers. I want Billy Wilcox to give you wide exposure to what goes on in local government. We're a growing community and you're in on the ground floor with me. We can make practical use of your college education. How's that sound?"

"Mr. Mayor, I have a great deal to learn, but I thoroughly enjoyed my first week. Thank you for the opportunity." In an unassertive manner and rubbing my chin, I added, "To be honest, though, I'm not sure how much I remember from those college courses that could be applied here."

"Don't worry about that," he said, setting aside my concern. "The main thing is to appreciate that public service has its rewards and it's an honor to serve. Never forget that, Drew. Look what's happening here as an example. We're putting Barnegat Junction on the map, but it takes hard work and dedication. The voters expect a lot from their elected officials and you have to deliver or else." He glanced sideways at me as if to assure I grasped his message.

"Yes. Quite a challenge."

"Okay then. Take it one day at a time and everything will work out. Good luck to you."

Standing to close our meeting, with his hand on my shoulder, he grinned and said, "Tell you what. Why don't you come with me this afternoon to a ground-breaking ceremony for the new shopping center?"

"Love to. Thanks."

Wow! I was already participating in local government activities, and at the side of the mayor no less.

I sat at my desk absentmindedly shuffling papers. My first impression of the mayor went beyond expectation. Jorgenson oozed personality. I was a bit in awe of the man, like no one else I had met. *No wonder he's been twice elected.*

When was Angie finally coming out of his office? She's the one who could tell me more about Jorgenson. Besides, it was an excuse for me to get to know her better. "Kill two birds with one stone," I mouthed.

Angie acted and looked distinct from Lauren or Carolyn. Her silky black, shoulder-length hair parted in the middle. The twinkle in her green eyes had a kinda sexy look when she was in a playful mood. Great figure and shapely long legs, like the women in the *Victoria Secret* advertisements. She must be five-seven or so, coming up to my chin. I bet she's a great dancer. She was the smartest and friendliest person on the staff and obviously loved her job. I was certain she was not married, at least not now.

I think I'll ask her if we could meet after work some day.

Since the mayor had been away for a week, Angie's workload was heavy, so she was busy the rest of the day. At one point she waved at me and smiled, but continued typing on the computer and handling letters or files in and out of the mayor's office. Combined with the phone calls, the day was more hectic than usual. Meanwhile, I completed a catalogue of letters from residents, assisted at the property tax record counter, and updated the donor lists until departure time with the mayor. It surprised me how many relatively small contributions came from out-of-state and north Jersey.

I watched as Mayor Jorgenson mingled with the crowd at the ceremony and traded high-fives with jubilant supporters. The sun had shown through the clouds as the large crowd cheered him. He gave the impression he knew everyone, and was accessible to all. *Everything but kissing babies.* His presence overshadowed all other "dignitaries" on the raised makeshift stage. A representative from Hallmark Cards described how delighted the company was to be in the community. He turned the microphone back to the mayor, who spoke with pride of this event fitting into a grand plan for Barnegat Junction. The response from the onlookers was boisterous. The mutual affection appeared genuine.

"Who is that gentleman on the stage to the right of the mayor?" I asked Sam, the on-call limo driver. Perhaps it was my military training, but I spotted him standing aloof, displaying a disregard for Jorgenson and his speech. No handshake, no clapping, no smile.

"That's Councilman Pitman," Sam replied above the noise.

What's his problem? He looks mad at the whole thing or somebody, like this is the last place he wants to be.

As the crowd dispersed, Jorgenson huddled briefly with a few storeowners. Ignoring Pitman, he strolled back to the car, waving to all, his charming smile much in evidence.

"All in a day's work," he said as the car pulled away from the new Center. "I have big plans for Barnegat Junction, like other towns that have grown up all across America and made this country great. At the proper time, I'll let the cat out of the bag."

"That was quite a show," I volunteered, not knowing how else to describe it. Mayor Jorgenson sounded to me like a visionary. With leadership qualities as well.

"It's a matter of staying focused on the subject matter and audience at hand," he said in an unequivocal firm pitch. "You do a good turn for people and they reciprocate. If you want to be reelected, you've got to work for and appeal to your constituents. Politics is a people business, but you have to have the stomach for it and be ready to fight for your political life. You and your family live in a fish bowl."

"It must be demanding being in the public eye all the time," I offered weakly. "I don't think I have the temperament, or the desire for that matter, to be a politician."

"Don't sell yourself short, Drew. Remember, you only have to get half the voters to like you."

No way could I live with the other half disliking me.

Jorgenson was quiet now, gazing at the passing stores and shoppers, some wheeling baby carriages. I felt like I was imposing on someone contemplating a grand strategy. He seemed to be in a world all his own. His eyes would light up and just as quickly a frown darkened his face, but for only an instant. I wondered if hubris was at the core of his political passion, as is the case of most politicians. Regardless, Jorgenson had every right to be proud.

"Before you go back to the office, I'd like you to pick up some material from the lawyer's office," he said without looking at me. "Sam, stop at the curb before parking at Town Hall. Mr. Baxter will get out there."

Driving home that night I couldn't believe how fortunate I was for my new position in life. I owed a big debt of gratitude to Doc Burkett not only for my demeanor and confidence, but also for aligning me in the direction of a meaningful career path. Iraq was a distant memory. Nevertheless, an unexplained tension continued to nag me, as if I were trying to reach perfection or a task was left undone.

Am I so different than everyone else? I don't want to be out of the ordinary, but there's something forcing me to be drawn into peoples' lives.

I have an opportunity to learn a lot from Hank Jorgenson, an astute politician, and this job. It was not out of the realm of possibility that he might become governor of New Jersey some day. It would be smart to steer clear of that rude Pitman character. Maybe I'll become a politician after all and run for office. Public service wasn't the worst thing I could do with my life. Hell, I've always been inclined toward helping people. *Not too much unlike a policeman or social worker, I guess.*

A comfortable position in bed quickly placed me in another world. However, that inexplicable basketball game kept interrupting my erotic dream with Angie Carswell.

CHAPTER 8

Time flew by the next few months. Besides becoming familiar with office procedures and my duties, my daily routine included morning coffee and afternoon breaks with Angie. We discovered common interests in movies, football, national politics and novels–Nora Roberts was her favorite–that enhanced a growing, amicable rapport. Even curious glances from Lena did not inhibit our leisurely or work-related exchanges. Despite the fact office gossip can be brutal, I hoped my attraction to Angie was reciprocated.

There was one unusual occurrence during this period. Two days ago I'd received a call from Mr. Cohen just as I was about to leave for the day. He sounded cordial to me for a change.

"Baxter, please hang on until I call you back. You might have to pick up documents in town."

At 6:30 he finally called. "Listen! There's been a legal complication so it will take more time than expected. Since the other party lives near the shore where you are, I've given them instructions to deliver a packet to your home tonight. Bring it to my office first thing in the morning! Thanks for waiting around."

My doorbell rang about 8:45. I turned on the front door lights and stepped outside to greet a young man wearing a baseball cap. He stated my name, handed me a legal-size packet and departed immediately. I called out to him, "Do I have to sign anything?"

He never looked back.

As ordered, I delivered the bulky packet to Cohen & Mahoney's office before 800 a.m the next morning. "Just go with the flow," I said to myself.

Reminiscing, it occurred to me I had never been this busy, and satisfied, in my life. Totally dissimilar, of course, from the military. Even Billy Wilcox complimented my job performance. On my daily runs to the lawyer's office, Cohen was nowhere to be seen, which was a relief. Best of all, Mayor Jorgenson's friendship with me endured, despite the mounting pressure he faced governing a new community. He was primarily absorbed in legal matters, which tied up Angie and added to her responsibilities.

Arriving at work early, I learned the mayor's calendar showed he and Wilcox would be out of the office most of the next day. No Friday staff meeting for Wilcox to show off his authority ...and high-fluting style.

"How are you doing, Angie, besides staying busy," I asked with a silly grin.

"It's been unbelievable," she replied. Resting her elbows on her desk, she gave me a lazy smile. "I haven't been ignoring you, Drew. Just trying to keep up with reports and the agenda for the next Executive Committee meeting."

"I sure wish I could give you a hand."

"That's kind of you, but you've already helped me with the mail and phone calls." She ran her right hand through her hair, highlighting her pretty face and a few freckles at the tip of her nose.

"How about we go out to lunch tomorrow? You need a break and the mayor will be out of the office."

"Well, I don't ..." I saw the hesitation in her eyes until finally she smiled and said, "You know what, that sounds like a wonderful idea."

I couldn't concentrate all the next morning, looking forward to lunch with Angie. I wore a new tie with my best shirt, even used more aftershave than usual. While my heart beat faster, I wasn't worried about how we would get along. *Burkett will be proud of me when I tell him.*

"How about going to the Olive Garden up the street? We can walk to it and get back on time; plus, it's a beautiful day."

"Fine with me," she said. "I need a change from Subway sandwiches."

"I know you're familiar with my background, Angie. How about telling me more about yourself?"

"Okay. You know I grew up in Cherry Hill. Liked the Seaside Park area and beaches better than Wildwood, so I moved up here after school. Went to Katherine Gibbs, a top secretarial school in Boston, for two years thanks to my parents and—"

"Which explains why you're so professional," I interrupted.

Her eyes widened in obvious appreciation. "Thank you. I was lucky to land the job at Town Hall. Mayor Jorgenson went through several secretaries before he hired me. Although it's wild at times, I enjoy the excitement and meeting the residents in town."

I held the door as we entered the restaurant. We were seated immediately and ordered diet Cokes. While she read the menu, I gazed at her in this casual setting. I felt relaxed in her presence.

"I think I'll have the Chicken Caesar Salad," she said.

"Make it two." I handed the menus back to the waitress. "Angie, if you don't mind me asking, what do you do for fun and relaxation?"

"Let's see. I have an older married sister, Maria, who lives in Chicago with her husband and my two nieces. I like to swim, read romantic novels as well as Patterson's detective stories, and go to movies, a host of things. I volunteer at the Junior Olympics and—"

"I bet you're a good dancer."

"Yes, I love dancing. Why would you say that?"

"Oh, just a guess," I replied, picturing her gorgeous, tanned legs.

"I follow sports a lot. Played tennis in high school. As I've told you, the Philadelphia Eagles are my favorite team."

"You enjoy contact sports then," I said with a chuckle.

"Excuse me?" She arched her eyebrows at me.

It was only an innocent comment. *Did I upset her*?

"That's probably from your high school days," I added as a clumsy attempt to soften the point. "Were you a cheerleader?"

"No." She glanced around the room, seemingly to ignore me, and then leaned forward resting her elbows on the table. "Can I ask you one question?"

"Only one? Sure." I took a drink of water, wondering if I was making a good impression.

"I admit to scanning your physical examination records. Was Iraq as bad as the scenes we see on TV?"

Although I expected she'd raise the issue eventually, my mind went blank. I forced a cough, uncertain of her views on the war.

"When you see soldiers on patrol through the streets, there are usually kids around and the adults are generally friendly. Sometimes we kicked a soccer ball back and forth. The unexpected is the problem. One minute you're walking along with your buddies, the next minute there's chaos and someone gets hurt."

"That must have been an awful mental strain."

"You're so right. That was the horrible part."

The food was served. *Perfect timing*. We ate in silence for several minutes. She smiled when she caught me gazing at her. It surprised me how at ease I felt with her. How is it possible she was on her own? Or was she?

"Do you like to travel?" I asked to restart trivial talk.

"I went to the Bahamas in May with ...er, yes I do. I'd love to visit places like Rome and Paris."

I felt a weakness in the pit of my stomach. Who was she with? A boyfriend? Oh, not again.

"Are you okay? You look like you just saw a ghost." She reached out and touched my hand.

"I'm alright. The anchovy didn't agree with me." My hand shook as I sipped more water causing drops on my chin.

"Drew, you should know that I'm coming off a bad situation with someone. I made a mistake and ..." Her innocent face faded away to a mask of gloom.

"Hey, there's no way it could have been your fault. If there's anything I've learned from my military experience, it's that I'm able to spot sincere people and those who are not. You're a friendly, straightforward woman without an inconsiderate bone in your body."

"That's sweet of you, but you've only recently met me. There's a lot more to it." She bit her lower lip.

Before I could comment, the waitress arrived to remove the plates and then pour two cups of decaf coffee.

I figured it was appropriate to change the subject. "How did you learn all there is to know about your job?"

She squinted as she reflected on my question. "Well, I did go to two civil service classes, one on local government personnel assignments and one related to newly-incorporated towns. Barnegat Junction falls under the Small Municipality form of government with less than twelve thousand people. It wasn't hard to adapt specific procedures to our town, particularly with the support of Mayor Jorgenson. He put up with my on-the-job learning."

She's smart as a whip.

"He's a fascinating man, alright," I acknowledged. "Not surprising he would succeed in business. Do you know his background?"

"His fortune was made when he sold his computer chip business to a Japanese company. Don't repeat this, but I believe he's been divorced twice. He moved from Toms River to property he owned off Route 751 at the same time the incorporation process was underway. When he ran for mayor, he outsmarted the former mayor with his aggressive vision for growth of Barnegat Junction. Won by a wide margin, too. I understand ..."

As Angie continued, I detected her admiration for Hank Jorgenson, which had been evident to me in the day-to-day office interactions. I wondered if there was a latent affection for the mayor.

When the waitress handed us the checks, Angie said, "This has been fun."

As she pushed herself away from the table, I abruptly jumped up, shoved the waitress out of my way, and rushed to the table directly behind Angie. I grabbed a middle-aged stout woman in distress and held her upright to perform the Heimlich maneuver. Her chair overturned, and knives and forks clang to the floor.

"Stop!" her husband shouted to me. "You're hurting her."

I immediately backed away.

"She's an asthmatic having an allergic reaction," he scowled at me while he removed an inhaler from her purse.

The woman's wheeze tapered off. Patrons stared at her and me as a waiter scurried to check out the problem.

"Sorry," I mumbled. "I thought ..." My lips moved, but no words came out.

I picked up both checks as Angie stood to leave.

She looks more embarrassed than I am.

As soon as we reached the sidewalk, she turned to me, eyes widened, but trying not to make a scene to a passersby. "My God, are you always that impulsive? And ...and so frantic?"

"Angie, I was trained to deal with people at risk. I honestly thought she was choking and couldn't breathe. You know, bright red face, hands flailing, gagging, all that."

"But you could have taken a second to ask her husband if you could be of assistance."

I gulped. My mouth went dry. "Right," I admitted in defeat. "That's what I should have done."

Walking rapidly back to work we chatted about the weather and some of the funny calls or requests from residents. Laughter, although forced, came easy on that topic. I was sure the incident was still on her mind and wondered what it would take for her to overlook the matter. It surprised me how much her opinion of me mattered. I sure didn't want to end our rapport because of a asinine mistake.

Town Hall was a modest one-story structure in the center of Barnegat Junction. Limited parking was available in front of this municipal building, but there was ample parking space in the back. Ten steps led to a wide front entrance, flanked by Roman columns, which added prestige to the original drab look of the location.

I halted at the first step and turned to face her. "If I'm not interfering with your plans for the weekend, would you like to get together?"

"Actually, I've got a lot to do, so I'll be busy the entire weekend."

"I understand."

"Maybe some other time." She took two steps, halted for a second as if to add an explanation, and then continued to the front door.

Lena, the oldest of the clerks, gave us a suspicious glance as we entered the atrium.

Sitting at my desk, I suddenly felt the blood draining out of me. I needed fresh air. I reversed my steps and found myself at the top step of the building entrance, all the while berating my performance in the restaurant and in front of Angie. Staring down the ten steps, I wobbled from fear of fainting and my mind blacked out, maybe for a nanosecond. The smoky sight of that house in Iraq and those ten steps directly below made me tremble.

I really blew it with Angie.

I hid behind the Roman column ...and puked.

My nerves were still on edge during the drive home from work. A wind-swept drizzle added to my dark mood. *Why is it that dull, dank days cloud the mind as well as the sky?* Other drivers seemed to be blowing their car horn at me, but I could care less.

I drove directly into my garage. The car motor was still running when I hit the remote to close the garage door. Random visions of my past whizzed through my head like the fast-forwarded frames of a movie.

Five seconds. Ten seconds ...

"No!"

I turned the ignition off and fumbled with the remote before pushing the green button. I used the side of the car to steady myself toward the creaking, sluggish garage door.

"Open up!"

Crawling on all fours onto the driveway, the night air triggered a coughing spell, which somehow cleared my mind as well. *I can't let this happen. Not again, God.*

Following a cold shower, a peaceful relief came over me. I decided not to tell Doc Burkett about this urge, fearful he might commit me to Walter Reed or a VA hospital. *Can't cope with that once more.*

11:30 p.m. that night.

Lying on my back in bed with my hands clasped behind my neck, I stared at the slowly rotating ceiling fan.

What's wrong with me? Everything I do gets screwed up. Maybe I should re-up in the army, except the freaking headaches come back just thinking about it. "Fallujah, what a pitiful place!"

I labored to scratch an itch in the small of my back.

I gotta do better at work and make an impression on Angie. That's it. That's what I must focus on. I know it'll work out if I just apply myself and act normal. I'm not a bad person and I'm not a coward.

I yawned and turned on my side. Maybe tomorrow would be different,

CHAPTER 9

"**Y**ou don't look well, Drew," Dr. Burkett said, observing my somber, pale appearance. "Are you okay?"

"I've got a lot on my mind, Doctor Burkett, so I'm glad I could see you this morning." It was the first time we were together on a Saturday.

"Just take your time, I'm free all morning." He placed the pendulum clock on the floor out of sight.

"First, I've tried to think back about any meaningful events with my parents like you asked me to do. Trivial things, you know, when I was caught smoking or my first drink, school grades and the like. We argued once when they didn't allow me to go with my friends on a skiing trip and—"

"Did you hold it against them?"

"Naw, in fact, one of my buddies broke his ankle. Regardless, I forgot the whole thing right away. Despite how I acted outside our home, I wasn't a rebellious kid."

"Please go on."

"One lesson I learned the hard way was acting selfish in school or with friends. Dad chastised me good, you know what I mean."

"Teaching values," he nodded his approval.

"I often heard my dad tell my mother of his experiences as a social worker. It was obvious how much pleasure he gained engaged with people in need. Also, he spoke highly of President Reagan for the fall of the Berlin Wall and how that gave millions of people freedom. Made me watch those great scenes on TV."

"So he wanted you to be aware of local and world events and the lives of other people. Sounds like he took a keen interest in your well-rounded development. "

"Yes, he did. Oh, on the other hand, there was tension when my grandmother lived with us. Frankly, she was a crabby old person who drank heavily."

"How did you feel about that?"

"It made me mad, seeing that my mother was always on edge. Her quality of life was not the best. Often crying."

"So what happened?"

"Well, that made my father real angry too, so they would argue and I ended up getting into it with him. I couldn't understand why he defended my grandma, his mother-in-law, all the time. He ..." Tears welled up and streamed down my face.

"What is it, Drew?"

"I don't know. I just can't talk about it. Please don't ask me!"

"Drew, does this have anything to do with your father's accident?" He leaned forward as if I were speaking too softly.

His question brought the tragedy to a head. *It's time I get it off my chest.*

"Mom and I had remained at the kitchen table after dinner discussing Grandma's drinking problem for the umpteenth time." I began to choke up. "Dad said he had a headache or the flu and went up to change for bed. I showed my frustration by raising my voice to her. It wasn't the first time, dammit, and—"

"How old were you?"

"Fourteen."

"What happened then?"

"He heard me shouting at my mother and came running back downstairs." I put my hand over my mouth. "I yelled back at him. And he ..."

"He tripped. Is that what happened?"

I could only nod my head, as the shocking sight overwhelmed me. I felt I was imploring Burkett for forgiveness.

"Why don't we take a break?" He led me to the bathroom outside his office. "It was an accident, you hear me, Drew. It was not your fault."

Returning to the couch in his office, I was still shaky, but had my wits about me. For some reason I accepted Burkett's conclusion more than the police who had investigated my father's death and reached the same judgment.

"Is there anything you want to tell me about your job after the first few weeks in Barnegat Junction?"

I welcomed the clever change of subject. "Up until yesterday, it was perfect. I enjoy the work and I'm very busy all the time. The people are nice and I've been accepted, especially by one young lady, and even the mayor. You sure sold Mayor Jorgenson on me."

"Not at all," he said with a quizzical look. He shrugged his shoulders. "So tell me, what went on yesterday that changed your view?"

I recounted to him the incident in the restaurant and surmised what Angie must have thought.

"I'd be quite surprised if she holds it against you," he offered. "How was it left between you?"

"I think, and hope, she'll put it behind us. After all, we have a friendly working interaction." My response to Burkett was more of a prayer than an opinion.

I closed my eyes for an instant and clasped my hands. "There's another matter, Doc. As I stood outside Town Hall at the top step staring out at traffic, my nightmare suddenly reappeared like a fog lifting before my eyes. The round object came so close to me I could almost touch it." I wiped away perspiration that coated my forehead.

"What else could you see?"

"I felt myself floating to the foot of the ten stairs and looking back up. The object kept getting closer and rolling on the stairs and—"

"Hold it! Stairs did you say? Were there stairs?" He sounded like a prosecuting attorney pressing for a confession.

I fell back on the couch, straining to distinguish the scene and terminate the vision.

Am I hallucinating?

"Are there stairs, Drew?" He held my shoulders rigid, intensifying my focus. "Please concentrate!"

His questioning jolted my visualization of the scene. "Yes, stairs and ...and the round ball. Background objects. Oh God. My father's looking straight at me. Reaching out. Oh no, no." I buried my head into a corner of the couch at the horror.

Burkett sat next to me and held my hands in a secure grip. "It's alright, Drew. It's over. You've allowed it to come to the surface."

Dubious about his conclusion, the shrewd analysis astounded me. Doc wasn't about to let go connecting my subconscious to how my father met his death.

My head drooped to my chest. I was emotionally wasted, but was able to rally my energy due to his genuine consolation. I needed to be excused to go the bathroom again. When I returned, my blood pressure was back to normal.

"Doctor Burkett, what does it all mean?"

"Listen carefully! For the present, I'll just give you a short, non-technical observation of your condition. The assault in Iraq brought out feelings of grief and guilt, rightly or wrongly. Your subconscious had suppressed a stronger guilt complex from the death of your father. Your brain subordinated the more recent military action to the family tragedy, which forced the concealed culpability to resurface in your dreams."

"So?" I hungered for an answer that made sense.

"So, the overriding issue now is why you have feelings of

guilt in the first place, as opposed to any actual guilt, and, more importantly, what drives you to act in a compulsive manner." He double-underlined the note in his pad.

His voice had notes of frustration and challenge. He searched my eyes and face as if I were a painting.

I looked at him stone-faced.

"Without exploring more details at this moment, the focus of your treatment requires a new approach. Today we touched the surface of your complex background." He turned away from me and searched his blackberry. "Here it is. I have a good friend who is an excellent clinical psychologist. This may be the right time for you to see him in the future and—"

"Please, Dr. Burkett, you know me and have improved my attitude over the last months. I beg you to continue as my doctor."

"Fine, if you wish. I just wanted to give you an option."

"One more thing. Will I continue to endure those nightmares?" I awaited his answer or opinion as if my life depended on it.

Wrinkles lined his brow He scratched his head. "With regard to guilt feelings pertaining to your father, I do not believe so."

The sound of my long sigh resonated throughout the small office.

<h1>CHAPTER 10</h1>

During Angie's visit to her sick mother on Monday and Tuesday, I bided my time, subduing my eagerness to strengthen our rapport. I had to speak privately with her, anxious to let her in on Dr. Burkett's news.

Since Saturday, I had reflected on the dramatic revelation and diagnosis of Dr. Burkett. While the full implication of his preliminary evaluation eluded me, I felt a weight had been lifted to the point where I wanted to broadcast my mental health to all. Although I recognized further development of my comprehension skills was necessary, the daily grind seemed more controllable. I simply felt better about myself.

Life is good. Well, pretty good.

Now I had to gain the affection of Angie.

"How have you been doing, Drew?"

Startled by Angie's welcome, I swung around toward her and grinned from ear to ear. I actually felt my heart skip a beat. *Should I tell her I care for her and want to start all over?*

"Hey, Angie, good to see you. How is your mom doing?"

"She's much better, thanks." A look of relief lit up her face. "Any problems or questions about your work the last two days?"

"It's coming along okay, I think. But I've sure missed getting to see and talk to you every day." I kept a serious look, hoping to detect her reaction to my subtle flirtation.

"How nice," she said without emphasis. "The mayor left me a bunch of instructions, so I'll be tied up for most of the day."

"Can I ask you something?"

"Of course."

"Actually, I wanna tell you …it's personal."

"Look, I don't think you and I should—"

"Angie, you read my medical history, didn't you? I just wanted to let you know some good news I received from my doctor."

She started to turn away, halted, and eased into the chair next to my desk. "I didn't mean to pry," she said, "it's just that I had heard the mayor and Wilcox talking about you, and I guess your military experience fascinated me."

"No need to apologize. That's why I believe you'll be happy to hear what I have to say."

"If it's important to you—"

"It is. How about we have coffee on the back patio this afternoon?"

"You are persistent." A slight smile curled her mouth. "Sure. Say about three o'clock."

Burkett was right as usual. She doesn't seem upset with me about the restaurant incident, so I'll avoid that subject.

"That's not the way it's done, Drew," Lena said to me before lunchtime. "Remember, you havta cross-check the lot number to the property tax file."

"Sorry, Lena, somehow I always forget that step each time."

"How we doing here?"

Over my shoulder, an inquisitive Billy Wilcox interjected himself in my training. As we were speaking, a female resident approached the Property Tax Record.

"We're just reviewing the procedure again, Mr. Wilcox," Lena answered. "He's starting to pick it up."

"Looks like you'll have to pay a lot more attention to all this, Drew," Wilcox said. He nodded approvingly to Lena.

"I'll work on it," I acknowledged uncomfortably.

I felt the resident's eyes peering at me as she tapped the

counter for service. My frustration at Lena and Wilcox rose a degree or two. *Calm down.*

As Wilcox walked away, someone burst through the front door and the security gate.

"I want to see the mayor right away," a man called out.

Based on his thinning grey hair, frail features and stooped shoulders, I guessed the man was in his mid to late seventies.

Wilcox marched directly to the man, grabbed his arm, and led him into his office. I couldn't make out the name Wilcox mumbled.

While the disruption was fleeting, ordinary activity ceased. The staff and the resident gawked at the glass-walled office to observe the confrontation, straining unsuccessfully to hear the conversation. I wondered if I should take charge and encourage the staff to resume their duties. As I walked toward Angie, I saw Wilcox pointing and shaking his finger at the old gentleman.

Meanwhile, the impatient resident departed, mumbling, "Typical bureaucratic incompetence."

"Who is that with Wilcox?" I whispered to Angie.

"That's Mr. Trotter."

Where had I heard that name before? Oh yeah. He's the gentleman who left a message to speak to the mayor. Three times no less.

"Do you have any idea what he wants? Sure seemed upset."

She shook her head. "No, but I know he's had a disagreement with Councilman Pitman and the mayor in the past."

"What about?"

"I don't know all the details," she replied, moistening her lips. "It had to do with a complicated eminent domain issue. There was an article in the paper last year that reported on a public meeting concerning Trotter's property and the mayor, and—"

The door to Wilcox's office opened and a downcast Mr.

Trotter shuffled out. He headed straight for the exit, unaware all eyes were watching him. I had a strong urge to reach out to the old guy, but figured it might affect my job. Nevertheless, I thought Wilcox was obnoxious, treating the old man with disrespect regardless of the reason.

Wilcox closed his door and, standing with his back to the inquisitive staff, he picked up his phone.

On impulse, I casually walked out of the building to track down Trotter. At his slow gait, he was only a half block away from Town Hall. I caught up to him with an easy jog.

"Sir, will you be okay?"

He turned and looked at me, then waved his hand from side to side. "I'm fine," he said, a touch of annoyance in his voice.

"I just wondered if you were alright after your meeting with Mr. Wilcox."

"That's nice of you to ask." He put his hand on my shoulder. "Son, I'm an old cranberry farmer who had to give up the farm that's been in my family for generations. My great-grandfather, Gus Trotter, started working that very land."

There was no question of the pride in his background. "I'm sorry to hear that. Why did you give it up?"

"A combination of things. An early frost the last two years. The floodgates of the reservoir were closed. My bad health during the planting season. Because of all that and legal trickery, they cheated me on the price."

While he rambled on from one issue to another, I thought it best not to ask any further questions. He became more perturbed the longer he spoke.

"Good luck," I said to him, as he turned to leave in mid-sentence.

The remainder of the day at my desk was business as usual. Ten minutes before my afternoon break with Angie, my phone rang.

"Drew, come on in and see me," said Wilcox, sounding solemn.

"Sure thing."

Motioning to me to close the door and sit in front of his desk, he scanned papers on his desk, ostensibly in deep thought. I wondered if he had a new assignment for me, or criticism of my performance. *Is Wilcox another George Parker out to bug me?*

"Let me get right to the point." He hunched forward, elbows flat on the desk and head resting on his hands.

I almost laughed at the sight of Shorty Wilcox's head seemingly affixed to the desk. A modern Napoleon. While he didn't chomp on cigars, Wilcox came across to me as the stereotype portrayal of a wheeler-dealer politician.

"Do you know the gentleman who left earlier today?"

"No ...well, Angie told me his name is Trotter, but I've never seen him before," I said in a composed tone, withholding the fact I had spoken to him.

"Correct. The poor man has a problem and he wants me and the mayor to provide advice and financial aid. It's a complicated matter that pertains to real estate transactions. Trotter feels he was cheated on the sale of his property."

"Really?"

"It turns out someone tricked him by making the price of the property erroneously based on eminent domain. Do you know what eminent domain means?"

"Sure. It's when the government acquires property over the rights or objection of the landowner and—"

"The property is needed for public use and the good of the community, and fair compensation is offered to the owner by the way," he roared. "How the hell do you think roads are constructed, pipelines are laid and shopping centers built?"

"I heard that the shopping center I accompanied the mayor to a couple of weeks ago was acquired by eminent domain."

"Did you also hear that the area was blighted. Look

what the mall has done for the economic development and aesthetics now!"

"Mr. Wilcox, wait! I'm not opposed to the concept of eminent domain." *What's his problem?*

He sat back and smiled. "I'm sure you're not. When you have the responsibility to run a town, you need tools to accomplish all the things the citizens want." He walked around and sat on the corner of the desk facing me. "So, do you know what actually happened to Mr. Trotter? And who deceived him?"

I held my palms up. *How the hell do I know?*

"I'll tell you. His complaint is against Councilman Pitman who advised his client, Mr. Trotter, he had no choice but to accept the lower value for the land."

The tone of his accusation had a trace of antagonism, as if I had to also share in the disparagement of Pitman. I wasn't sure what I was supposed to say and was more confused than ever why he'd told me about it.

He stood, signaling our meeting was over. "Now you know why we've suggested that you avoid contact with our councilmen."

Back at my desk, I saw Angie look my way, but I shook my head in the negative concerning our get-together. The meeting with Wilcox consumed my thoughts. I tried to rationalize why he invited only me to learn of Trotter's problem. Perhaps, everyone else already knew ...or he wanted to reemphasize my link to councilmen. After what I saw of Pitman at the groundbreaking ceremony, it didn't surprise me that he had a chip on his shoulder. Maybe this explained why he disliked the mayor and visa-versa. Chances are it's the last time this issue would come up as far as I was concerned. *Although I wonder.*

I overheard Lena say that Angie was leaving early, so I decided to write her a note.

Dear Angie,

Sorry I couldn't get away to have our talk. Is there any way we might meet this weekend? Maybe at the beach followed by a bite to eat. Gives you some needed relaxation time as well. I do want to tell you the news from my doctor. Let me know tomorrow, okay?

Sincerely,
Drew (your pupil)

I no sooner had placed the note on her desk than Angie emerged from the bathroom. I watched her read the note, twice. She glanced toward me and clearly mouthed, "Yes, yes."

I felt like climbing on my desk and doing a dance. It hit me that this is what the good life is all about. *If I don't screw it up.*

CHAPTER **11**

We were fortunate to get a somewhat quiet corner table on Saturday night in the Sail Inn restaurant away from the locals, who were absorbed in their usual banter on sports and politics.

"I love the ambiance of this place," Angie said to me. "Just what you'd expect to see at the shore."

"Glad you like it." I ordered a California Merlot for her and my usual, an O'Doul's.

The day had gone perfectly. For the first time I got a glimpse of Angie carefree and playful. We took advantage of the warm September afternoon on the beach. I believe she felt as comfortable as I did, enjoying the ocean air and our companionship while making small talk. She even went for a dip in the ocean up to her waist. Boy, can she ever model a bathing suit!

As she caught her breath after sprinting back from the surf and rested on a beach blanket, I couldn't hold in my news any longer. Once I confided to her Dr. Burkett's opinion about guilt feelings and controlling my behavior, withholding from her the details of my father's death however, she was sincerely elated.

"That's wonderful news." She held my hand and kissed my cheek. "I'm so happy for you to be free of the strain you've endured and—"

"Well I'm still on medication, and therapy with Dr. Burkett will continue, but I feel more secure than ever with my life." I paused to ponder my next admission. "It wasn't too long ago that I was so messed up I had monologues with myself. I—"

"You don't have to tell me anymore. That's not the Drew I know. So I understand." With a sympathetic nod, she volunteered, "And you're doing so well at work."

Coming from her, the remark didn't sound patronizing.

We sat in silence watching the high tide come closer and closer, as the setting sun no longer warmed our backs. I draped my windbreaker around her back and put my arm over her shoulders to shield her from the late afternoon breeze. All too soon, it was time to get ready for dinner. We returned to my home to change clothes.

The drinks arrived and we touched glasses, toasting our jobs and friendship. I had the feeling I was the most important person in her life. After seeing her most days in a sweater, or blouse with a vest, and skirt, she looked striking in a blue dress cut low at the neck. *What a knockout!*

"I'd like to add to our conversation on the beach, if you don't mind. There's another explanation for my improved outlook and hopefulness."

"Oh." Her raised eyebrows gave away her curiosity.

"Ever since I met you, there's been a glimmer of optimism in my life that didn't exist before. I look forward to seeing your pretty face each morning and something's missing when you're not—"

"I don't know what to say," she said.

Even her blushing drew me to her. *Irresistible.*

"Yes, I do like you and you are a special person, but—"

"Angie, I know you've only known me a short time. It's just that I wanted you to understand how I felt. This is not a childish crush."

"I'm very moved by your affection. Remember though, I told you at our luncheon about an earlier hurtful relationship that—"

"Look, I don't have to know anything about that. The only thing I'll say is if the other guy cared for you as much as I do, it would never have ended." Without any forethought, I blurted out, "My love would never fade."

She sat back, shoulders down. She was trembling as her right hand concealed her eyes. I thought she might cry. An uneasy feeling broke my self-confidence. Did I come on to her too strong and too fast?

The waiter showed up for our food order. I waived him off while we read the menu. She whispered she'd have the salmon. I selected the crab cakes and gave the waiter our orders.

"If I've said anything wrong or made you feel uncomfortable, I'm truly sorry." I shifted my body as far forward in my chair as I could. "I guess I wanted to share the status of my health with someone and you're the only one I—"

She raised her hand to interrupt and took a deep breath, obviously struggling with what she would say. I watched her with my heart in my throat, now afraid I might hear words of rejection.

"Drew, you didn't say anything wrong and ...and I'm struck by your openness and sensitivity. I've had my guard up so I would ignore advances from anyone." She reached out to hold my hand. "Right from the first time I met you, I've admired you to the point where I had to control my emotions."

She admires me. Awesome.

"I can understand you had to set up defenses to avoid another predicament, so I'm not surprised—"

"Let me finish what I started to say," she said softly. "I didn't want to get involved with anyone so soon, and you don't know everything about me."

"I know what qualities are important and I've seen how you interact with others. From the first day I met you, I knew you were special."

"Drew," she whispered.

"Yes."

"No one has ever told me they love me the way you did. I believe it came from your heart."

"Angie, this is serious for me."

As she held her breath and placed her hand over her mouth again, the food arrived. We ate in silence pretending to listen to the raucous arguments between Yankee and Met fans at the now crowded bar.

"Would you like coffee and desert?" I asked.

"No thanks."

She looked self-conscious. *She's shy.*

"Drew, I do like you a lot."

"It's time we go back to my place," I said gently. I stood and put my arm around her shoulder as she came close to me.

"Let's go," she sighed.

The difference between intimacies based on love matched against raw sex exceeded my expectations in a profound way. Thrilling. Emotions I had not felt in years, if ever, poured out of me. As we undressed each other, I was spellbound at the shape of her body and the white smoothness of her skin. Her touch warmed my body and soul.

She turned on the nightstand lamp. "Drew, let me see the injury I read about in your employment papers?"

As she lightly ran her fingers down the scar on my leg, my concern that it was repulsive proved to be unfounded. Her touch upgraded the doctor's prescription. Our first consummation of love came shortly thereafter.

"Is this when I'm expected to have a cigarette?" I teased.

She giggled. Like two kids, we laughed aloud as she tickled me on the back of my neck.

After lowering the bedroom air conditioning, she slid under the covers next to me and said, "That's a picture of your parents on the credenza, isn't it?"

"Yep."

"I can see the resemblance with your father. Youthful-looking innocent face, high forehead. Did he have blue eyes, too?"

"I honestly don't remember. I can say he was a wonderful dad."

"This bachelor hangout is not too bad at all," she said, her eyes scanning the room. "You're a lot smarter and more independent than expected."

"Is that so? What makes you say anything like that?"

"Oops, I shouldn't have said that. Sorry."

"Now you have me wondering." I leaned my elbow on the pillow and awaited her response.

"Well, before your first day at work, I overheard Wilcox say to the mayor that, because of your head injury, you would be slow to pick up the procedures and be in awe of the workings of government. I heard them laugh about it."

"You're kidding. They've never mentioned that to me. Why the hell did they laugh?" I reflected on her remark. "On second thought, Wilcox kinda insinuated that it would take more time for me to pick up governmental procedures, but—"

"Don't let it worry you. As far as I'm concerned you've done great at work and I certainly know you better than anyone else."

Later, I was exhausted and Angie fell off to sleep. I lay on my side facing her. Perhaps all my misfortunes in the past were erased in one night with this wonderful woman. The future seemed bright and I had never been happier.

I tried to sleep, but couldn't get Wilcox's statement out of my mind. Is that why he didn't want me talking to the council members? Strange! Why was it necessary to inform me about the problem with Trotter? Did Doc Burkett actually spout everything about me? What happened to doctor-patient confidentiality?

I'll prove to them I'm not slow. Angie certainly doesn't think so.

I'm not paranoid, but I have to find out what they expected and why they hired me in the first place.

The same basketball game at the Rutgers gym appeared in my sleep. Very hazy this time.

Who is that with me?

CHAPTER 12

A ngie and I agreed to keep the lid on our relationship at work. We devised hand signals to communicate our feelings for one another. I felt like a third-base coach and had to take care she wouldn't bust out laughing for no apparent reason. I had doubts my pent-up emotions could wait for the weekend, but accepted it had to be that way "for my sake," she had said.

The proverbial light bulb finally went on in my head at work. My grasp of the job improved to the point where I inquired about handling additional assignments. Wilcox gave me a quizzical look and said, "We'll see." He cast his head back signaling for me to come closer and held my elbow. "We're happy with the job you're doing. Just continue to be a team player and you'll be rewarded. Take my word for it."

This job is not rocket science, for Pete's sake. Or am I becoming overconfident? Maybe it's an escape from past doldrums! Will I be rewarded by a raise or promotion?

On the pretext my Ford Taurus needed servicing, the staff knew I would not show up for work until after lunch on Friday. My bewilderment about Wilcox's comment concerning my learning ability and my natural curiosity refused to let it go away. It led to a plan to get some answers by starting with old man Trotter's dilemma. It still bothered the heck out of me how the old guy was treated ...and I did nothing about it.

There were few people in the Toms River Public Library after the 9:30 opening. First, I picked up a book on New Jersey's history. A major industry in the state has been cranberry farming dating back to the 1800's, and NJ was third in the nation in cranberry production, primarily in Ocean, Atlantic and Burlington Counties. The cultivation required wet marshy land with sand and a peat soil base, prevalent in the famous Pine Barrens, or Pinelands, of Central Jersey. Floodgates from local reservoirs controlled the flow of water to the bogs. Planting began in April and harvesting ran from Labor Day to the end of October.

"Interesting! Cranbury Township is on the northern edge of the Pinelands and has no cranberry farm." Wow! The Inn in the historic downtown area was alleged to be a stop on the Underground Railroad.

I located the section of the library containing back issues of newspapers, following up on Angie's informative tidbit. It took me fifteen minutes to find the weekly issue of the *Toms River Times* that referred to the mayor, Pitman and Trotter on page six, which contained news and social events of Barnegat Junction. I sat in the back of a spacious room so as not to be disturbed.

At the recent public meeting of the Mayor and Council, a local resident, Harold Trotter, raised an issue regarding the sale of his cranberry farm, which, he understood from local officials, would be acquired by eminent domain. A lengthy discussion followed.

Councilman Pitman claimed the property in question was originally to be acquired via eminent domain for the purpose of widening Route 751 to relieve traffic congestion heading to the Jersey shore at the Toms River-Princeton connection.

The mayor's position was that an opportunity presented itself to purchase the property from Mr. Trotter at a fair market appraisal without waiting for the extended period necessary to obtain approvals for widening 751, which has lowered the Town's property tax rates. He cited the long delay at the state level in the consideration of widening Route 9, a much publicized, higher priority project. As a result of a negotiated agreement between the Town and Trotter, he added, Condemnation documents on Trotter's land were never filed with the Circuit Court in Toms River.

Trotter claimed he had been misled. He pointed at Councilman Pitman and proclaimed, "Your law firm gave me bad advice." Before Pitman responded, Mr. Cohen, the town attorney, informed Mr. Trotter and those in attendance that, "The matter was a good-faith transaction marked by just and fair compensation at the time, and that it met standard business conduct for real estate dealings."

Mr. Trotter has not been available for further comment.

Councilman Pitman later explained that his firm had represented Trotter for only this transaction, fully two months prior to the negotiated settlement, and their advice was based on the Town's intended filing under eminent domain. He further stated that Trotter discharged his firm verbally before the transaction took place, and that he recused himself from consideration of Trotter's property.

Once the town acquired the parcel, the zoning of the land changed from farm usage to commercial. The land was subsequently sold, at a substantial profit to the town, to the Outsource Data Corporation, a Philadelphia data service company, that constructed an attractive two-story building on the property located in...

"Oh my God." I sat back and clasped my hands behind my neck. First of all, I thought my old company was located in Toms River. Second, was this a weird coincidence for me or what?

Driving back to Town Hall, I mulled over the news article. If the finger of blame pointed at Pitman, why had Trotter continued to bother the mayor about his problem? I guess Wilcox gave me the straight scoop about Pitman's involvement in all this, although I still didn't know why he told me. What the hell? Why should I care about what had happened? I'd just work harder and do the best job I could. My main purpose now was a life with Angie.

Rather than wait until Saturday, Angie showed up at my place unexpectedly on Friday night. I ordered a pizza and we watched an old movie, "The Firm", until midnight. The intimacy we shared was like a breath of fresh air for me. I had a flashback to a college course reciting Elizabeth Barrett Browning's poem, *How do I love thee? Let me count the ways,* which came alive magically. I visualized the words of each line as if they were my own.

Lying in bed next to her, I stared at the ceiling fan reflecting on how I had spent countless nights discouraged and depressed about my life. In so short a time everything had changed beyond my wildest expectations.

"You're deep in thought," Angie said as she snuggled up to me.

"I was thinking about my mom and dad."

"Why so sad?"

I rolled over with my back to her and closed my eyes. "I didn't tell you one aspect of what Doc Burkett observed about me. My dad's accident was partly my ..." I began to shake.

"Oh Drew, I knew there was more to your guilt complex than you confided to me on the beach. I'm sure it truly was an accident and not your fault. Isn't that what the doctor concluded?" She leaned over and rested her cheek against mine.

Her comfort was the proper antidote, as effective as any medication. I realized my past grieving was selfishly for me, not my father ...nor my mother.

"I can only imagine how devastating the accident must have been for your mother."

That thought made me twinge. If a conscience had flesh and blood, the ache would be unbearable. *I miss my mother and her last days.*

I put my arms around Angie and held her tight. My entire being was locked up in the all-to-brief moment.

I returned from the kitchen with two diet Cokes.

"Drew, you've told me many times how I've made you so happy. Well, your influence on my life has been just as significant."

Except for the ticking clock and sipping our drinks, the room was quiet as we were lost in reliving the pleasure of our liaison.

"Is everything okay with your car?"

"What?" I asked without a clue.

"How did the servicing of your car go?" she asked again. "I missed you this morning."

"I intended to tell you about it tomorrow."

"So what's the big deal? Tell me about it now!"

"Angie, I went to the Toms River library this morning."

Her chin protruded forward as she gawked at me. "What in the world for?"

"I remembered you told me there was a story in the paper concerning the mayor and Mr. Trotter."

"Right. So?"

"I just had to find out more about Trotter's problem in order to—"

"To what?" she interrupted rudely. "It isn't any of your business. I thought you felt the same way."

"I didn't get a chance to tell you but, for no real reason, Wilcox filled me in on the issue with Trotter the day he showed up at Town Hall demanding to see the mayor. It wasn't that important until you mentioned last weekend that I was viewed as a slow learner."

"But, honey, you did have a serious injury, and I don't see the connection. I think it's best if you just forget the whole thing."

I sat up and took a sip of soda. "Well, you may be right, but at least let me tell you what I found out today. Very unusual."

She rested on her elbow and said, "Let's have it!"

"I know you're familiar with the change in zoning to Trotter's old property. Well, the company that now occupies the land is Outsource Data Corporation."

She thought for a second. "I recall that name appearing on the agenda for an Executive Committee meeting regarding the zoning. I've passed the building a number of times on my way to Princeton."

"I worked for that company," I said emphatically.

"Oh, of course. It was on your employment resume." She patted her chin. "But it's only a coincidence, right?"

"I guess so." I got out of bed to exercise a leg cramp. "I wonder why Pitman didn't inform Trotter that eminent domain ultimately didn't apply to the transaction," I said, grunting through the pain.

"Funny thing," she said, sitting on the edge of the bed, "I never received a file copy of the Condemnation documents on the Trotter land. The original was given to the mayor to review with Cohen prior to the scheduled meeting with Trotter."

"Do you usually handle the files for such matters?"

"If the subject has been formally approved at an Executive meeting, Cohen provides copies for the mayor's office."

I shrugged my shoulders. "Oh well, maybe it's a paperwork screw-up."

I reflected on the news article and said, "I still feel sorry for old man Trotter. I wish there was something that could be done for him."

"Look, you shouldn't think that way. It's nice of you to be concerned, but in your job you can't get in the middle of disputes of the residents. Believe me, you'll go crazy."

I walked to her side of the bed and kissed her. "You're right. Nevertheless, it bugs the hell out of me and I know what

I have to do. I want to hear what Pitman can do for Trotter to compensate him, at least in a modest way."

"Oh my," she said, shaking her head. "You don't give up, do you?"

"No. You should know by now that's the way I am." I couldn't give her a better explanation.

Once Angie left my place before noon on Saturday, the remainder of the weekend was boring. The Yankee's game against the Red Sox in Boston was rained out. Nothing held my interest throughout the day. Then it occurred to me Jorgenson might ask me about eminent domain like Wilcox did. Maybe I'd show off by disclosing some details on the benefits to the community when property is taken by eminent domain. After spending twenty minutes reviewing information on Google, I gave up. References to the Fifth and the Fourteenth Amendments to the Constitution were too difficult and obscure to use as simple talking points. *What is 'just' compensation anyway?*

All the same, I remained committed to cajoling David Pitman next week.

Before lunchtime on Monday, I left Town Hall to drive to Veterans Fair Grounds, the largest park in Barnegat Junction. After checking Councilman Pitman's appointments, Angie informed me he intended to inspect the mayor's proposed rezoning in the area of the park by the late morning.

My cell phone rang. "Hello."

"Drew, it's Angie."

"Yes, what's up?"

"Mr. Wilcox was looking for you. He wanted to know where you were and became upset when no one knew how to contact you." A lilting announcement followed. "I didn't tell him I have your number."

"Thanks for letting me know. I'll think of an excuse before I get back." *What's so important for him to want me?*

I recognized Pitman as he walked alone to his car. There was a parking spot right behind his car.

"Councilman Pitman, may I speak to you?"

He looked me over. "Sure, I have a few minutes. What's on your mind?"

"I wanted to talk to you about Mr. Trotter's claim."

"Who are you and what's your name?"

"My name is Drew Baxter and I've become familiar with the town's purchase of Trotter's property. I believe he was cheated on the sale. The land substantially appreciated in value when it was rezoned to commercial only months after the transaction. Don't you feel an obligation to help him based on the bad advice you gave him?"

He motioned to a nearby park bench for us to sit.

"Listen, Mr. Baxter, you better gets your facts straight. I don't like the way Trotter's been treated, but he wasn't misled by me. You should—"

"I read the newspaper article where he blamed you at a public meeting."

"I'm not going into a lot of details with you, so you should speak to Mr. Trotter about the transaction." He paused and asked, "Don't you work at Town Hall?"

"I intended to tell you that I'm employed there. As recently as a week ago, Trotter visited Town Hall to ask the mayor for relief. I did speak to him, for your information. And, by the way, I observed your peculiar behavior toward the mayor at the ceremony for the new shopping center."

"Look, there's more to this than I'm in a position to discuss. You're acting naïve and ought to understand how politics works. The mayor has taken advantage of his—"

"Don't pass the blame on to him," I said, raising my voice.

"Oh really. Let me tell you why I'm here today." He pointed to the far end of the park. "You see how the inlet comes right up to Bay Street next to the park."

"Yeah."

"Well your mayor has contracted a firm to dredge the inlet in order to permit yachts to dock on both sides of the inlet."

"So."

"This park, the only one of its size in town, will be rezoned to commercial to support the needs of boaters. A marina, restaurant, shops, etcetera will occupy this plot. If you waited here until school is out, you'd see hundreds of kids using this area." He stood, scanning the width of the park, and shook his head.

"Won't it be beneficial for the town?"

"The town doesn't need that kind of help. However, it sure advances Jorgenson's reputation in the county and state, and who knows what else."

"Okay, I've made my point," I concluded, disappointed I was no help to Trotter. "You can live with your conscience as you see fit. Now I have to get back to work."

If Pitman was a reasonable guy, my last jab might sting.

"I suggest you keep your eyes open and mind on town matters." He shook my hand and walked to his car.

I drove back to work with mixed views of Councilman Pitman. He appeared to be a sincere guy, but I had a nagging feeling he was holding back on the facts. Was he putting the onus on the mayor for Trotter's problem? His decent style didn't convince me he was blameless.

I'm going to ask Dr. Burkett to explain how people rationalize their sense of right and wrong if an injustice has been committed. Some people, politicians for sure, have no shame. My conscience bothered me all day even for insignificant things. Heck, I remember when I failed to give a waiter a tip. Once I realized it, I made a special trip to the restaurant to relieve my guilt.

I'll get Angie's view on this, too. She's probably right again that I'm getting in over my head or chasing windmills.

Why did Pitman have to say that I'm naïve?

<h1>CHAPTER 13</h1>

"Do you like your job here?"

An angry Billy Wilcox threw that direct question at me. He had waited until quitting time on Monday afternoon to order me into his office after Angie and the clerks left for the day. Jorgenson's schedule called for all-day meetings with developers out of town.

He must know about my meeting with Pitman. So what!

"Of course, I like my job, Mr. Wilcox. It's important to me, and I admire the mayor and what he's accomplished for the town." If I continued talking, maybe it would placate him.

"Oh yeah. Then why do you disobey clear instructions?"

"Whaddaya mean?"

"Don't bullshit me," he shouted. "You met with Pitman today. Either you're hard of hearing or—"

"Wait a minute! It was personal and had nothing to do with work." The tone of my voice almost matched his.

"Hey, nothing's personal that concerns this administration and the councilmen. You got that straight, once and for all?"

"Look! I wanted him to own up for his bad advice to Mr. Trotter. You told me about it right in this office."

He stared at me for a few seconds and a smile crossed his face. "Who the hell do you think you are? Are you naïve, or stupid, or what?"

My face turned red, and I repressed a strong inclination to give him a fat lip.

That's the second time today I was called naïve.

"Is that all you talked about?" he asked, toning down his irritation.

"He mentioned the mayor wanted to change the zoning of the Bay Street Park to commercial use. He didn't like the loss of recreational land one bit."

"And you believed him? I can see it in your eyes. Without checking with me or the mayor? You really are naïve."

"Don't say that to me again!" I gritted my teeth and clenched my fists, advancing toward him. My jaw began to tremble.

"Alright, back off, I'm sorry. Sit here and let me tell you this." His initial anger had changed 180 degrees. "The mayor plans to expand the area around the new school for a sizable park with an up-to-date playground and all. But you go off half-cocked because I fill you in on the old man's financial problem, confidentially remember, and now you blindly accept what that arrogant Pitman says."

I felt like a sucker.

"I'll tell you something else in absolute secrecy. We have evidence that Pitman charged excessive legal fees to the old guy. Cohen is checking into Pitman's background and the way he's handled other zoning applications filed with the town. All very suspicious! Are you finally getting the message?"

"You're kidding." *Is Pitman a crook?*

Wilcox moved papers on his desk and pitched several sheets into the trash. "I'm going to forget what happened this time and the mayor won't find out about it. But, it's the last time. Understand?"

"Yes sir."

On my way to Lavallette, I decided to call Angie at her home for the very first time. She still wanted to be cautious about our togetherness, particularly since Lena had been asking leading questions about me. Despite Wilcox's demand of secrecy, I felt she should know what he told me.

"Drew, what a surprise!"

"Angie, I wish Saturday and Sunday were the only days in the week. I just had to talk to you."

"I feel the same way."

"After you left work, Wilcox cornered me in his office. Somehow he learned I met with Pitman."

"Sweet goodness. Let me get comfortable on the couch and tell me all about it. Don't leave anything out!"

I quickly proceeded to fill her in on both encounters. It was easy to tell she was also caught up in the uncertainty of where this led.

"My God, I can't believe that Pitman is involved in misconduct like that," she protested. "In any case, please don't do anything rash to lose your job because of Trotter's trouble! One word from Wilcox to Mayor Jorgenson and you'd be fired."

"You know, I think there's a bigger issue here than the eminent domain question. Pitman's at the heart of it all."

"If that's the way you see it, I won't argue with you, except to say you're getting more and more embroiled in matters beyond your job or expertise."

"We'll see about that. See you tomorrow. Love ya."

I dropped my cell phone on the passenger seat and stepped on the gas pedal.

"My expertise?" I shouted at the rearview mirror, trying to control road rage. "Of all people, I never expected Angie to put me down. I'm fed up with references to my intelligence and ability. Like I'm immature or worse."

The main issue is something's wrong in Barnegat Junction. It wouldn't be the first time there's an abuse of eminent domain transactions. But, what the hell do I do to get to the bottom of it?

After a frozen meatloaf dinner cooked in the microwave, I turned on the TV to relax and uncapped a second O'Doul's, hoping to get Pitman out of my mind.

It wasn't ten o'clock yet, so I took a chance and called Dr. Burkett on his private number.

"What's the problem, Drew?" The interruption was evident in his voice.

The mention of my name gave me a start. Caller ID, obviously. "I apologize for calling so late, Doctor Burkett. I—"

"Is there anything wrong?" he asked.

"Not at all, at least not what you're thinking. I'm feeling fine and ... by the way, I've met a wonderful girl at work."

"I'm pleased. So what can I do for you?"

"First, I like my job. No more nightmares, either."

"Wonderful. Is that it?" he asked, uncharacteristically conveying exasperation.

"No, Doc, there's more. I think there are peculiar things and innuendos swirling around Town Hall, possibly illegalities."

"Drew, please! For God's sake, politics is a tough business and you're a novice in the workings of government."

"I realize that, but I'm convinced there are shenanigans going on with one of the councilmen."

"Look, you've gone through a traumatic experience over the last few years and your self-control is back. You know you can't make charges about someone without ascertaining all the facts. Please don't feel compelled to inject yourself into what you perceive to be underhanded. Frankly, it may backfire on you." He pardoned himself to cough.

And I thought he would understand.

Back on the phone, his voice lowered, he said, "I intended to discuss a new treatment with you at our upcoming session that addresses your behavior with regard to other peoples' problems. I'm anxious to examine this subject with you."

"Doc, can I just sit by and do nothing when there might be a serious ...let me ask you, Doctor Burkett, have you ever felt helpless?"

A shrill laugh quickly became silent.

"Doc, can you hear me?"

"Yes, I heard you," he responded, obviously irritated.

Have I hit a nerve?

"In my line of work, doctors often wish they could do more to assist patients. We're not always successful and we—"

"What about you?" I interrupted.

"Drew, I utilize my training for all my patients. I maintain a detached approach in order to offer my best advice and care. Each situation is different." A weak cough followed. "The fact is my interest in you and your case is strong, perhaps more so than others. I sincerely want to find the cause of your trouble. You must know that."

"I'm glad to hear it, of course. Fact is I've sensed your concern beyond the norm. It's much appreciated."

"Tell you what," he interjected, "let's move up our next appointment by one week and we can explore your predicament more closely."

"Have you heard of whistle-blowers, Doc?"

"Certainly."

 I reported to him the substance of my conversations with Pitman and with Wilcox concerning Mr. Trotter.

"You can't go by his—"

"I've researched what my obligation is and possible retaliation so I know the risks. Please accept my strong belief that there's misconduct in Barnegat Junction." I started to hyperventilate, uncertain of his feedback, as well as the effect on my ultimate decision.

There was silence on the other end.

Finally, he said, "Drew, I've come to know you as an honest person with admirable qualities. Your intuition about right from wrong is sound, and you don't want to hurt anybody. You admit you don't have all the facts, right?"

As he paused briefly, I thought, *Here it comes. Another put down.*

"You're obviously determined to act on your presumption of irregularities. Okay. I'll just caution that whatever you do, you shouldn't feel guilty about your action or the outcome. But, good or bad, you'll bear the responsibility."

Relieved, I said, "Thank you again for listening, Doctor Burkett."

I now knew what I had to do.

Tomorrow it would begin.

CHAPTER 14

As I watched TV while dressing on Wednesday morning, I was prepared to take the next step in the plan immediately after work. Angie didn't have to know anything about my intention, just in case it backfired somehow.

An unexpected procedural problem came to light shortly after I arrived at my desk.

"Take a look at this, Lena," I said. "There's a mistake on the Proposed Tax notices."

"What are you talking about?" Her indignation was a typical reflex action.

"The tax rates from last year's final budget were used to calculate the proposed property tax for the new year."

Lena grabbed a handful of sample notices from the printer and returned to her desk to compare them to last year's notice. "Oh my. Somehow the computer didn't pick up the revised rates I inputted. We've got to stop the printing immediately."

When Wilcox heard of the error, he became overly excited, fretting about the delay in mailing as well as the extra costs. "You'll all have to work overtime tonight to catch up with the schedule," he announced, leaving no doubt about the staff's compliance.

The frowns on the clerks' faces conveyed their reaction, but I knew there was no alternative under the circumstances. Unfortunately, the directive from Wilcox also changed my plan for the that night.

I had checked out the address of the nearest FBI location and intended to appear unannounced to speak to an agent. This was a better approach than submitting a crime tip to the FBI on Google. All my free time on Tuesday had been focused on itemizing the potential misconduct by Councilman Pitman. I'd leave Angie out of the questionable undertaking. "Is there truly a case here?" I had asked myself, weighing the merits of the accusations.

The mayor appeared in front of my desk. "Drew, I want to personally thank you for spotting that mistake this morning," he exclaimed. "That would have been an embarrassing situation for us all, particularly me."

"Your welcome, Mr. Mayor."

For all to see and hear, Jorgenson shook my hand. "You've been an asset to the department. Keep up the good work."

"Thank you, sir."

The clerks, especially Lena, glared at me while Angie gave me the high sign of her affection. I felt a chill from the compliment from the mayor as well as Angie's wink.

Everyone pitched in to correct the mistake on the tax notices and to print and sort them for mailing the next day. We completed the assignment at 8:45.

Too late now. I'll visit the FBI tomorrow night.

Even with one more day to think it over, my course of action was unchanged. Despite the consequences, it seemed the only way to resolve a potential problem and satisfy my instinct. I can't answer what drove me to step forward, but someone had to do it. Thankfully, Thursday was a routine workday.

At home on Wednesday evening, I had read a paper on federal laws protecting whistle-blowers. While I considered contacting the media, that approach would add another layer to a possible investigation. Furthermore, there was no way I'd inform the IRS of probable tax evasion in order to collect a bounty.

Hollywood has profited through highly-acclaimed movies of true whistle-blowing acts. "Serpico" dramatized police corruption in New York City. The case against Big Tobacco and the use of carcinogenic ingredients was portrayed in "The Insider" and on "Sixty Minutes". Closer to home, an employee finally was successful in his efforts against the United Medical and Dentistry of New Jersey, despite personal retribution. He disclosed the culture of bureaucratic incompetence, overbilling and major fraud. No movie royalties for him.

Perhaps the most sensitive and politically controversial disclosure concerned the Pentagon Papers in 1971. The *New York Times* reported on secret Pentagon reports, over several administrations, that concealed the government's intention to continue and expand the war in Southeast Asia, notably Vietnam and Cambodia.

Those examples and many other whistle-blowers had stepped forward in the past to identify wrongdoing. *Why shouldn't I take the plunge?*

I arrived at the FBI office in Red Bank at 7:30 p.m., Thursday. I decided that it might be too risky for me to go to their Trenton office, given the number of state agencies and the conspicuous presence of politicians and lawyers. *Just my luck that the wrong person would see me there and asks questions.*

The FBI office was only several blocks from Dr. Burkett's office, so I had no difficulty locating the place. After the door opened for me to enter, I approached a reception desk located behind a glass-enclosed area, noting the overhead camera staring down at me.

"I'd like to speak to an agent."

"Please pass me your I.D. What is the subject?"

"I have information about activities of a local councilman."

Ten minutes later, a tall, well-built gentleman with a friendly face approached me and said, "I'm Special Agent Steve Walsh of the Public Corruption Squad. Please come with me to a conference room."

As I walked beside him and we talked, I felt at ease by his soft-spoken manner. His jet black hair and deep-set blue eyes easily set him apart in a crowd. At over six feet tall, his posture was straight and stiff, perhaps from the starched white shirt. *Friendly face, but standoffish.*

For the next twenty minutes, I spoke of my background, the job in Barnegat Junction, and the story of Trotter's property. I checked off each potential charge on my list:

--Malpractice representing Mr. Trotter on the eminent domain issue regarding his cranberry farm;

--Charging excessive legal fees;

--Improper handling of zoning matters;

--Lying to the public.

Walsh listened politely, but didn't seem impressed with my list. He even stopped taking notes.

When I referred to Councilman David Pitman by name for the first time, a noticeable squint suggested he was troubled with my information. He picked up his pen and notepad, and resumed writing.

"Mr. Baxter, do you have any physical evidence or are your charges based on hearsay?"

I debated with myself if I should mention Wilcox and his official position.

"Well, other than Mr. Trotter's complaints, not really. I—"

"Have you spoken to local or state authorities about this matter?"

"Er, well, no." I leaned forward in my seat. "Agent Walsh, I hope this doesn't sound crazy, but I sense there's more to this that meets the eye." I ran my fingers through my hair several times realizing I lacked credence to make such accusations.

"Sir, I want to thank you for bringing this information to our attention. However, I'm afraid the FBI cannot investigate this matter. You have to understand we need more concrete facts to take jurisdiction on a case. We're always concerned about unproven or unjust allegations leaked to the public for political reasons."

"Sure. I'm just trying to do my duty." I felt unwise and juvenile.

He stood to shake my hand and said, "Thanks for coming in."

In route to Lavallette on Route 35 in light traffic, I was confused. Walsh didn't give me any encouragement at all. Should I have gone to state law enforcement in the first place? *Will it cause trouble for me like Burkett said?*

It dawned on me that my action may have been idotic and I was out of place in the FBI's office. One more thing to occupy my mind.

"Hey, it's done. I can't worry about it anymore," I spoke into the rearview mirror. Regrettably, my decision seemed more convincing when I had rehearsed it aloud the previous night.

Thankfully, a song on the car radio sparked my attention. I turned up the volume to hear the lyrics, which had more meaning to me now than ever before.

I've been waiting for a girl like you, "To come into my life," I crooned. Whistling the tune was easier on my ears than vocalizing.

Just one more day and I'll be with Angie again.

CHAPTER 15

I procrastinated all Saturday morning expecting Angie at any minute. Each time a car passed or families headed to the beach loaded down with gear like gypsies, I went to the front door only to be disappointed once again.

She finally arrived after lunchtime. We kissed and gently dropped on the couch in an embrace. We lounged in front of the TV before going to dinner and catching a late movie. We were in a secure zone with each other.

"I wanna tell you what I've done, but don't get mad at me," I said in a sheepish manner.

"Oh no, that's not a good start," she smiled.

"I decided to get Doc Burkett's advice about my reaction to the Wilcox and Pitman meetings."

"Good move."

"I informed him of my intention to expose possible irregularities committed by Councilman Pitman. Recognizing how serious I was, he concurred with my objective, with a firm caveat, but, in effect, gave me a green light."

"A green light to do what?"

"I went to the FBI and—"

"Oh Drew," she gasped. "I hope to high heaven you're not creating an even bigger and new problem."

"I did the best I could covering each potential offense with the agent in charge of public corruption," I explained rapidly. "Nevertheless, this Special Agent Walsh indicated it was all hearsay and, without any hard evidence, the FBI couldn't investigate the matter."

She reached out and touched my face. "Whatever happens now, you know I'll support you one-hundred percent." She paused. "I'm not suggesting it, but maybe you should have gone directly to the office of Attorney General McGrath."

"In Trenton?"

"Yes. I have a handbook at work of all New Jersey governmental agencies. Actually, I remember there's a phone number of the Division of Criminal Justice to report complaints against elected officials."

"Do you have to give your name?"

"I don't know." She bit her lower lip. "Regardless, you realize you're putting your job in jeopardy." Her eyes had the look of a Basset Hound puppy.

While I had thought of that possibility, it hadn't occurred to me I'd no longer see Angie everyday. *No way do I want that. I should have discussed this with her first.*

"I know I'm way out on a limb. I …I just can't change the way I am."

"Maybe we should both go see Doctor Burkett next time and you can tell him about what's happened. I'm sure he can suggest a feasible approach."

"We'll see."

I argued silently with myself if I should pursue with her a bothersome unsettled point. *Here goes.*

"First, please hear me out about one more thing, okay Angie?"

She nodded; her face went blank. She folded her arms.

"When I prepared for my meeting with the FBI, I realized that there's a missing piece to all this. It may be tricky, but I would love to get my hands on a particular document. The only way it can be done requires your help."

"My help? How?" she asked. Her expression reflected a blend of anticipation and alarm.

"You told me you never received the Condemnation documents on Trotter's land. And you usually do, right?"

"Yes, but—"

"If you can find that document in the files, we might discover why Trotter sold when he did and Pitman's role in it."

"Mayor Jorgenson does have a file cabinet in his office under lock and key," she acknowledged, peering up to the ceiling in thought. "He keeps private papers and some proposals under consideration in his desk or the cabinet."

"Are you willing to take a shot at it?" I held her hands.

Is it fair of me to get her in deeper? What about her job, too?

"Do you honestly think a draft document that was never officially filed will prove anything at all?"

"I'm not sure." *She has a valid question.* "I only know this is driving me nuts. It just doesn't add up."

While I tried to make a case for her participation, there was a limit as to how far I would go to convince her. There was no way I wanted to get her in trouble ...and jeopardize our relationship.

A long pause followed.

"Yes, I'm willing to do it," she answered.

The firmness in her voice reminded me of a heroic soldier's acceptance of a perilous mission.

The remainder of the weekend was blissful. It would be as impossible for Angie to grasp my unconditional tenderness and yearning for her as it would be for me to intelligently define the essence of my love to her. And I'm certainly not a poet.

Mayor Jorgenson exhibited a rare public display of his temper Tuesday afternoon. He stood in front of Angie pounding on her desk. "Cohen said he sent the Memorandum of Understanding over here on Monday, just yesterday. Where is it?"

"Mr. Mayor, I'm certain I never received it. I'll check my—"

"This doesn't make sense. You better look in every drawer and—"

The mayor's private line rang. "Mr. Cohen, yes, the mayor is right here," Angie answered.

The mayor listened for only seconds before interrupting. "Dammit, Fred, how did that happen? I'll be right over to your office."

Immediately after the mayor left, Angie approached my desk, coffee cup in hand. "Thank the Lord Cohen located the Memorandum when he did. In his haste, the mayor left the cabinet in his office unlocked. This may be our chance to search—"

She hesitated until Lena passed by, failing to hide her inquisitive glimpse our way.

"Okay, but be careful and do it quickly," I agreed, but my nerves began to act up. "I'll keep watch."

Angie left the door to the mayor's office open as she entered. Since the file cabinet was in a corner of the room hidden from the outside, I was unable to see her as I strolled casually around the atrium.

Time was passing; what seemed like an hour to me was only ten minutes.

"Angie, please come out," I whispered. *This is as nerve-racking as the patrols in Iraq.*

"Could you lend a hand with the deposits for today?" Lena asked.

I feigned I didn't hear her, but I had no choice. As Lena and I were copying checks at the cashier counter, the noise at the front door attracted our attention.

Oh no, he's back already.

Angie was nowhere in sight. I wanted to shout her name, but my vocal chords emitted no sound. The mayor had returned with Wilcox, and they walked slowly toward the mayor's office in obvious disagreement about their meeting with Cohen. They detoured into Wilcox's office to continue their discord.

My stomach was churning and perspiration soiled my shirt. *Where are you, Angie? Please come out!*

The mayor exited Wilcox's office, looking upset, and walked quickly toward his own.

"Welcome back, Mr. Mayor," I blurted out from my desk to the rear of the atrium. "Is everything alright?"

The unexpected high-pitched sound of my voice jolted everyone, including the mayor. Taken unawares, Jorgenson gazed at me for several seconds, as if he prepared to discipline my office decorum. He took two steps toward me. "Everything is fine."

With bulging eyes like a bullfrog, I watched as he turned toward his office. My beating heart was out of control.

At the same split second he reached the door, out popped Angie carrying two oversized folders.

"Pardon me, Mr. Mayor. Finally cleaned up the material from the last public meeting." Breathing hard, she brushed by him and dropped the folders on her desk with a thud.

I shrunk down in my chair gasping for air. Whoa.

Before quitting time, Angie placed a file of campaign pledge letters on my desk. I noted her sly glance as she walked away. An index card clearly in sight read: *Meet me at the Shore Diner near the movie theatre on Rt. 37.*

An hour later, I spotted Angie in a booth at the diner in Toms River. This was the first time we had met anywhere close to Barnegat Junction, and on a weekday.

I gave her a peck on the cheek. "What's up?"

"I got it," she said, grinning at her success.

"You're unbelievable," I responded, amazed at her daring escapade. "I thought I was going into cardiac arrest, so I can only imagine your anxiety."

"Sure, but it was exciting. I recalled how the actress pulled off a similar exploit in the movie we watched the other night."

She removed an official-looking document from a large manila file. "Look here," she said, pointing at handwritten notations at the top of the document.

Rather than face her, I changed my seat and sat next to her.

"This is Billy Wilcox's handwriting and initials under the words that there's no need to proceed with the Condemnation filing."

It was difficult for me to read Wilcox's writing. "Who's this?"

"That's J. Wilson Hannigan. He's a local appraiser who has curried favor with Wilcox for town business. Wilcox's note says, *'Hannigan will set the market price as we discussed.'*"

While I accepted Angie's interpretation, my interest focused on the next notation directly below.

She continued. "This clearly shows that the mayor supported Wilcox's recommendation, and he would quote 'get Cohen on board.' That's Jorgenson's initials."

"That would take Pitman off the hook. Oh, then he did advise Trotter in good faith." I recalled my meeting with Agent Walsh and felt dejected for my false accusation.

"There's more, Mr. Whistle-blower. Take a look at this." She directed my attention to the dates on the notations.

I squinted at the scribbling. "Isn't that—?"

She interrupted by raising her hand to my mouth. "They killed the condemnation proceedings ...the day *before* the contract was settled with Trotter."

"Is this what they call the 'smoking gun'?" My mind needed unscrambling. "So poor Mr. Trotter was indeed deceived and cheated. This is like a conspiracy right out of John Grisham."

"There's a more important question for us to think about now," she judged.

I detected a spiteful tone in her statement.

"I'm the one who's casting an accusation this time," she

stated firmly. "Did the mayor or Wilcox intimidate the old man into thinking he had no choice but to accept the appraised value for his soon-to-be condemned property?"

"Wow, I can't believe it. Mayor Jorgenson? Is there another explanation for all this?"

We ate our hamburgers and chips in silence. I guessed her mind was racing as was mine. To what conclusion?

"I have to figure out a way to return the file to the mayor's cabinet," she said, apprehension contorting her face. "What do we do after that?"

"You mean what do I do?" I sipped water to give myself time to think. "One thing you can do is go to Office Depot or some place like that and get a copy of the document." I sensed there was no stopping her once she set her mind to it.

With the startling disclosure fresh in my mind, I almost forgot to raise the subject of Bay Street.

"Let me ask you about the Bay Street Park rezoning. To your knowledge are there plans or an intention to expand a park at the new grammar school?"

"Er, I haven't heard any mention of that. In fact, the playground was described as barely adequate for the student body."

I sat back in a state of disbelief, not knowing what to say or think next. Was Wilcox bullshitting me all along ...or worse?

"Angie, you were right to warn me about becoming entangled in political matters. I feel sick about suspecting Pitman." My initial weekly visits with Burkett many months ago at a time of deep depression flashed before me.

"Drew, honey, we're in this together and we'll work it out." She put her arm around my neck. "You were right all along that activity was improper. I'm proud of you."

Her soothing perspective returned me to reality. How lucky I was to have her at my side at a time like this.

"I have no idea what the FBI will do when I admit I was mistaken about Pitman. I sure put my foot in it this time."

"Let's not worry about that now. The question is what do we do with this new information? Can you go back to the agent in Red Bank?"

"I'll have to give it some thought."

Two customers slid into the booth behind us.

Angie put her purse, which had been on the seat, on the table and opened it. "By the way," she lowered her voice, "the mayor has a ticket for you to the Chamber of Commerce event this Thursday and—"

"It isn't formal, is it?" I grimaced at the thought.

"Black tie optional. He insists that you attend so just grin and bear it. You'll probably enjoy it." She handed me the ticket.

"Seven at the Toms River Ramada. I'll be there."

A formal event was not my cup of tea, but I didn't want to disappoint Angie. Under the circumstances, it would be damn awkward to witness an honor bestowed on Jorgenson. Maybe I'll pick up some gossip about him.

"I wish you were also invited so ...Shush! Keep your head down!" I nudged her elbow.

I held a menu partially in front of my face, peering at the cash register . "Lena and a man are checking out. I'm not sure if they saw us or not."

"Damn," she whispered. "I hope they didn't."

"It's only a question of time before everyone knows or ...we make a big announcement," I said, holding in a smile, which didn't change her gloomy appearance. *Makes no difference to me who knows.*

She held her chin, resigned to the fact we couldn't keep our love a secret much longer.

"Why don't you leave first?" I suggested, after verifying Lena had left. "I'll think about how we handle your last question, understand?" I mouthed the name McGrath, which seemed to please her. "Enjoy your two vacation days off and I can't wait to see you Friday."

I squeezed her hand as she glided by me. "I love you."

She bent down and whispered in my ear, "Love you, too."

Angie's right. This is not the time to worry about my accountability to Pitman, but to accept that Jorgenson is the true culprit.

After a few minutes, I paid for the meals and headed for my car as my mind labored to unscramble the implication of Angie's discovery.

The full moon over the ocean guided me home. Many a night I sat by myself on the sand dunes gazing at the moon and stars. I never realized at the time that my reflections were prayers to God that I accept whatever comes my way. *Thy will be done.*

Quite often, this place of solace was the most meaningful time of day for me. When the moon reappeared from behind a cloud and cast a glimmering passageway toward the end of darkness, I wondered if it beckoned me to pursue a new course.

What is still missing in my life?

CHAPTER 16

Wednesday had been a routine day at work, except for my dull headache. Thankfully, the staff was busy in their own concerns as we all went about our duties.

I set up a tray for supper in front of the television that night. I needed a temporary diversion from angry feelings about Hank Jorgenson. Since I expected an elaborate meal the next night at the banquet, a personal pizza and diet Coke would do me fine. What a treat!

The six o'clock news reported on troop reductions in Iraq. Simultaneously, the Pentagon announced another army division received orders to beef up current troop levels in Afghanistan due to the escalation of fighting by the Taliban. A political commentator articulated insightful skepticism at the timing of the withdrawal from an unstable Iraq.

"While we take our eye off the ball in Iraq, the in-fighting between the generals and the administration's civilian leadership in Afghanistan makes success problematic, not to mention the affect on the troops' morale," he opined. "The teams gotta get their act together with respect to strategy and tactics."

A scene of foot soldiers on patrol burst across the TV screen. Except for the uniforms, equipment and the terrain, the picture was just as vivid as the GI's in World War II, in Korea and in Vietnam all over again.

"Ooh." The old tremor in my leg acted up again.

"What happens if there is renewed violence, supported by Iran?" a guest asked the host. "How do we mobilize to protect the democratic country of Iraq, which costs the US lives and money?"

While a debate among the panel ensued, their questions made me think. Political decisions can fly in the face of common sense and justice. Legislators become beholden to special interests at the expense of others. Suppose a Jorgenson type became a national leader. *Well, I did my part to expose him and I'm proud of it.*

I thought of a second tour of duty, but quickly dispelled the notion as nonsensical. While I get choked up at the singing of, *My Country, 'Tis of Thee,* the truth is I'd miss Angie much too much and that decision would be an escape.

As bad as the terrifying duty in Iraq, I thought of the return to civilian life after Walter Reed. A new low in my life. Loneliness can be as devastating as bullets whizzing overhead or as demoralizing as my awful lifestyle in Vegas. There was no fanfare upon my return from Iraq. Unlike WW I and II, there were no celebrations or parades. I'm not sure about the post-Korea public sentiment, but 30,000 troops are still stationed in South Korea. Hard to believe. Of course, veterans returning from Vietnam were viewed with sadness or contempt. Many survived that war only to live in their own private hell. Hail the conquering hero, *nice title for a movie,* was a fantasy in my case.

My lonesome existence then was unbearable. I lived in a void, not knowing a soul, no job, no conversation with anyone, in dreary Bronx motels. Wandering the streets was like patrol duty in Baghdad. My door and windows were bolted closed not only to keep out thieves, but also to lock me in. I often found myself crawling around on the floor from my dreams. No idea how I got there.

The juxtaposition of the house in Fallujah, various

unrecognizable faces and innumerable round balls all slowly rotating in my nightmare was like Chinese torture.

It was combat without weapons; combat with an abstract enemy.

That period lasted six weeks. Desperation left me no choice. With my military severance pay, I made the stupid decision to head to Las Vegas and find some army buddies.

Maybe I should have been more forthcoming to Burkett about how bad this time was as a civilian. At least it made sense of why I opted to go to Vegas. The alcoholic's serenity prayer was of no help. In any case, he was already aware how often loneliness and despair had been part of my adult life.

The TV newscast switched to a protest rally against the war. It reminded me of a letter I had received last week from an old Bronx friend, Russ Williams. His story made me somewhat upset and jealous, I regret to admit. While I served in the military in Iraq, he made it big in business and was now a corporate attorney with IBM after graduating from Manhattan College and St. John's Law. He has a wonderful wife and two kids, and a big house in Scarsdale. Wow, season tickets to Yankee games as well, he bragged. A far cry from our youthful aspirations to be astronauts when we watched the space lab launch of *Columbia*.

Oh, what the hell. More power to you, Russ. We never visualized that kind of success when we were growing up, that's for sure.

Come to think of it, I'm not doing too badly with my job. Working the counter in Town Hall and assisting new residents in particular gives me a high, like a dope addict must feel without the bad side effects, of course. The point is I know my job. They say I like to kibitz, which is the way I was in college. I bet my dad would be proud of me, too He often repeated the old saying, it's better to give than to receive. Perhaps, that's how I've compensated for the loss of my parents and being a wise guy when I was a kid. *Who knows?*

Angie. I can't describe the joy she brought to my life. It's made everything before worthwhile. She accepted me for who I am. What more could a man ask for?

I guess I was lucky after all. Look at all those guys who returned from Iraq minus a limb or worse. All I have is the nonsense in my head. Big deal.

All of these indiscriminate distractions and musings caused me to miss the baseball scores and the local weather report.

As I stood to carry the tray to the kitchen, I felt weak. I leaned against the kitchen door to steady myself and closed my eyes.

Suppose Angie left me or wasn't around any more? Suppose this job didn't work out? Suppose there was another 9/11 attack?

After all this time, I'm still isolated in this crummy old house. No male friends. What happens to me then?

The tray slipped from my hands and fell on the floor; pizza crusts danced across the tile. The anticipated nausea produced sweat from every pore, like a diabetic occurrence.

Doc Burkett has to be there for me. I can't go it alone.

Total exhaustion conquered my desolation.

CHAPTER 17

I entered the lobby of the Ramada, relieved that my previous night's depression and ailment were under control. By phone, Dr. Burkett had determined that the combination of missed medication and TV images of troops on patrol in Iraq triggered a spontaneous fear of losing what I had achieved to date. He moved up the date of my next appointment and explained that bouts with anxiety might be expected, given my rapid increase in social contacts. "That's a good thing," he said.

The main ballroom was as elegant as any establishment I had seen. A magnificent chandelier hung from the ceiling in the center of the room, adding a glow to the impressive gathering at the annual Chamber of Commerce affair. The décor matched this hotel's reputation for impeccable service and presentation. A centerpiece of yellow roses and greens on a mirrored plate adorned every table. Since most guests wore formal attire, the entire atmosphere was best described as glittering.

"What am I doing here?" I mumbled to myself. My blue blazer and grey pants stood out, as I noted raised eyebrows in my direction.

Screw it. I ordered a second vodka and tonic on the rocks, light on the tonic, in the final minutes of the cocktail hour. Maybe this would get me through the night. *It wouldn't be so bad if Angie were here as well.*

There were hundreds of locals in attendance, some of whom I recognized from their visits to the Town Hall. However, the more predominant crowd, dressed formal of course, were the politicos from Ocean County and around the state. Angie had informed me that all the high profile lobbyists in the state would attend. This was their night to network and protect careers. The reason was simple-- a rising political star, Hank Jorgenson.

I strolled through the large reception room, acting casual with a forced smile that caused my cheeks to ache. I felt incompetent to engage in their topics of conversation, which did nothing for my self-confidence.

Approaching a circle of local folks, I noted Councilman Pitman among them holding court. I returned his friendly gesture. If I got a chance, I should apologize to him for my insinuation at our meeting at Bay Street Park. The doors to the ballroom opened wide, saving me from an introduction to the guests glancing my way.

My assigned seat was at a table in the back of the room. As I searched for it, five officials marched out on the dais, including a dapper Mayor Jorgenson. He seemed quite gregarious as he waived to associates in the room, and his smile was a definite attraction. *I guess that's what's called charisma.*

I introduced myself to the seven other guests already seated. There was the outgoing mayor of Seaside Park and his wife, two attorneys with their spouses, and a member of the Ocean County Board of Commissioners, Miles Trowbridge, who sat next to me. The opening chatter encompassed the weather, upcoming baseball playoffs, and the financing of the new football stadium in the Meadowlands. All a prelude to their first love, that is, political banter.

"Mr. Baxter, I understand you work at Town Hall in Barnegat Junction," the female attorney said to bring me into the conversation.

"Yes, I've been there about five months."

"It must be thrilling to see the growth of a new town, and witness the operation of Mayor Jorgenson and his administration."

"Well yes, but I haven't been around long enough to appreciate what it took to get where the town is."

The male attorney raised his hand to make a point. "Sure, but you're aware of all the jobs created and the relatively low property taxes. Quite an accomplishment, which of course is why we're all here tonight." His smile reminded me of a toothpaste commercial.

"As I said, it is exciting, and the staff is very proud of the town's reputation as well as—"

"Mr. Baxter," the Seaside Park mayor interjected, "we refer to Mayor Jorgenson as a mover and shaker. His ability to gets things done is extraordinary. Even the opposition party can only nitpick to diminish his achievements." He winked at Commissioner Trowbridge and added, "He just may become our governor one of these days."

"I understand that and I'm a strong supporter of the mayor and his goals. I know he believes it's essential that elected officials act ethically to preserve the trust and confidence of our citizens during the start-up years."

Commissioner Trowbridge, a veteran of political wars I was given to understand from the opening introductions at the table, placed his hand on my shoulder as he directed his remarks around the table. "Young man, you've hit upon what public service is all about. We all aspire to earn the goodwill of the voters. Just recognize, however, what it takes to get reelected by a super majority twice, as Mayor Jorgenson has, and be grateful that you have a nice, good-paying position because of his success and patronage."

I felt out of my league with these career politicians. Suppose

I told them how Jorgenson and his pal, Wilcox, operate in reality. What the hell would they say or think then?

"Sir, I'm all for public service and glad to be in my position. I recognize the progress made by the mayor, but I don't want to be considered a party hack." Immediately, I wished I could take the characterization back.

Damn that vodka and tonic.

The reaction at the table ranged from shock to visible discomfort. The three women, wide-eyed and open-mouth, looked at their spouses. Trowbridge removed his fatherly hand, staring at me like I had insulted his best friend. I didn't want to be so blunt, but my opinion of Jorgenson couldn't be masked.

"You're way off base, mister," Trowbridge chided. "I suggest you rethink your role in local government and the people who do the heavy work to make it operate." He turned his back on me.

The male attorney spoke in a condescending tone. "Perhaps, you should consider a different career path instead of—"

A screeching noise from the microphone at the head table distracted him, which turned everyone's attention to the speaker, the Chamber of Council President.

"Sorry about that," he began, adjusting the microphone. "Ladies and Gentleman, welcome to our annual gala event and thank you for coming. Tonight we are pleased and honored to ..."

His words no longer penetrated my understanding. I was distraught over the needless reference to my civil service appointment, whether it had strings attached or not. Had I forgotten that I was hired partially due to my military service, thanks to Jorgenson and Burkett? And what would Doc think about my inappropriate words? While my table watched the dais, I felt like I should run away and hide.

What will Angie think of my remark?

The Council President's words came through again. "He made the new list in *The New Jersey Monthly* of the 101 most influential persons in the state. I'm delighted to present our honoree, Mayor Hank Jorgenson."

The applause was loud and long. Our table stood like everyone else. My distress inhibited me from absorbing Jorgenson's opening remarks. H regal mannerisms broadcast he was reveling in this distinction. Thank God, the focus at my table was now on him rather than me.

"I believe our success is based on the realization we are in competition. A competition against New York and Pennsylvania. A competition against our detractors, who have no vision, who are reluctant to act on behalf of Barnegat Junction. We have adopted sound business principles to set goals and manage our growth. The voters have responded with a clear message for us to continue on the path we've chosen. As elected officials, we can do no less." Jorgenson paused to sip water.

Mild applause followed at his words espousing professional competence and responsibility in civic duties. For the most part, jealousy aside, he was preaching to the choir.

"Ocean County has the highest growth and employment rates in the state. We can all be proud of these records. Closer to home there have been no, zero, home foreclosures in Barnegat Junction I'm pleased to say. I believe a free market economy is our best approach to insure our freedom and prosperity not only locally, but also nationally."

Trowbridge bumped my knee, accidentally I assumed, while the audience gave the mayor spirited applause. Feeling uncomfortable, I wondered if this was an opportunity for me to sneak out, as the acclaim prompted a standing ovation. While the mayor continued with a compelling story about how he dealt with a specific resident's hardship, I looked about the room. The guests were engrossed in his speech and ...*Is that ...?*

"I don't believe it," I whispered.

The male attorney turned toward me and asked, "What did you say?"

"Just thinking out loud."

I stretched to get a better look at a table in front of the dais. Billy Wilcox and Cohen were easily spotted chatting with bigwigs from Trenton.

Who is that sitting next to Wilcox? It's ...George Parker, of all people. What the—

I was too flabbergasted to make the connection. Now I decided no matter what I had to leave as soon as possible.

The audience stood once again when Jorgenson completed his monologue. This was my chance to slip out the back door without even saying goodnight. I regretted that it was impolite, but the sight of Parker and my earlier inane reference to party hacks left me no choice.

No one at the table noticed me leave.

I drove home blaming myself for drinking alcohol for the first time in months.

Besides Angie, what if Wilcox or even Jorgenson learned of my conduct at the event? Burkett would be rightly disappointed with me.

I knew I was in deep trouble this time.

I parked the car in my driveway and hurried to the front door, keys in hand. All the way home, I was dismayed by my faux pas at the banquet. My mind was muddled by the troublesome events in Barnegat Junction and the suspense of the ultimate outcome. *It's all too much for me to handle, so I better see Doctor ....*

"Who's there?"

A voice behind the hedge said, "Mr. Baxter, it's—"

"Come out of there!" I shouted as I jumped back; the door keys fell to the ground.

"Hold on, FBI, it's Agent Walsh." He pushed aside the hedge where he now could be seen by the light from the outdoor lamp.

"Good grief, you scared the crap out of me. What's the idea?"

"It's time we talk." He gestured toward the front door. "Can we go inside?"

It was clear from the inflection in his voice that I had no choice. His tone was entirely different than at our first meeting. If this is how the FBI operated all the time, they'd ruffle a lot of feathers with the ACLU and others.

I led him to the living room and offered a soda, which he declined. He removed his suit jacket and sat on a sofa opposite me.

"Agent Walsh, I'm glad we're together because some new facts have come up since we met last week that—"

"Allow me to interrupt you first."

"Yes, of course." I felt relieved by his more cordial approach.

"I figured you wouldn't come to see the FBI again, so I want to bring you up to date on the matter of Councilman Pitman."

"Listen Agent Walsh, I had no idea this would come to a head so soon, and cause trouble for Pitman. Besides, I didn't think you were that interested." My regret was sincere; hopefully, he accepted it.

"Let me explain, Mr. Baxter! First we had to verify you didn't have a political axe to grind or a history of filing complaints against authorities. Except for a dismissed charge in Las Vegas, you have no arrest record. We know you were awarded the Purple Heart and spent time at Walter Reed Army Medical Center and the Trenton VA hospital."

I shook my head in astonishment at his information about me.

"As for your accusations, let me inform you that Councilman Pitman is cooperating with the FBI on an investigation regarding Barnegat Junction. He has made allegations of misconduct against Mayor Jorgenson."

I fell back on the cushion of my chair dumbfounded. My world had turned topsy-turvy in an instant. Running my hands through my hair, I could only respond in a weak voice. "That can't be."

"For the last four months, he's been an informant for us to uncover more about the Jorgenson administration. He came to the FBI rather than the state AG because he was concerned of Jorgenson's political connections in Trenton."

"That's incredible."

"He told us about the Trotter land deal and admitted his firm did not serve him well, but he had been assured by Jorgenson that eminent domain was the only proper way to acquire the property for re-routing Route 751 and—"

"Hey, I've got a story to tell you about that." My energy level went up a couple of notches.

"Okay, just hold it for a second. Pitman's information about Jorgenson's methods corroborated an ongoing inquiry based on charges of kick-backs and illegal campaign contributions from a company on Route 751."

"On 751? What's the name of the company?"

"The Outsource Data Corporation."

"I worked for that company up until earlier this year. This is unbelievable!" *What the heck else am I going to hear?*

"The General Counsel of ODC informed the FBI Philadelphia office of suspicious transactions involving their employee, George Parker, and Billy Wilcox. An internal audit disclosed undocumented cash payments through Cohen & Mahoney. Their goal was to acquire the land as soon as possible."

"I'll be," I reacted, completely amazed. "Parker was my boss at ODC." *They were sitting together at the banquet.*

"Okay, Baxter, so what changed your mind about Pitman?"

"I sure owe him an apology to begin with."

I related to him the frightening effort of Angie to remove the Condemnation document from the mayor's personal records. "The dates on the notations showed they never intended to file it or extend 751 through the property. Then they pressured Trotter to sell before the rezoning and the value increased."

"Baxter, you may have committed an illegal act, and it wouldn't be admissible in court. At the proper time the FBI will subpoena all relevant documents and telephone records."

"The secretary will return the document first chance she gets ...after she makes a copy. Okay?"

Is what we did considered stealing?

"Is this secretary, Miss Carswell, the same woman who visited your home over the weekend?" Walsh exhibited a new side of himself with a wide grin.

"Oh my God. You're kidding. The FBI spied on us." Despite my surprise, it showed me that the FBI was serious about the investigation.

"You can show me the copy, but I can't guarantee how the FBI and a prosecutor will use it."

"Fine with me."

"Here's why I've told you all this, Baxter. You're very important to us and the investigation as our only insider."

He stared at me as if he were reading my expression. I wasn't sure what he expected me to say or do.

"Are you familiar with the Bay Street rezoning?" he inquired.

"Sure. Pitman filled me in on the dredging and rezoning; then Wilcox tried to explain it away with a lie."

How gullible was I?

"I want you to be alert to any discussions or reports and correspondence that come across your desk relating to Bay Street and how the dredging contract was awarded. Also, make a note of unfamiliar visitors with the mayor and Wilcox, and any references to Pitman. Please be careful about including your girlfriend in this any further."

"I'm happy to do it, but I usually don't see or know about

critical transactions, although I pick up legal papers from Cohen, the town counsel."

"Just keep your eyes and ears open. You've been an asset to the FBI so far and smart enough to spot something wrong." He headed to the front door. "Let me give a word of advice. Don't rub Wilcox the wrong way. He's a tough and possibly dangerous man to cross."

"I appreciate your confidence in me, Agent Walsh ...and thanks for the warning."

My spirits were buoyed by his reliance on me and by my role in an abuse of public trust case. It was exciting to be thrust into a law enforcement drama. How things might have been different in my life had I become a policeman?

Forget it. I would never have met Angie.

CHAPTER 18

After a decent night's sleep, my remark to those political junkies was still on my mind. And that pompous Trowbridge. However, I no longer gave a darn about what Jorgenson and Wilcox might think. The FBI was on my side. How Angie would react was more important.

"How was the banquet?" Angie asked as she poured coffee for both of us Friday morning at the mini-kitchen in Town Hall.

"I'll tell you tomorrow at my place, but let me know if you hear anything about it or about me last night."

She brushed against my shoulder and whispered, "I did make a copy of the Condemnation file notations." A sly smile accentuated her natural appeal.

"Wonderful." I gently touched her hand, containing my enthusiasm.

Out of the corner of my eye, I caught Lena staring at us. She abruptly stopped whatever she was doing and approached us. My pulse rate inched up. *Oh-oh!*

"Good morning to both of you." She smiled and whispered in Angie's ear, "You make a lovely couple." She placed two fingers over her lips and glanced about the office, presumably to see if the two clerks had heard her. "Your secret is safe with me," she said quietly with a motherly look on her face.

Angie blushed, but I was happy someone finally knew about us and who obviously approved. Had I misjudged Lena from the start? Each of us went directly to our desks, so I wasn't sure how Angie felt about Lena's awareness of our bond.

I brought in a large pizza at lunchtime to share with Angie and the three clerks, somewhat as a reward for Lena's endorsement. Angie and I used the conference room to eat, away from the others so it was an opportune time for me to speak freely.

"I had a visit from the FBI last night. I'll tell you about it tomorrow at my place." Regardless of Walsh's admonition, Angie deserved to be kept in the loop.

"I thought they weren't going to look into the case."

"Let me just say there are new developments." I couldn't wait to see her face when she learned of Pitman's cooperation with the FBI.

"I assume you told them about Jorgenson and Wilcox's dishonesty."

"This is a more important issue to discuss right now. Do you know where the Bay Street rezoning files are?"

"Let me see. I don't think they've been sent to the temporary archives in the Public Works Municipal building yet, so they must be in storage in the basement." She went to her desk and returned with a set of keys. "The long one will open the door to the storage room; the others open file cabinets if needed."

"Thanks."

"Tell me, what do you expect to find in those files?"

Her eager look convinced me she enjoyed the intrigue of all this, like it's an Agatha Christie mystery.

"I just want to see if Pitman told me the truth about the park." Let Agent Walsh take the blame for my white lie to her.

"Please be careful," she warned.

Ten minutes later I opened the door to the storage room. I flipped through files in the cabinet nearest the door. "Nuts, they're not in alphabetical order," I murmured. "Nothing in this one." I tried to estimate how much time I had to locate what I needed. Since the mayor was in Trenton and Wilcox out to lunch, I figured I had a half hour at most.

The last of four cabinets was locked. After trying different keys, the cabinet slid open with ease. Several folders labeled as *Bay Street and Veterans Fair Grounds* stood out in the partially full upper drawer. However, my interest was drawn to a file headed *Mayor's Trip File*.

"Let me take a look at what he's been up to," I whispered to myself. "What the hell, the information is not private if it's town business."

I turned pages of correspondence and expense reports quickly, not knowing what might catch my attention. *I still have fifteen minutes …ample time.*

"What's this?" The title of a thick binder was, *Conference of New Mayors of Small Municipalities—Program, Mayor Hank Jorgenson, guest speaker, Atlantis Resort, the Bahamas, May …*

As I read further, my heart seemed to stop beating. I held onto the cabinet to steady myself.

"Oh my God, Angie! No." *She was there with him.*

My cell phone rang. *It's her.*

"Wilcox just called. He's on his way back and—"

"Thanks." I hung up cutting her short, unable or unwilling to say another word.

My mind couldn't digest the meaning of this finding, and I struggled to carry out the purpose of my mission.

Did Angie have a relationship with Jorgenson? Yeah, they did seem too chummy during my first days on the job.

I leaned against the tallest cabinet, tempted to bang my head against it.

How am I going to face her?

"Why is this happening to me?" I sneered between my teeth.

I ran my shaking fingers through the Bay Street data. Clipped to a public notice for a zoning change, there were two bids for dredge work on the inlet. Without thinking, I removed them and closed the cabinet. It was easy to stuff them inside my shirt. Any other pertinent material could wait for another day.

I just want to get the hell out of here and think.

Minutes later I sulked back to my desk as Wilcox showed up.

"Just the person I want to see," he said, with a smugness I found irritating. He probably took delight in belittling me. "I hear you were inebriated last night,"

"Yeah, I guess I overdid it. I'm sorry."

"No need to say you're sorry to me, man. Save your apology for the mayor." He grinned at me and walked away humming a tune.

I volunteered to work on sorting tax notices for the rest of the afternoon, pretending to ignore Angie and her hand signals. The more I thought of them in the Bahamas at the same time, the more upset I was, and my dejection became unbearable. She looked my way when she left at five and I returned a casual wave without emotion.

Once everyone departed Town Hall, I called Agent Walsh.

"I have documents on the bids for dredging the inlet."

"What? Please don't remove them from the office. I'll let you know what to do next." He cleared his throat. "You don't sound so good, Baxter. Are you okay?"

"Yeah, sure. Everything's just great."

I banged the phone down on the cradle and pitched a pencil clear across the atrium floor to Angie's desk.

A quick stop in a local tavern and one beer, my limit, only added to my anguish. I must have driven past Angie's apartment ten times, debating if I should resolve my heartbreak tonight or wait until she came to Lavallette in the morning. At one point I thought I'd throw up. Darkness was nearing as house and streetlights brightened on cue at the Azalea Park Development's apartments and condominiums. I wondered whether Dr. Burkett would encourage me to face the issue head on or view the visit as too hasty and allow time to compose myself.

I finally knocked on the door.

"Drew, I can't believe it." The door opening was limited by the latch. "What a nice surprise!"

"Can I come in?"

"Of course." She led me into the living room, straightening up the couch and a coffee table before offering me a place to sit.

Even in jeans and a loose-fitting sporty blouse, she was alluring. In spite of that, I evaded her attempt to hug me.

"Would you like coffee or tea?"

"No, I only wanted—"

"I bet I know why you're here."

"You do?"

"You want to talk about Lena and when we go public with our romance?" Her eyes sparkled at the idea. "I was going to suggest how we handle it when I'm with you tomorrow."

"That's not the reason at all," I scoffed. "I'm here about our relationship." My voice sounded sharp and harsh to my ears.

She sat across from me with a blank face. She wet her lips, a look of confusion on her face until her eyeballs enlarged.

"Have you ever been to the *Atlantis Resort*?"

She studied my dour look as surely as I examined her reaction.

"When I was in the Bahamas earlier this year, as you know, I stayed there," she replied in a slow cadence. "Why do you ask?" She crossed her arms beneath her breasts.

"The mayor was there at the same time, wasn't he?" I wished I'd spoken in a softer tone, but my emotions got the best of me.

At first she looked stunned. Moving about the room, her face turned red. I wasn't sure if it was from rage or shame. A flood of tears gave away her reaction.

"I told you before I had a bad time with someone," she sobbed. She sat back down, running her fingers through the full length of her hair.

"But you never told me who it was and that you had an

affair with him." I fidgeted with the buttons on my shirt. "Did you love him?"

"Love?" she screeched. "I never loved him."

"You went with him to a resort and—"

"It was supposed to be for town business, Drew. You men equate respect or ...or admiration for an opportunity to take advantage of a woman."

"Is that how it was?"

"I'll admit to an initial infatuation with the manner in which Jorgenson treated me in the new job. I accepted his kindness as genuine. And he is charming, dammit." She wiped her nose with a tissue, and confessed, "But that didn't give him the right to manhandle me, tear my blouse and try to—"

She couldn't complete the sentence, but it wasn't necessary. My stomach tightened into a knot as I pictured that bastard, Hank Jorgenson. I wanted to go to her and hold her close, but the pangs of guilt restrained me.

Good God, I came here to accuse her?

"Angie, I had no idea it was anything like that. Please forgive me for igniting your pain all over again. I—"

She raised her hands for me to stop. "I tried to warn you ...I didn't want us to become involved." Her crying had turned to a whimper. "I thought you loved me and trusted me."

I felt devastated. I couldn't utter a word while past feelings of remorse compounded my shame at letting down the one person in the world I cared for. I leaned forward with my elbows on my knees; my chin rested on joined hands.

"There's got to be a reason we came together," I sighed. "God knows I needed you, and, yes, you had to find someone who could love and admire you for who you are. Please don't allow my jealous mistrust about this to separate us. " My eyes clouded up from shame.

She rushed to sit with me and put her arms around me.

We embraced, weeping, until we finally looked at each other and kissed over and over again.

"I'm glad you came here tonight," she said to break the silence. "I want you to know this. Remember the night we dined in Lavallette?"

"How could I ever forget?"

"Do you recall what you said about your feelings for me?"

"Well, not the exact words."

"You said your love for me would never end." Her eyes became watery again.

I kissed her cheek and said, "I meant every word of it, but it must have sounded like it was right out of a Hollywood movie."

"Well, the suddenness did startle me. However, I'm a believer in love at first sight, so the attraction was mutual."

We held each other close, so close that the scent of her hair and softness of her body rendered me defenseless.

She went to the kitchen for glasses of water. There was an open question I wondered about, but did I dare bring it up?

"Angie, mind if I ask how you put up working with Jorgenson every day and looking him in the face?"

With legs crossed underneath her on the couch, she got comfortable to divulge the full story. "Before you came along, I intended to quit my job the end of this year and go back with my parents in Cherry Hill. The mayor had apologized to me, blaming his transgression on having too much to drink. He promised nothing like that would happen again. Nevertheless, I had made up my mind to leave ...until I met you."

"That makes me feel like a million bucks." I moved to her and kissed her softly on the lips. We caressed for too brief a moment.

She flipped strands of hair off her face and said, "It was a big surprise to me when I was promoted, but I'm sure the reason was for me to stay on the job and keep my mouth shut. A scandal would ruin his political career."

"It's a peculiar environment there for you." I placed my hand on her shoulder to show my empathy.

"Why do you think I agreed so readily to get those documents from Jorgenson's private files? If there was a chance he's guilty of misconduct, I loved finding the evidence so he gets what's coming to him. I could care less if he goes to jail. That goes for Wilcox, too."

"And I sure have an added incentive to take down the phony...eh, I think cad best describes him."

"Amen to that." She raised her right hand to do high-fives with me.

"Speaking of doing just that," I said, "I removed two bidding contracts on the Bay Street rezoning, but the FBI wants me to return them right away." Laughing, I added, "By the way, we better be discreet. The FBI is watching us."

"Let them watch." Now she giggled. "I want you to stay here tonight with me. Let's go check out my bedroom. It's make-up time after our first quarrel."

I lifted her up and carried her into the bedroom. "Would you really move away without me?" I asked lightheartedly.

"Not on your life. I'm not letting you get away."

No more caring words had ever been spoken to me. She wanted me not because she needed my help, and I felt no obligation to smother her with kindness in order to retain her love.

Forgotten was the foolish comment at the banquet and my childish jealously.

I don't know what I would do if I ever lost her.

CHAPTER **19**

Angie and I arrived at my home about eleven on Saturday morning. During the twenty-five minute drive, I filled her in on Pitman's role with the FBI.

"This is all so unimaginable," she confessed. "To think that you accused him of misconduct!"

I'll never live that down.

Parked in my driveway was none other than Agent Walsh.

"We eluded your surveillance, didn't we?" I exclaimed in a cocky manner.

He didn't think it was so amusing, but smiled at last when we sat at the kitchen table to enjoy coffee and crumb cake.

"I want you to return these bids as soon as possible," he said after reading the dredging contracts I'd turned over to him. "Although I don't recognize one company, the other is owned by Wilcox's brother-in-law. In fact, that's the company we suspected will be awarded the project."

Angie and I observed the agent as he scanned the notations on the Condemnation document. His raised eyebrows, mumbling, "Hmm, hadn't heard the name Handgun before," disclosed its significance as evidence. "Please return the original Condemnation document as well as the bids," he ordered.

"How does the FBI know so much about this case in so short a time?"

"Actually, long before Councilman Pitman and you, Mr.

Baxter, came to us, the Bureau was investigating Wilcox on real estate conspiracy charges in the Princeton area. He was the alleged mastermind. We were about to move in when his association with Hank Jorgenson began. Once Jorgenson entered politics—"

"When Barnegat Junction was to be incorporated," Angie interrupted.

"That's right. That's when the case became more complicated as questions of kickbacks and corruption arose. The investigation was transferred from the White Collar Crime Squad to my Public Corruption Squad in Red Bank."

I wondered how the FBI managed to keep their myriad probes throughout the country under wraps. Fantastic discipline and loyalty; beyond remarkable.

"Barnegat Junction grew through sweetheart deals with developers, and the mayor prospered. We weren't absolutely sure how Jorgenson attracted the businesses."

"Probably Wilcox did the negotiating on behalf of the mayor," I interjected.

"You hit the nail on the head. Once the Outsource Data Corporation allegation came forward connecting Parker and Wilcox, we knew that it was just a question of time before the pieces fit together for an indictment."

"I always thought it was out of the ordinary how the mayor was able to acquire land off 751 ...with Wilcox's know-how, of course," Angie added, clearly pleased to participate behind-the-scenes. "However, I'm still confused how a smart individual like the mayor got hooked up with Billy Wilcox."

"That's an interesting story, which became another piece of the puzzle and kept the case expanding. Wilcox got wind of how Jorgenson secured the patent of his software company, which he sold to an international Japanese technology company at a substantial profit. Wilcox had represented Jorgenson's partner in numerous real estate transactions. The partner, an unsavory character to begin with—who had developed the software in the first place—confided to Wilcox that he had a falling out with Jorgenson and he might be cheated out of his share of the business. Rather than support the partner, Wilcox went to Jorgenson and they conspired together to blackmail the partner."

"Why didn't the partner go to the authorities?"

Walsh grinned. "Because of his shady past and, more significantly, fear of bodily harm from Wilcox."

"You're kidding. So how did the FBI uncover the details of their collusion?"

"The partner committed suicide and—"

"Jesus," Angie gasped.

"And he left a suicide note describing the whole affair." Walsh casually added, "We kept the note a secret from the public. The implausible affiliation of Jorgenson and Wilcox began then and is linked directly to a crime."

I threw my hands in the air. "The more I know of them, you've got to wonder how they pulled the wool over so many people's eyes for so long."

"I can make a good guess," Angie said.

Her tone and contorted facial expression conveyed a strong message of contempt for Jorgenson.

My emotion spiked again at the thought of Jorgenson's conniving as well as molesting Angie. *Am I capable of killing the sonofabitch?*

"As it turns out," Walsh continued, "The Trotter deal may be the final straw to seal the case against Jorgenson and Wilcox."

"I feel sorry for the old guy," I mumbled.

" Baxter, you threw me off at first when you implicated Councilman Pitman. After all, you are the one and only insider to come forward."

"I still regret that. Like so many others, I was manipulated by them." I glanced at a sullen-looking Angie.

"How did you happen to be hired for a job in Town Hall?" Walsh inquired.

"Mayor Jorgenson is a personal friend and college roommate of my psychiatrist, Doctor Timothy Burkett. There was a vacancy to fill, and Jorgenson apparently wanted to offer a job to someone simply to help out a worthy individual. Burkett recommended me as most qualified. That's it in a nut shell." I looked to Angie for confirmation.

"Frankly, I wasn't aware they intended to hire anyone, but it was a welcomed addition to the staff," Angie said.

"Other than clerical duties and back-up duty, I was the courier from the mayor and the town counsel—"

"You're referring to Mr. Cohen?" Walsh interrupted.

"Yes."

"The FBI suspects Cohen was the bagman for the mayor in numerous transactions."

"Him too? Barnegat Junction's a freaking cesspool. Unbelievable." I wondered if Angie and I might be tainted with guilt by association.

"I'd like to meet Doctor Burkett with you as soon as possible, Baxter," Walsh said. "Can you arrange it?"

After one phone call, a visit to Burkett's office was set for 2:00 p.m.

I was curious what Walsh might learn from Burkett, but resented the time away from Angie. Weekends were our personal time to share.

"A pleasure to meet you, Agent Walsh," Burkett said, eyeing the agent as if he were a patient. He led us to his private office, roomier than the one to which I was accustomed.

"Drew indicated it was important we meet right away, so what can I do for you?"

"Thank you for making the time, Doctor," said a courteous Walsh. "Please be advised that this interview is confidential, but obviously bears on Mr. Baxter here and your practice."

"Understood," Burkett affirmed.

Burkett stroked his chin and glanced at me. *I bet he imagines I'm in some kind of trouble related to my talk of a whistle-blower.*

"Perhaps we could start, Doctor, with your connection with Mayor Jorgenson and the circumstances which led to your recommendation of Baxter for employment in Barnegat Junction."

I held back a smile when Walsh removed a notepad from his suit jacket. I thought it ironic that the shoe was now on the other foot. As for Burkett, he seemed relieved by the innocuous subject matter.

"Yes, let's see. Hank Jorgenson and I were college buddies for our first two years at Rider. Although we hung out together in the dorm, we didn't socialize or get mixed up in the same activities. In fact, he was a dynamic take-charge student on campus, and everyone expected him to be a success in business ...and he knew it. Very popular guy and, in all candor, quite conceited. We only saw each other occasionally after graduation and—"

"So how did Baxter's name come up?"

"We ran into each other at Homecoming Week earlier this year. After catching up on our careers, he asked if he could visit me in my office. I wondered at the time if he were having psychological or other health problems, since I hadn't seen him for several years."

"Jorgenson has no such health issues to your knowledge, is that correct?" Walsh looked intently at Burkett.

"As far as I know, that's right, and, as it turned out, that wasn't the reason for coming to see me. We talked about the growth of the town and the hard work it takes to establish a new community. He was quite proud of his success and being elected mayor twice by a large majority. I congratulated him."

"Did he mention the role of Billy Wilcox?"

"Not that I recall, but I have seen his name in the press as Jorgenson's right-hand man."

"Go on."

"Well, he brought up the matter of staffing at Town Hall and how difficult it is to get the right people. He didn't feel an obligation or desire to hire any more supporters, or leeches to use his term, from his campaigns."

Walsh looked at me. "Are the current employees active in politics?"

"Not that I'm aware of. Angie certainly isn't." I wondered if Lena had been hired because of connections to the mayor's campaign.

Burkett continued, "He asked if I knew of candidates to work in a non-challenging clerical position. Prior experience didn't matter. I was reluctant to accommodate him initially, but he persisted. In the end I concluded it was good thing that would both support him and one of my patients."

He glanced my way. *Makes sense to me.*

"I listed four people who have had forms of psychological stress or learning weaknesses and are progressing nicely with minimum medication."

"Did you describe the backgrounds of each?"

"I did, Agent Walsh, but within the bounds of patient confidentiality."

"Did Jorgenson know that Baxter worked at the Outsource Data Corporation?" Walsh leaned forward, elbows clamped on the table, awaiting Burkett's reply.

"I can't remember for sure. In any case, I didn't see it as improper to disclose the educational and business histories of each possible job candidate."

"What did Jorgenson do with the information?" Walsh asked.

"He took the list and left my office. About a week later, he called me to say there was a job opening in Town Hall and he selected Drew as best suited for the position."

"And?" Walsh continued to press Burkett for all the details.

"Jorgenson asked me to inform Drew the job was his and I indicated I'd be happy to do so."

"Then you didn't specifically recommend Mr. Baxter, did you?"

Burkett's face reddened as he looked at me for a second and turned back to Walsh. He hesitated, as if he were conjuring up an excuse.

I held my breath, awaiting his confirmation of what actually happened. *Why has he paused? Someone turn on the air conditioning!*

"No," Burkett admitted. "I just gave him four names and that's all."

"Then you didn't actually recommend me like you said?" I butted in.

He moved his chair to face me, scrapping the tile floor. "Let me explain my thinking to you, Drew. You had just lost your job and showed signs of renewed distress. This opportunity was a natural based on your educational background. For your good and in my professional opinion, I felt it was imperative I convince you to accept the job offer."

My right hand slapped my forehead. Burkett no longer had the upper hand on me. My verdict of his action produced a tension between us, with Walsh as an innocent observer.

Initially I reacted with shock that the one guy I trusted didn't level with me. After a pause for reflection on Dr. Burkett's impact on my life, I nodded to indicate my acceptance of his motive. However, his opinion of my real qualifications for the job persisted in my mind. The doubt hurt.

"When you called me at home a short time ago," he continued, "I knew you were in a difficult situation, and I trusted you would do the right thing. It was my judgment from the start that you would do well in public service, but I had no idea when you mentioned the term whistle-blower that the FBI would—"

"The Bureau is grateful to Mr. Baxter," Walsh broke in. "He's to be commended for his civic duty."

"Of course, I totally agree." Burkett appeared burdened as he reached out his hand to me.

I shook it and said, "Doc, I'm still obliged to you for all you've done for a nutty guy like me, and thanks a lot for the push for me to take the job."

"I appreciate that, Drew, more than you know. For your benefit and Agent Walsh, I'm confident you can, and will, regain a perfectly normal life."

"I appreciate hearing that, Doctor."

He nodded at us and added, "If you don't mind, Drew, I'd like you to bring your girlfriend with you to your next appointment. It's very important I see you both."

"I'd like that very much." It occurred to me I wanted a chance to tell Burkett I was off base by my question on the telephone about his feelings.

As we stood to leave, Burkett vigorously shook my hand once more.

We drove from Red Bank to Lavallette mostly in silence. Whenever Walsh did speak, his words couldn't get past my distraction. I longed for Angie. Since I had not made plans for this evening, I got a tingling sensation at the thought we could just sit on top a sand dune, enjoying the cool ocean breeze. Our love affair, which seemed like it began only yesterday, started right there.

"Did Jorgenson or Wilcox ever tell you why they chose you to fill the vacancy?" He took his eyes off the road for a second to watch my reaction.

"Well, Jorgenson made a point of my interest in Political Science courses. Thought it would be germane to learning each function in local government." I scratched my head, searching for a more definitive response. "But there was no indication why they chose me or that other candidates were considered."

We stopped for a red light about a mile from my house.

"For your information, Baxter, I've discussed the status of the case with the District Director in Newark and the US prosecuting attorney. They believe we can indict Jorgenson on lesser charges, but the consensus is we need more real hard evidence on him."

"How much more dirt do you need for God's sake?"

"You may have to confront the mayor to get him to admit to the Trotter swindle or lose his temper, which may cause him to act in an unguarded manner."

"You're kidding. I can't fathom how the hell it would be possible for me to pull that off." I wished he had mentioned the intrigue to Burkett.

My apprehension eased, like I had dodged a bullet, when he didn't say a word for a few minutes. I mumbled to him, "Turn at the next corner."

With the car motor still running in my driveway, he spoke in a stern tone. "Look, you are the one insider the Bureau needs who can uphold an air-tight case against Jorgenson on the bigger corruption charge. That's the only reason we took you into our confidence so soon. I took a calculated risk that we could rely on you, and you were committed to work with us."

"Suppose I refuse to do anything further." *What would my father do?*

He faced away from me. "Of course, the Bureau could ask your lady friend, Miss Carswell, for assistance. Do you want us to do that?"

I jerked toward him in the seat, upset at the implication. No way is he putting Angie in harm's way. They just don't take no for an answer.

"This sucks. What the hell do I have to do?"

"First, we'll tell you what you have to say. Most likely, you'll be wired. Of course, we'll be close by."

If it weren't for my hatred for the corrupt Hank Jorgenson, I might have told Walsh and the FBI to forget it. With all the facts they had about the mayor and his buddy, I couldn't believe they'd put me through this.

Civic duty, sure. Angie is priority one in my life now, so nobody can force me to play this game of gotcha.

I exited the car and slammed the door closed.

I didn't tell Angie about my conversation with Walsh, who promised without a doubt he would contact me soon.

"How did it go with Doctor Burkett?" Angie asked.

"I'm sure he was somewhat helpful to the FBI, except—"

"Except for what?"

"Angie, did Jorgenson or Wilcox ever indicate why they hired me to fill the vacancy rather than someone else?"

"Not at all. I didn't even know there was an actual vacancy, but we were all glad somebody was hired, because the workload had increased substantially."

The weekend further strengthened our union. We planned how to return the two files undetected, and agreed to keep our relationship secret a little longer. The subject of a marriage proposal entered my mind. I decided I'd wait for the right, romantic time. Even the thought of a lifetime with Angie was an exhilarating feeling.

As we watched the first quarter of the Giants-Eagles game on Sunday Night Football, the phone rang. "Hello," I answered.

"Mr. Baxter, it's Agent Walsh."

I moved to the far side of the living room, hoping to hear a change of plans. My gut told me it was my duty, but I didn't want to risk a life without Angie if something went wrong.

"Yes."

"We're ready. I'll meet you tomorrow night at seven. Park directly across the street from the Sail Inn."

Why me?

I gazed at an animated Angie relishing in an Eagles' touchdown to take the early lead 7 – 0.

"Okay, okay. I'll be there."

We set the alarm for five-thirty the next morning so I could drop Angie at her house to get ready for work. I went to the one Starbucks in town, had a black coffee and a danish, and squandered time ogling the pretty young mothers, who had deposited their children at school, before driving to the Town Hall ten minutes away.

Flashing lights suddenly appeared behind me.

"Oh shit, the police," I grumbled. As I parked at the curb, I observed Police Chief Campbell finally exit the police car.

"Good morning, Chief Campbell. I'm Drew—"

"I know who you are, Baxter." His demeanor was unfriendly to say the least, while I handed him my license, insurance card and registration. "You didn't stop at the stop sign before the turn onto Main Street and you were driving erratic."

"Oh my God, I thought I did stop, Chief. I mean, I wasn't in any rush this morning to get to work so—"

"Please step out of the car."

"But Chief—"

"Now!"

I exited the car. "Chief, I usually don't travel this route to work, so maybe I missed the stop sign."

He directed me to stand against the fender as he searched the front seats.

What the hell is he doing that for?

"What's this?" he asked with a smirk on his face.

He produced a small plastic bag of white powder.

"I don't know what it is and I don't know how the hell it got there." His tightened chin and lips reflected his reaction to my raised voice.

"Hey pal, don't get aggressive with me or you'll find out what trouble really is!"

"Sorry, but this doesn't make sense," I said in a mild tone.

"Okay. I'm going to let you get to work while I have this material analyzed at the lab in Toms River. Then I'll be in touch with you. Understand?"

"Yeah, but I still don't get it." I labored to control my irritation ...and confusion. "It's all a mistake."

"Whatever," he said with a stoic smirk on his face. He dropped the car documents on my lap after I sat back in the driver's seat. "My deputies and I will be watching you, you hear?"

He followed me for two blocks and made a right turn.

This is crazy. I distinctly remember stopping at the sign. And where did that bag of powder come from?

CHAPTER 20

There was only one person that came to mind to contact for legal advice. A consult with Frederick Cohen was out of the question. First thing Monday morning I called Russ Williams in his White Plains, New York office of IBM.

"Great to hear from you, Drew. What a surprise!"

Foregoing small talk, I described my encounter with Chief Campbell, noting every detail of the puzzling occurrence.

"You've got to be kidding. He knows you work for the town! What the hell did you do to put a bug up his butt?"

"This is serious, Russ. It could affect my job."

"Okay, I understand. From what you've told me, he can show cause for pulling you over—simply his word against yours regarding the stop sign. However, rummaging around your car sounds illegal on the surface. Did he indicate on what grounds he was permitted to conduct the search?"

"Not at all."

"Why in the world would he plant the stuff on you?"

Damn good question.

He coughed and inquired, half joking, "Are you sure you didn't leave that stuff in the car when you were shopping or ...or were you with someone who was using coke?" The cough turned to a chuckle.

"Hey man, you're not with me on this." My frustration was heading toward rage. "Can I sue him or ask for an investigation?"

"Drew, you know I only deal with corporate law and contracts, things like that. Forget suing the police! Let me check with some colleagues who handle criminal and civil cases, and I'll get back to you. Meanwhile, I'm sure you don't want to put your job in jeopardy any further, so why don't you wait for the results of the analysis?"

I felt my old buddy was giving me the run around. "Thanks loads, pal," I said; the sarcasm in my voice was purposeful.

Monday was a complete blur at work. I went through the motions to keep my paperwork current and desk clear. Lena informed me of a computer glitch, but I just nodded as if I understood everything she said. Nothing could possibly distract me from what might be a life- changing event.

"Aren't you hungry?" Angie wondered when I didn't order any lunch.

"I ate too much at Starbucks this morning." No further response was necessary, as I caught the twinkle of understanding in her eyes.

I bit my tongue wondering how I would keep my meeting with Walsh a secret from Angie as well as the outlandish episode with Chief Campbell. There was no point in worrying her about what was ahead. *It's scary enough for me.*

I made one run to Cohen's office in the afternoon. When he saw me, the grin on his face was unmistakable. I left his office in a hurry to deliver a large file to Angie. The afternoon didn't end fast enough for me. Time moved so slowly I thought my watch had stopped.

I decided to get to the Sail Inn earlier than seven for my FBI rendezvous. No need to go home first and hang out. A hamburger and an O'Doul's settled my stomach ...and my nerves. I brushed off several patrons who wanted to join me. One called me, "Unsociable." I found myself staring at the second hand on the wall clock wondering why it moved so slowly.

Then I walked across the street to my car.

And waited.

"Hello, Mr. Baxter," Walsh said, slipping into the passenger seat. He had parked down the street behind me.

"Yeah, hi."

"The Bureau believes we have a workable plan."

"I hope I can handle it."

"I'm sure you can." He changed his position to face me. "We've learned that Jorgenson has been invited to meet with the governor and other party officials concerning his future. The word is he may run for the US Senate in two years, bypassing New Jersey state senator. They believe the opposition party candidate is vulnerable."

"Jeez, are they in for a surprise about their bogus superstar."

"We'll see. The meeting is this Wednesday night in Princeton. A limo will take him directly from the Town Hall, so we want you to stay late. You'll have to pick the proper time to get to him while he's waiting for the pick-up." Walsh hesitated for a second to view the heavy commuter traffic. "We think it's the most opportune time and place for you to confront the mayor and catch him unaware."

"Okay, but what about how I catch him on tape and ...and what about Wilcox hanging around?"

"Right. First, the State Police will detain Wilcox late Wednesday afternoon about a traffic issue, unrelated to his association with Jorgenson. Second, two agents and I will be located in a television repair van a half block south of Town Hall. We want you to leave the building alone at the regular time and meet us in the van."

"That will give me enough time?"

"The device we use now only takes a few minutes to cut-on and adjust. You'll have no problem returning on time."

He reached into his jacket inside pocket for a single sheet of paper. "Here are a few topics as a start for you to incite

Jorgenson. Use your own words. The Trotter property sale is the main objective to stress and get him to talk."

I glanced at the notes, but my mind focused on the face-to-face exchange with Jorgenson. *Can I stand up to him?*

"Wear a dark-colored loose-fitting shirt with a breast pocket! The device works best that way and is undetected."

"Okay."

"Are you ready to do this, Baxter? You know better than anyone what's at stake." Walsh looked dead serious.

"Yeah, I'm ready, I guess. Suppose you tell me. Doesn't the FBI do this stuff every day of the week? "

"I know you'll do the best you can."

He handed me a release form to sign approving my voluntary participation. Even the FBI believes in the need to CYA.

"See you Wednesday night," he said, closing the car door.

Fortunately, I had an all-day assignment on Tuesday inputting receipts on the tax rolls. I masked my apprehension by softly whistling Broadway show tunes. Angie shook her head at me a few times, holding in a chuckle. While I didn't speak directly to Jorgenson or Wilcox, I noticed them look my way several times during the day.

Am I too suspicious?

As I ate that night and watched TV, I was surprisingly calm. Even the prime time news was devoid of calamities, scandals and war reports for a change. However, my composure changed once I lay back on my pillow in bed, unable to screen out wild thoughts. *The medication better kick in fast.*

What happens if Jorgenson avoids my attempts to aggravate him? Suppose he just fires me on the spot? Maybe he'll spy the wiring? Or threatens me ...or calls the police? The enormity of the task flooded out my mind like a raging river.

I remembered my sudden deep depression the night before the Ramada banquet and kicked the covers off the bed.

No, not again.

Angie.

"I can't let her down," I whispered, sitting up ready for action. "I never got cold feet on patrol duty in Iraq, so bring on Jorgenson."

A restful night's sleep followed.

CHAPTER 21

Through the open door of his office, I watched Mayor Jorgenson adjust the cummerbund of his tuxedo. The invitation to the Governor's Drumthwacket Mansion in Princeton on Wednesday evening was a black tie affair. A limo was scheduled to pick him up from Town Hall at 6:30 p.m. sharp.

I had left the office a shortly after five as instructed and met Walsh and two other FBI agents in the television repair van for last-minute instructions. He fitted me with a pocket digital recording and transmitting device inside my shirt pocket. What technological advances! I expected wires wound around my body.

"Are you sure this thing works?" I asked. Jitters consumed my emotions, ever conscious of the metallic device half the size of a cigarette pack.

"Don't you worry about that! Just don't rub against it or get too close to anyone. No hugging your girlfriend."

I forced a smile. Although his objective was to calm my nerves, I was concerned with the unexpected.

"Remember, Baxter, you've got to be aggressive to make him talk on point. If you see an opening, keep after him. Don't let him off the hook." He looked at me with empathy for my situation, then patted my shoulder and said, "Listen, for reasons out of your control, the deception may turn out inconclusive."

I appreciated Walsh's pep talk, but I had my own motivation.

I had respect for Jorgenson at first, but he turned out to be another crooked politician. The residents of Barnegat Junction trusted him and deserved better. But there was a more pressing incentive to do my best to provoke him into a confession. The torment Angie went through because of that egotistical charlatan had to be redressed.

It's up to me.

I squirmed in my chair sneaking glimpses into the mayor's office, building up the courage to initiate the trickery. The mayor had been too busy to see me leave or return. The wall clock became my impetus to act, but the seconds hand could not keep up with the beats of my heart.

"Excuse me, Mr. Mayor, may I take a minute of your time?"

"Drew, you surprised me." He replaced his pen in the holder. "What are you doing here at this time?"

"I wanted an opportunity to speak to you privately."

"Uh-huh. Can it wait until tomorrow morning? I'm due to be picked up in a few minutes." He checked his appointment book and diary expecting me to leave.

"It will only take a minute or so, sir." *Be persistent, Walsh insisted.*

"Drew, it's important I finish this letter, so I'd appreciate it if—"

"We have to talk now!" My harsh interruption signaled our conversation would be anything but routine.

"What do you want?" he growled, clearly taken aback.

Leaning back in his chair, I felt like he was looking right through me, unaccustomed to hearing such a tone from anyone.

"What did you do to Angie in the Bahamas?" I hoped that humiliating experience would throw him off-guard.

His face turned grim. He held his chin and stared at me. "First of all, it's none of your business," he said, enunciating each syllable. Now his jaw jutted out. "Angie and I have a wonderful working association, so how dare you even suggest something obscene." He stood and walked around his desk toward me.

"The great Hank Jorgenson tried to make out with her, and I've had her in bed a dozen times." My own words sounded foreign to me. "You were going to rape her."

Walsh was right to egg him on forcefully. Jorgenson's conceit was offended, as his wrinkled brow and mean look might have been his ugly twin.

He stepped back and rested on the edge of his desk. "Look, Drew buddy, you better cool it right now. I'm not going to forget this, so get out of my office this minute and sober up."

"I haven't had a drink and I'm not finished." I matched his stern demeanor, unfazed by the tricky reference to the hotel banquet.

He looked outside his office to see if anyone was there. Slipping into his tuxedo jacket, he started to leave.

"Hold it! Why did you cheat old man Trotter? The eminent domain threat you and Wilcox orchestrated was a sham."

He smirked at me like I was dirt. "Who the hell do you think you're talking to? I've done all I can for the old guy." Pointing a finger at me, he snidely said, "Why don't you ask your friend, Pitman?"

"Why don't you tell me instead how Wilcox's brother-in-law was awarded the dredging contract at the Bay Street inlet?"

The squint in his eyes conveyed surprise at my thrust. "Now you're an expert on the bidding process for capital projects? It was a perfectly legal transaction." He laughed. "Is that what's bugging you? You've had too much to drink again, like last week. Not very appreciative of my administration, are you? Ingrate. Who the hell else do you think would have hired you?"

I hesitated. *What do I do now*?

"I know how you and Wilcox acquired your property on

751 and about the payola from Charles Parker of Outsource Data Corporation."

Once again his stricter profile returned as he checked his watch and stared at me for several seconds.

"Your administration stinks with corruption. You're a fraud."

He advanced toward me, nostrils flaring. "I can sue you for charges like that." He shook his head and added, "You're even more stupid than Parker said and I thought. He told us about your short fuse when you caused an argument over a slow-witted babe. We knew you had a screw loose, pal."

I promised Agent Walsh I would control myself and stick to the plan, but Jorgenson's words stuck in my craw. I felt my face redden and wanted to punch the fake in the jaw.

"Maybe I'm not so smart, but I can report what I know to the authorities."

"Oh you can! Without any proof, how far do you think you can get with Chief Campbell? Come on, Baxter, your hands are not so clean."

Now it was my turn to be shocked. "What are you talking about? You can't scare me."

"We have a photograph of you taking a kickback on a zoning matter at the front door of your house and—"

Cohen set me up?

"I delivered that packet to the lawyer's office the next morning."

"Sorry, buddy, there's no record in Cohen's files of receiving any packet from you. If you check your next bank statement though, you'll find a nice deposit in your account. How will you explain that to the authorities or," he chuckled, "what the police found in your car?"

My knees buckled. It was now clear why they hired me. I was their mentally impaired puppet. Jorgenson even deceived Dr. Burkett.

Thank God, the FBI has this on tape. I hope.

I forced myself to appear unruffled. It was essential I get Jorgenson to admit his misconduct. *Time's running out.*

"Angie thinks so much of you that she took the Condemnation documents on the Trotter property from your personal files." I concluded she was the catalyst to infuriate the mayor and cause him to lose control.

I pointed at the locked cabinet. Jorgenson pushed my arm away and moved back to his desk, opening the front drawer. He dangled the cabinet key to taunt me.

"Angie wouldn't do anything like that. She's a loyal employee and knows there are confidential files in—"

"She hates your guts."

His jaw trembled and he raised a fist at me. He walked around to the front of his desk.

I didn't give him a chance to respond. "Suppose I tell you that you authorized a discontinuance of the condemnation proceedings the day before the deal with Trotter was finalized. You tricked him into accepting a lower price for his land based on a low-ball appraisal. You knew all along my old company wanted the property once it was zoned commercial."

"Listen, you dummy. The greater good was achieved by the deal we arranged, okay? So who gives a damn about one miserable old man? Get the hell out of here and don't ever come back again."

I got 'em.

"Sure, I'll go."

I started to leave the office, but couldn't resist one more chance to rub it in good. "I'm going right to Angie's place and make out."

He walked slowly toward me. "I could care less," he said with deliberate aplomb, as he gently rubbed the palms of his hands together.

Next thing I knew, his fist caught me direct on the cheek and spun me around.

The sucker punch dazed me. "Crook," I sputtered, as I tried to get my bearings.

As he charged forward swinging rights and lefts, I protected my chest and head, but he pushed me hard into a bookcase. I dropped to one knee, wiping blood from my nose. His strength went beyond my expectation, as I tried to pull myself up by his jacket lapels to no avail.

He howled from the pain in his fist from hitting the top of my head.

It gave me an opening to scramble away on my knees, but he grabbed me from behind and started to choke me. I knew if I could gain leverage to reach my arms back around his neck, I'd yank him over my shoulder and pin him on his back.

As I struggled to stand, the transmitter device fell out of my shirt pocket and rattled on the floor

"What's that?" Jorgenson stared in utter astonishment at the curious-looking device. "You no-good idiot," he screamed.

Oh no.

Before he could reach for it, I threw a surprise right hand to his cheekbone. He reeled backward and held himself against his desk. Recovering quickly, he pushed himself forward at me and landed a punch on my temple. As he went for the transmitter, I limped ahead and tackled him. We rolled on the floor until he jammed me into the bookcase again. Several books fell off the shelf, which hindered me from fighting back against his blows to my head and chest.

"Oow," I groaned, as he banged my head against the wooden shelf. I thought I'd black out from the pain when another wild swing got by my guard and hit my shoulder blade. His hands grasped my throat again.

I couldn't breathe and felt light-headed.

Using all my strength, I kicked him in the crotch and held

him back with both feet. He bent over coughing. Although shaky, he stood over me, his eyes filled with rage.

"I could kill you, you stinking jerk, but you'll get yours when I tell the police what's happened."

"FBI. You're not going to kill anyone." Walsh burst in not a bloody second too soon.

"Agent, arrest this man," Jorgenson ordered, regaining his mayoral authority. "This neurotic drunk accosted me after everyone had left and—"

"Please sit down, Mr. Mayor," Walsh ordered. He read Jorgenson his Miranda rights and warned, "You have a lot of explaining to do."

"This is an outrage. He attacked me." Jorgenson stood, waving his arms in all directions. "I want my lawyer."

"Sit back down now!" Walsh blocked the mayor from exiting, or escaping, the office, leaving no doubt who was in charge.

As a second agent handcuffed Jorgenson, he cast a vengeful glare my way, mouthing, "I'll get you for this."

His words were surreal to me, like we had acted out a scene from *High Noon*.

I gawked at the mayor in his disheveled tuxedo as the agent led him out the door. For a solitary moment, my weariness faded away at this reassuring sight.

Although Jorgenson protested and insisted he speak to his lawyer, his gloomy appearance conveyed a picture of complete despair. The veins on his neck and swollen right hand looked made up for a horror movie. The small town empire he had built from scratch was crumbling down around him.

An agent led me to a couch outside the office. My nosebleed had stopped, but my face was puffy from that first punch I absorbed. My ribs hurt like hell, but I wasn't sure why or how. Despite feeling battered and bruised, with a bump on the back of my head, I had the unique satisfaction of a victory following a rough, physical football game.

A beaming Steve Walsh gave me a thumbs-up, smiling like a proud, triumphant coach. A crowning achievement for a law enforcement professional.

A resurgence of fulfillment swept through my body. I realized that my curiosity, an insatiable desire to aid a person in need, and intuition, had uncovered the worst kind of misconduct. Elected officials should have a higher standard of morals, but reality seems just the opposite. What was it a 19th century Englishman said? "Power tends to corrupt, and absolute power corrupts absolutely."

"I've got to see Angie." I tried unsuccessfully to stand

"An ambulance is on the way," Walsh said. He restrained me and advised, "We have it all on tape. You did a great job." He shook my hand and added, "I'll call Miss Carswell so she can go and see you at Toms River Medical."

In my stunned state, I relived awakening amid rubble and carnage from the safe house explosion in Iraq and visualized Lieutenant Munson, with tears in his eyes, saluting me as they carried me by stretcher from the charred building.

I rested comfortably in the Intensive Care Unit after doctors examined me in the emergency room. To my surprise, I had three broken ribs. A slight headache persisted, but it didn't subdue the contented feeling I had for terminating the Jorgenson regime.

"Drew, oh my poor Drew." Angie rushed to my bedside and kissed me.

"Ow. That's my ribs, but don't worry, I'm not going to die." I hoped she would appreciate a sense of humor.

Her eyes glistened as she inspected my facial appearance until a tear or two appeared. "I'm so sorry this happened to you. I love you very, very much and ..."

"Angie, no reason to be sorry or cry. We, you and I together, got him."

"Why didn't you tell me what you were going to do?"

"Blame the FBI for that." Grinning, I jested, "Besides, I didn't want you to see me get beat up."

When I yawned, she straighten the blanket over me. I mumbled, "You'd make a terrific nurse."

"From now on, no secrets between us, you hear me," she said as a demand. "We're going to be together forever." The sincerity and joy were back in her beautiful face. "I'm very proud of you."

"I've got that statement on tape too, and—"

"Stop kidding! I'm serious." She turned the lights out in the room and walked to the door.

"Now I *am* serious," I whispered in the dark. "You've changed my life. Everything I went through before this, whether at home, in Iraq, and leading up to tonight, it was all worth it for me to find you."

As I faded off to sleep, I heard myself cheering at the Rutgers-Connecticut basketball game. The stinking dream was back.

CHAPTER 22

We delayed the appointment requested by Dr. Burkett for three weeks following my confrontation with Hank Jorgenson. Other than heavily taped ribs and a bruised face, the soreness in my body had eased, and my sense of accomplishment was euphoric. My inevitable appearance as a witness at the corruption trial seemed a minor inconvenience at this point.

The interim was time well spent. Angie and I became devoted friends as well as lovers. Temporarily, she agreed to move into my place. The fact that our interests were compatible made the 24/7 companionship easy. We shared simple things, like food shopping, quiet time reading, house chores. Personal quirks were shrugged off. As examples, she overlooked my fixation with checking my watch and meeting schedules, and I held in laughter when she looked up answers to the daily crossword puzzle and then boasted when it was completed.

To deal with or avoid monotony, we planned short trips. Driving in the treasured Pinelands, we stopped at a functioning cranberry farm, bringing back fond memories of Harold Trotter. Further south, we toured Batso Village. This iron works site, in the National Registry of Historic Places, operated in the seventeen and eighteen hundreds and supplied the Continental Army.

On a day trip to the Barnegat Lighthouse, I learned more about this special woman.

"How did you get to know so much about the Jersey coast?" I asked after she rattled off numerous facts worthy of a trivia contest.

"My dad and I went by car to all the tourist spots one summer. The history from Sandy Hook and Asbury Park to Wildwood and Cape May fascinated me. Before Atlantic City had its rebirth as a gambling mecca, the rich and famous chose the grand resort hotels on the boardwalk for their vacations. A 1944 hurricane started the city's decline. Shipwrecks off the coast were common in the late eighteen-hundreds." She threw me a quick glance as she drove and added, "It was a special time for me to connect with my father. I'll never forget it."

And I only went to Yankee games with my dad.

I let her knowledge sink in as we passed towns with cool names on Long Beach Boulevard: Surf City, Ship Bottom, Harvey Cedars, and, best of all, Loveladies.

"No, I've never heard of the *Morro Castle* disaster," I responded defensively to her insistence.

"The ship was travelling between Havana and New York City, caught fire and burned killing hundreds. It eventually beached in the surf off Asbury Park, although some survivors made it all the way to Spring Lake in the storm."

"When did it happen?"

"I think it was nineteen-thirty-four. The reason it's a significant event has to do with stricter rules for maritime safety of luxury liners and new regulations for ship construction materials and fire drills, and the like."

"You're just trying to impress me," I kidded her. "Seriously though, the more I know about you, the more I surrender to your qualities ...and smarts. You are a whiz."

Even her self-conscious smile was distinctive. I wondered how Dr. Burkett would describe Angie once he met her. Perfectly normal, I'm sure. From my standpoint, she combined an outgoing, warm personality with a levelheaded respect for everyday issues and personal interactions. Pleasant with others, but firm in her positions. Despite the stress of the incident with Jorgenson, she has coped better than I with my issues.

When we reached our destination, I groaned at the lighthouse signage.

"Two-hundred-seventeen steps too much for you to climb? You'll be amazed at the panoramic view across Barnegat Bay and up and down the coast."

She was right on both counts. Despite difficulty breathing, the effort was worth sharing the experience with her.

We stopped for a late lunch at the nearby Plantation restaurant. After placing our order, she whispered, "Can I tell you what's been on my mind?"

"No way," I replied in jest, continuing to move the salt and pepper shakers like checkers.

"Don't do that."

"Sorry, just being playful."

"Stop checking your watch and listen!"

Whoa! What's this sudden melancholy all about?

"I want you to know this. It hasn't been easy for me to get too close to any man. Maybe I'm afraid after what happened to me with him in the Bahamas."

I squeezed her hand. *She can't even say his name.*

"When I was in high school, I had wild thoughts about becoming a nun. Even after I graduated and was dating, my life was empty. I wasn't happy. It took going away to school to Katherine Gibbs, with my parent's encouragement, to change my outlook."

The emotion in her voice amplified. I sat rigid, not knowing what to expect.

"Then you came into my life. It's all different with you. When we're apart, I'm not the same. Jumpy or worried. I just want to be with you all the time."

My heart stirred. I could only sigh, "I feel the same way," as I clasped her hands together in mine. "Look what we've been through together. How you got those condemnation documents took a lot of courage."

"Yes, but I did it also to get back at him."

"Understood." I smiled and added, "My gut feeling about wrongdoing at Barnegat Junction turned out to be one hundred percent correct. I—"

"This isn't about you or the town, dammit."

"Yes, right." The blood rushed to my face and ears.

"Are you bored with me?"

"What? Absolutely not."

"Do you truly love me?" Her piercing eyes were evidence of a serious plea.

"Of course I do!" I leaned across the table and gently kissed her on the lips. "You touched my heart right from the start. Please get rid of any doubts! Okay? The last weeks together have been wonderful. Before I met you, I drifted in and out of trouble or raced in all directions, almost drowning in insecurity. As I told you in the hospital room a couple of weeks ago, you've changed all that. There's not another person like you."

That's all that had to be said. The serene face I love returned.

While our comfort level with each other grew during these weeks, and my attention on Angie was constant, our upcoming meeting with Burkett lingered in the back of my mind. He had insisted she be present for the first time. Would she learn things about me that might diminish her feelings about us as a twosome? Is the price of gaining a healthy, stable outlook worth losing Angie? *Unintended consequences.*

As the visit neared, the tension was as if it were the bottom of the ninth inning with two outs, my team was losing by one run, and I was at bat once again with the bases loaded.

I'm not looking for her sympathy either.

CHAPTER 23

An eager Angie held my hand as we entered the doctor's office.

"I'm pleased to meet you, Miss Carswell," Dr. Burkett said. "I've been looking forward to it for some time."

"Thank you, Doctor. And special thanks for all you've done for Drew."

"Doc, am I a fortunate guy or what?"

"You're more than fortunate." He motioned for us to sit on the couch. "Your attitude and demeanor now are directly attributable to your employment in Barnegat Junction and a relationship with Miss Carswell. I'm proud of your advancement ...with her incredible backing." He shook my hand a second time and nodded to Angie.

"I understand the Barnegat Junction disgrace is one of the biggest scandals in New Jersey history," Burkett announced, "and your—"

"True," I interrupted, "but it doesn't compare to the widespread corruption and money laundering involving Bergen County mayors and other officials. Add to that the backroom dealings of Hudson County to the state's reputation."

"The state has definitely had more than its share of shame," Burkett observed. "The role you played should enhance your self-esteem."

"Yes, I feel it has." I glanced at Angie for confirmation.

She nodded with eyebrows raised.

"One thing for sure though," he continued, "New Jersey doesn't hold a candle to the corruption in Illinois politics," he continued. "I'm afraid quid pro quo is so ingrained in our political system that elected officials can't distinguish right from wrong."

Angie was quick to add, "I'm happy for Councilman Pitman, an honest man. As senior councilman, he's been named Acting-Mayor."

"I misjudged Pitman at first," I admitted, hitting my hand lightly against my forehead, symbolically, "but he has put the interest of the town first. His first act was to veto the zoning change at the Bay Street Park. Regaining all the trust that's been lost—a real tough assignment for him."

"One more time," Angie said, teasing me and my gesture. "But you don't have to be so modest about your part in cleaning up the mess."

"Doc, the thing is, I'm still in the middle of this mess." I felt a touch of anxiety, so I reached out to hold Angie's hand. "I've been subpoenaed to appear before a Grand Jury and—"

"I believe that's the normal process," he said. "Don't worry! It's your opportunity to tell all you know about the mayor, Wilcox and Cohen." He closed one eye and confided, "Frankly, I thought at first you were unreasonable about your attitude toward George Parker. Turns out you're one-hundred percent correct."

"Thanks for telling me. But, Doc, what I'm concerned about are the details on tape of my fracas with Jorgenson, and his lawyer's defense of entrapment."

"Well I'm not a lawyer, but based on what I read and your account of what happened, the evidence appears airtight. In fact, his blatant scheme to blackmail you, or whatever it's called, should be enough to convince a jury of his misconduct."

"The doctor's right," Angie added. "Remember what Agent Walsh told you. Wilcox and Cohen plea-bargained about their conspiracy from day one to take advantage of a new, growing community. The prosecution's case is very strong against Jorgenson."

"Walsh confided in me," I volunteered, "that the prosecutor needed the testimony of Wilcox, but the Bureau is hopping mad that he's getting off with leniency. In fact, the FBI will continue to investigate Wilcox's egregious past. According to Walsh, he'd sell out his own mother and throw Jorgenson to the wolves to save himself."

"Well then, without question we can expect a jury should find Jorgenson guilty," Burkett concluded, and Angie nodded her concurrence.

"I know, but that's not what's bothering me." I had decided that it was best Angie heard the whole story when I told Doc Burkett of my concern.

"Then tell me about it," Burkett said, turning serious.

"Okay." I faced Angie. "The tape will disclose how I baited Jorgenson to lose his usual poise. It was the only way I could think of to follow Walsh's directive to agitate him."

She looked at me without emotion.

"I made an assumption that Jorgenson's still attracted to you. In other words, and it's not hard to imagine, he has the hots for you."

"You're kidding."

"I bruised his ego by suggesting you and I are a twosome and we see each other after work, so—"

"Well we are," she interrupted instantly. "So what's the problem?"

I looked at Doc Burkett, who was listening in his usual intent way. I felt embarrassed.

"I told him I was getting you in bed ...many times."

"God, was it necessary to be so honest?" She slumped down and meekly glanced at Burkett, presumably looking for him to rebuke me.

"There's more to it," I said, picking at the fingernail on my pinky.

She half stood, like she was frozen in place.

"I kinda made it sound like it was nothing more than a sexual thing, you know, like one night stands."

"Drew, how could you say that?" She stood and stared out the office window.

Once again, I felt I let Angie down.

"Hold on, Miss Carswell," Burkett said. He beckoned her to sit back next to me so we both could listen to him. He picked up his ever-handy notepad.

"I wanted you to hear what I would tell Drew today. I know you're aware of the trauma that he has gone through." His voice was calm and unhurried. "The guilt complex due to his father's accident and the horrific incident in Iraq were a result of unforeseen circumstances in his life. His reaction was understandable, and he has overcome those guilt feelings."

By raising old wounds, I wondered where Burkett was taking us. I peeked at Angie, who was absorbed in his narrative.

"He had shown definite symptoms of post-traumatic stress, but there's a more fundamental reason that has driven Drew's behavior throughout his life. His case should not be confused with personal idiosyncrasies or habits. It's more serious than inoffensive peculiarities we all have. The mental health professionals and sociologists call it by different names, and the science of the workings of the brain is still evolving. Okay so far?"

"Yes, Doctor," Angie said.

I breathed a sigh of relief to see the placid look on Angie's face. I felt an unexpected calmness to hear what Burkett would reveal about me next, positive or negative.

"The simple description is compulsive helping, although there are several versions of this behavior. It's a less severe form of obsessive-compulsive disorders. Some are difficult to understand—"

"You mean they're uncontrollable," Angie broke in.

"Oh, not at all," he replied. "Let me give you some easy examples where treatment is available if the individual makes a commitment to stop; the alcoholic's need to drink; the drug addict; the compulsive gambler. Each has serious consequences on the individual's ability to lead a normal life. What drives the sex deviates is another unique derangement. Without treatment of these addictions, the body is powerless to fight back against the brain's desires."

"But, Doctor, helping others doesn't have the same harmful meaning as the disorders you mentioned." I tried to soften the implication of my condition.

"Well, let's talk about it and find out. First, I'll digress and refer you to the rather simplistic illustrations of obsessive-compulsive disorders of Jack Nicholson in the movie *As Good as It Gets,* and the TV show *Monk*. Also, you've heard of chronic lying and—"

"And eating disorders," Angie suggested. Her body shivered as she added, "I recently saw TV shows about compulsive hoarding of garbage."

"To go to the extreme, there's a neurological disorder known as apotemnophilia, a compulsion to amputate a perfectly healthy limb. Now forget I told you about it."

"Weird," Angie said, holding her nose. "I couldn't even pronounce or spell it."

"How about someone being obsessed with power? Can you tell me who might have that problem?"

Angie and I responded simultaneously, "Jorgenson."

"Right. Based on newspaper accounts, I believe Jorgenson is a classic case of someone with a compulsive disorder to control events, even if it requires manipulation. He masked his problem through what was attributed to ambition and the strength of his personality. Furthermore, a person so consumed with power or lofty status can believe he's immune to being caught at wrongdoing; actually common in all walks of life, even the superstars of sports. The Greeks call it hubris."

"You don't have to be a shrink to figure that out," I joked. Neither Burkett nor Angie laughed.

"Drew, the fact is there are detrimental aspects of an addiction to helping people with their real or perceived problems. In your case, I can point to your protection of Carolyn, which cost you your job. Another example, that Miss Carswell witnessed, relates to the incident in the restaurant where you mistakenly attempted to perform the Heimlich maneuver."

"What you're saying, Doctor," Angie said, "is these incidents prevent his confidence from growing. Is that right?"

"Absolutely."

I remained silent, but I knew they were correct.

"There were occasions where you exhibited an unhealthy helping tendency as a caretaker. As a kid you were obsessed with taking over as captain and pitted yourself against your competitors, as if it were your duty to shelter your buddies and take everything on your shoulders."

"Yeah, and I got kicked in the pants for it."

"Unfortunately, you were a caretaker to your roommate in Las Vegas where he abused your friendship and duped you out of all your money. From what you told me, the fella had a compulsion to lie."

"Gee, I hadn't heard of that before," Angie mumbled. She gave me a questioning look.

Damn, does he have to humiliate me in front of her?

"Taking responsibility for others has been evident throughout your life. In fact, when there is no opportunity whatsoever for you to exert your compulsion, your behavior often becomes erratic, for example, you're more apt to show irritation or worse."

"That may explain the miserable couple of weeks in the Bronx before I went to Vegas."

"Right. However, before you think this is all negative, there have also been examples of constructive non-intrusive caring prominent in your conduct."

Thank God for that. I shifted my position to alleviate a sudden uneasiness at the openly personal analysis.

"Are you referring to Mr. Trotter?" Angie asked.

"I'll get to that in a minute." Burkett smiled at her and leaned forward toward me, relishing in his trained proficiency.

"Your father played a supportive if not genetic role in your condition. His job as a social worker; his obliging position toward his addictive mother-in-law and so on."

"So you can't say for sure what the root cause is?"

"You see, Drew, because compulsive helping is the least offensive to third parties and, while the disorder can be debilitating to patients, the research hasn't advanced that far."

I took his clarification as an encouraging sign.

"So any number of good and generous acts by your father, as a role model, may have influenced you as a child. Words of wisdom, you might say."

"That's entirely possible. Angie, I wish you had met him. My memories of him, excluding the accident, were a source of worship as I grew up."

"I've told you on several occasions that your responsibility to duty is commendable." Burkett continued. "Your basic instincts of right and wrong combined with your compulsion to help led you to join the Army as a result of nine-eleven. You've confided to me how law enforcement work was one of your earliest wishes and—"

"And," I interrupted, "I feel real comfortable in public service. I enjoy meeting and talking with the residents to resolve whatever issues they might have. As far as my tour in the military is concerned, they do call it military *service*, don't they?"

"Exactly. Clearly, there are sound and rewarding patterns of your conduct, which we want to encourage and manage without provoking the intrusive, meddling aspects." He sat back, sipped his water, and clasped his hands together. "In fact, research has shown that obsessive-compulsive people have been quite successful in their chosen fields. As one example, TV game host and comedian, Howie Mandel, has struggled with an obsessive-compulsive disorder."

I bet Angie was thinking the same as me. *What's next?*

"This brings me to you and Miss Carswell; Angie, if I may." He referred to a specific page of notes. "Drew finally found someone with whom he could share and experience mutual respect, and yes, love. His past misfortunes have magnified his caring for you and his devotion or attachment, call it what you will."

Placing her hand on my knee, I felt Angie's fingers tremble in stops and starts. My hand reached out to hold hers as if it had a mind of its own.

"The Trotter affair became the basis of a dramatic partnership for you both to achieve a satisfactory outcome. In Drew's case, his resentment for an apparent injustice drove him to inform the FBI, the ultimate civic duty. Let's disregard you were misguided to point at Pitman. Angie supported you because she has compassion for you to begin with, and believes in you, but, more significantly, I think she found someone who truly loves her, a love she desired to return and—"

"I love him with all my heart, idiosyncrasies and all," Angie interrupted. "I comforted him because he deserved it, and his determination turned out to be correct." She tightened her hold on my hand.

The passion in her voice equaled a moving recital by a

Shakespearean actor. Instinctively, I blew her a kiss, yet was confused how Burkett would connect his analysis to my crude statements on tape concerning her.

"At this point Drew reluctantly agreed to compel Jorgenson to divulge his misdeeds, which coincided with his caring for you, Angie, and his concern for truth and duty. Rather than a collision of these goals, they meshed and complimented each other. How could he help not just one person, whether Trotter, or you or himself, but thousands of people in Barnegat Junction all at one time?"

Angie and I looked at one another. *He's making me seem like a lifesaver.*

"Your craving to overthrow the mayor," Burkett deduced, "and clean up the corruption in Barnegat Junction required aggressive or outlandish assertions."

My emotion spiked at his insight about my handling of the skirmish.

"Your non-intrusive caring and love of Angie provided you the trust to use her as a catalyst to goad Jorgenson. In other words, you were comfortable with her love no matter what."

"Do you actually see it that way, Doctor Burkett?" Angie asked anxiously.

"Positively! And guess what? It worked in two ways. Jorgenson has been exposed, and Drew demonstrated clear, smart thinking of priorities."

Angie gave me a bear hug.

He raised his hand indicating there's more to come. "There's another issue, however." Burkett's facial expression turned grim.

What now?

"Some time ago, Drew, you told me you were at a basketball game when your mother died. In fact, the game has appeared often in your dreams. Did—"

"Yeah. It was a big game against the UConns on the Rutgers campus. I ..." My hands began to feel sweaty.

"When you arrived at the hospital, I understand you were quite upset."

"Of course I was. I left the game at halftime when I got the call from the hospital. It took me almost two hours to—"

"You could have gone to the hospital sooner, but you had made a choice to see the game rather than—"

"Enough." I couldn't listen to his inquisition any longer. The vision of my mother's deathbed overwhelmed my senses. *I should have been there with her!*

"Are you okay, Drew?" Angie asked.

In a halting voice, I answered Burkett, "My mother needed me, but ...but I didn't get there in time." That nagging churning echoed once again in my stomach.

Angie put her arm around my shoulder as tears ran down my cheeks.

Burkett excused himself for a minute.

"Angie, I should have been there with her. But I went to the lousy game instead. I wanted to tell her I loved her."

Angie cemented her lips together. She wiped the tears off my face and stroked my head.

Burkett returned and stood in front of me. "I mentioned earlier that compulsive helping is not as hurtful as other disorders." He spoke in a low-key calm manner. "However, when you are unable to benefit someone close to you, the very thing you're compelled to do, it became the basis for your inner conflict. A single powerless feeling left a void in your life."

Oh my God. That feeling of helplessness had been held inside me all these years. I wished that miraculously I could have one minute, sixty seconds, to hold my mother close. Why didn't I get to know her better? Her likes and dislikes? The color of her eyes?

Is that why I still feel the emptiness?

"Drew, we've raised this turmoil in your consciousness and you have to come to grips with it. You're compelled to come to the aid of others, which you failed to do for your mother in her final hours. To undo that disappointment, you've pushed yourself to the extreme in the opposite direction." He paused and placed his hand on my shoulder. "We all miss loved ones, but we have to move on. It's what your mother and your father would want."

I allowed his meaning to sink in. My last conversation with my mom came to mind. She apologized needlessly for not always being there for me when I was growing up. I remember her final words were, *"I'm proud of you attending Rutgers and I love you dearly."*

"You do realize that your mother has forgiven you," Burkett closed. "You must know that by now, Drew."

Tears welled up in me on cue. I needed to hear those words. "Thank you, Dr. Burkett. I do believe you and I know they would wish for my happiness."

Walking about the room and reading the plaques on the wall, I overheard Burkett tell Angie that she should be alert to odd changes in my behavior and contradictory actions.

"Signs to watch for may be a rush to interfere in others' problems or if he becomes anxious about what to do to contribute or resolve a mundane issue. Overly impetuous. You must realize that when Drew first came to me, he was psychologically frail. He's come a long way."

She accepted the responsibility unconditionally by nods of her head and whispered, "I can offer observations to critique him like he helps others ...in a caring way."

"Wonderful. You are great together." A smile lit up his face. "I intend to reduce his medication," Burkett continued as he reached for his prescription pad. "You know, under different personal circumstances, Drew might have been a much-admired philanthropist. A Good Samaritan. Unfortunately, his character trait has made him a magnet to respond to atypical circumstances."

"If you knew him like I do," she confided, "you'd also see a real sentimental person. I bet if he saw someone drowning, he'd try to save the person even though he can hardly swim."

I was oblivious to the remainder of their conversation. They were both smiling, clearly pleased about our progress, which wrapped up the nerve-racking session in a relaxed atmosphere for us all.

Thanks to them, my road to recovery was assured as sure as the certainty that morning follows night. My mental state was free, albeit my sensitivity to others' needs, real or imagined, remained a constant part of my personality. All the difficulties in my life were a distant, but indelible memory. Happy occasions with my parents surfaced. A precipitous wide smile on my face probably made me look like a blooming idiot. At the same time, however, my brain couldn't come to grips with my relieved outlook.

If Burkett's analysis is correct, why is that gnawing sensation holding me back from relishing in the moment? Is my nightmare all over?

Angie excused herself at my request. I needed private time with Burkett.

"Doctor, I must apologize for putting you on the spot when I called you at home, and, you know, asked if you ever felt vulnerable like I do at times."

He nodded with a pensive look on his face. "Drew, it was a valid, but unexpected, question. You had me reflect on my career and ...would you believe my interest in mental health started in my high school American Literature course?"

"Is that right?"

"We studied Herman Melville and his classic tale, *Moby-Dick*. The insane obsession of Captain Ahab to track down the white whale, which led to his symbolic death, intrigued me. I explored similar novels of addiction, like *The Lost Weekend*. My college major was pre-determined from then on."

"Marvelous beginning for you."

"Over the years, I've counseled many patients, including military personnel. There are occasions, too often I'm afraid, where my efforts don't achieve a full or partial recovery." He stood next to me, arms folded. "It hurts, but I've reconciled myself to the fact I've done my best, keeping faith in my ability and a continuing education program."

"I can attest to that."

"Thank you, Drew. Your case has reenergized me, and I'm pleased with the results we've accomplished together. It will guide me to assist others."

"You chose a worthy profession." *Sounds like he has a compulsion, also.*

No sooner had I exited Burkett's office, Angie threw her arms around me and held me close. She choked up and said, "I'm so lucky to have you and I love you just the way you are."

"You mean everything to me," I whispered in her ear. "We're a great team, aren't we?"

Her innocent smile was back. "Yes, and you're the captain," she teased.

"Why don't we make this a permanent arrangement?"

"Is that a proposal, captain?" she asked. Her green eyes lit up like shamrocks on St. Patrick's Day.

"You better believe it is."

I tugged at my right ear.

Her body shook with laughter.

Later that night, as Angie slept beside me, I pondered the events of the last few months. The achievement and related publicity, mostly attributed to me, were too incredible to grasp. I couldn't judge if the public's cynical view of politicians had changed in any way. In fact, corruption and infidelity were endemic to the system. My integrity, as Dr. Burkett made clear, had augmented the trust in public life of so many. In all humility, it gave me a marvelous proud feeling.

I prayed that Angie and I would now enjoy a normal life.

I'll be glad when the trial is over, and Jorgenson and Wilcox get what they deserve. It isn't easy to forget the look Wilcox gave me as the FBI led him away. Now I know how Sheriff Will Kane must have felt.

CHAPTER 24

The national publicity over the scandal, as well as the jury trial in Trenton, propelled me into the limelight for at least a month's worth of fame.

The US attorney presented compelling evidence under the Hobbs Act of wrongdoing in Barnegat Junction. The fake Condemnation documents and my taped conversation were admitted into evidence. The prosecutor was confident that Wilcox's plea bargain against Jorgenson would seal the case.

Conversely, a clever rebuttal of entrapment by the FBI was weaved by defense attorney Robert Rickman in defense of Jorgenson. He blamed Billy Wilcox as the mastermind of a conspiracy aided by Frederick Cohen, and charged Wilcox with abusing his authority without the full knowledge of the mayor.

There wasn't an empty seat in the courtroom on the afternoon I was called to the witness stand. Despite my command of the facts, a queer fidgety feeling gripped my movements, like a golfer getting the yips on a short putt; a unique pressurized moment in front of a captive audience when time stood still.

The prosecutor carefully led me through my role in uncovering the corruption without a flaw and in accord with the testimony of Potter and Pitman. I was pleased. Then Mr. Rickman took over cross-examination.

Rickman eyed me for several seconds before grilling me.

"Isn't it true you suffered a serious head injury in Iraq and have been under a psychiatrist's care for several years?" he asked in an accusatory manner.

"Er, yeah—"

"Didn't a judge commit you to a mental institution in—?"

"Objection, your honor, foundation."

"Sustained."

"Are you dating Miss Angie Carswell, the former secretary of Mayor Jorgenson?"

"Yes." My knuckles turned white at his mention of her name. I gripped the witness chair hard to prevent me from getting in Rickman's face.

"In fact, you have a very close rapport with her, correct?" Rickman faced the jury as he asked this question.

"Yes, we're engaged to be married."

Abruptly striding toward the witness chair, he pointed at me. "Isn't it true you were upset that she went to a resort in the Bahamas with the mayor?"

"I had not met Miss Carswell at that time so—"

"Weren't you jealous they had a secret relationship and you were afraid you would lose her if—?"

"Objection," shouted the prosecutor.

"The witness will answer the question."

I stared at Jorgenson. "I loathe the man for his attack on Miss—"

"No more questions, your—" Rickman shouted.

"Carswell," I spoke over his voice.

"Your honor," he ended. "I have nothing further for this witness." Rickman shot a coy glance at the jury and returned to his seat

"You may step down, Mr. Baxter. You're excused."

I bristled at the cocky look on Rickman's face. No courtroom television drama could exceed my emotion.

Shaking my head, I implored the judge to let me speak. The

jury had to know Angie and I love each other unconditionally. To my chagrin, I left the witness stand.

The jury deliberated for four days. The world came to a stop as the wait consumed our lives. When the judge instructed the foreman to read their verdict, I held Angie's hand to ease her apprehension …and mine.

The foreman announced in a deliberate, loud voice, "We find the defendant, Henry Jorgenson, guilty on all counts."

An electrifying shock touched every part of my body at the foreman's words. I wondered if anyone noticed my shiver. *How else should vindication feel*?

According to statute, the judge was permitted to sentence Hank Jorgenson to eight to twelve years' jail time plus a stiff fine.

"There's not an ounce of humility in his body," I whispered to Angie, as an unrepentant Jorgenson was led out of the courtroom under guard. However, Wilcox's scowl turning to a smirk directed at me was unsettling.

"No different than most politicians," she volunteered. "They have no shame."

I had lunch with an upbeat Agent Walsh several days after the trial ended. However, to the dismay of the FBI and Walsh, Wilcox got off with two to four years based on no prior criminal record and his plea bargain. Cohen received a five-year sentence and was disbarred from practice. Chief Campbell was suspended without pay pending a full inquiry into alleged police money scams in addition to his complicity with the mayor's office to discredit me.

With the assistance of the FBI, Outsource Data Corporation terminated George Parker and had filed suit for misappropriation of funds. Parker, with knowledge I was under psychiatric care, had fingered me to Wilcox as a perfect patsy for their scheming.

"I'm apprehensive about Wilcox's smug outward demeanor,

and we still don't have solid evidence in our ongoing investigation about his shady past," Walsh decried as if he were apologizing to me. "I have a hunch he's seething on the inside, but will control his emotions until he's free. Then he's bound to make a mistake. It's clear now that Wilcox actually manipulated Jorgenson, who became enamored with gaining higher political office in New Jersey and nationally."

Walsh's intensity about Wilcox revealed feelings that overshadowed his normally dispassionate self. I wondered if he had a personal vendetta to conduct against Wilcox, with or without supervisory knowledge.

We said our goodbyes outside the restaurant. His parting comment to me was, "I'll keep you informed if there are new developments."

Angie and I gave Mayor Pitman notice we would resign once a replacement as secretary was hired and trained. While we valued our experience and new friendships in Barnegat Junction, our notoriety was a distraction.

When we announced our engagement, she moved in with me in Lavallette to save on expenses. I met her parents and we hit it off well. A mutual respect grew right from the start; their interest in Angie's happiness was paramount.

Our church wedding, elegantly orchestrated by Angie, was attended by her family and a few guests, including Mayor Pitman and his wife, Lena, Dr. Burkett, Harold Trotter and my buddies from the Bronx, except Russ Williams who indicated he was too busy on a special project. *Oh sure.* With money from wedding gifts, we planned a one-week honeymoon in St. Croix in the US Virgin Islands.

My joy was indescribable. I revisited in my mind the good times with my father and wishing things could have been the same with my mother. *If they could see me now.* I was a lucky guy despite how close I'd come to destroying my life. It was as if Angie was sent by my guardian angel to steady my course and show me what real love was all about. I guessed I had paid my dues sitting on the Lavallette beach so many nights without a clue how my life would change. *I'm truly blessed.*

I received a job offer from the law firm of Dickson, Dickson and Pennington in Point Pleasant the day before we were to leave for St. Croix. On a phone call to the Human Resource manager, she scheduled a meeting in their office on the day after we returned from our honeymoon.

Off Angie and I went, like two kids starting a summer vacation in paradise.

Never had I spent so much time without a care in the world. Angie felt the same way. As with all things in life, tempus fugit.

Unfortunately, the economic downturn in the States had substantially reduced business for the local restaurants and club owners. We only ventured into town at night once instead of dining at our beachfront hotel. The Beachcombers Club is located on a main, narrow street in Christiansted, which is a tourist attraction exhibiting a quaint European charm. "I never knew young Alexander Hamilton lived here," Angie said, reading the small plaque on his statue.

"I wrote a paper on him in my senior year in high school. He left the island at age thirteen to attend Columbia in New York. Might have become president if Aaron Burr didn't kill him in a duel. Legal in those days, can you believe?"

"What a nice idea to spend our last night in St. Croix at this club," Angie sighed. We swayed to the tune of *At Last* on the small dance floor. "I didn't know you enjoyed slow dances."

"Whatever it takes," I admitted. We held each other close, oblivious to the presence of a dozen or so patrons.

"My love has come along, my lonely days are over, and life is like a song," Angie sang softly in my ear. I put my arm around her waist until the music stopped and led her back to our table. To respond in kind, I thought of the words, *I only have eyes for you.* We sipped our Pina Coladas while the three-piece calypso band went on break.

"Who's in charge here?" A shout came from the other side of the room. All eyes turned in the direction of two guys whose table was littered with several beer bottles. "Service! Another round, pronto."

I had noticed the two gesturing at a Caucasian teenage girl sitting with a local young man at a nearby table. Their insults showed disapproval of her partner. *A pair of bullies.*

"Hey, honey, do you know where we can go for some action?"

The girl turned her back to them.

"They have some nerve," Angie said.

"Troublemakers," I said. "There's a bar down the street where white girls go to mix with the local black guys, so this couple must be here together by choice and should be left alone. Those characters are off base."

The taller man with the loud voice stood up and waved dollar bills at the local man, who ignored the heckling.

"It's getting late and this is the right time to leave," Angie said. "First, I have to go to the ladies room."

Once Angie closed the door, I stood and meandered over to the two guys' table.

"How about giving that couple and everyone else a break, fellas? Could you please tone it down?"

"Who the hell are you? Go mind your own business!"

"I'm asking real friendly, okay?" I placed my hands on their table and stared at them.

One pushed my hand off the table while the other stood and slurred, "Let's show this smart ass what we think of him." He stepped toward me.

In a flash I overturned the table sending beer bottles clattering on the floor. I landed a right on the jaw of the quiet guy, who fell backwards off his chair. The loudmouth lunged at me, and we wrestled to the floor. He caught me with a blow below the left eye, but I buried my head in his chest and rolled with him until I was on top, punching away at his face, which was smeared with blood from his nose and lip. As he rose, my uppercut sent his head to the hard floor. He was knocked out.

My senses picked up the shouting and shuffling of patrons getting out of the way.

The room seemed to be rocking as I pushed myself off the floor to stand.

"Watch out!" The voice sounded familiar. *Angie's?*

"Filthy pig. I'll get you for that!" the quiet guy growled.

I jumped away at the sight of a broken beer bottle swished back and forth in front of my face. My adversary, in a crouch, advanced toward me with the jagged edges glistening. The weapon was ready to do its dirty work, commanded by a drunk with rage in his eyes. He faked a low attack, and then swung at my chest, followed by a thrust at my left arm. As the glass sliced my shirt, I instinctively reached out with my right hand, grabbed his wrist and twisted.

"Noo," he groaned. "Stop."

I circled around with him as my hold tightened, employing a military maneuver. Before flipping him on his back, I gave him a karate chop to the neck and kicked him in the groin. He barely whimpered as he hit the floor. The fight was over.

Applause and cries filled the room. The bartender announced the police would show up in a matter of minutes. "Get out of here quick," he ordered me. "I'll take care of everything."

Angie didn't say a word until we reached our room at the hotel. "Drew, I've never seen you like that before. You were unbelievable." Her green eyes were as big as marbles.

"Those two deserved it, didn't they?" My heavy breathing had subsided finally. "Let's finish packing and get a good night's rest."

I didn't have to prove a thing to Angie by getting into a

fight, but it didn't hurt for her to know I could take care of myself ...and her when it was necessary.

"I'm still shaking," she said flopping into bed. "Are you hurt at all?"

I smiled at her. "Just a minor ache. Remember, I told you once before, there's no way I wanted you to see me get beat up."

Her trembling stopped. Her eyes expressed her admiration.

As the saying goes, all good things must come to an end. The return from island living to reality in New Jersey shocks the system. Surprisingly, I had fun shopping with Angie for new furniture, particularly a bedroom set, and settling in. Her female touch gave the modest home a great new look. As a bonus for me after all those frozen dinners, she was a culinary artist in the kitchen.

My anticipation of joining Dickson, Dickson and Pennington only made me more edgy. Regardless, Angie and I were eager to start on a new career.

Chapter **25**

The second day back home after our thrilling honeymoon, I visited the office of DD&P to meet the senior partner. My throat was dry, reminding me of the days I needed a drink. Not so now.

"Mr. Baxter, we adopted a policy earlier this year to hire more non-legal staff," said Franklin Dickson. "All of us at DD&P know of your role in Barnegat Junction, and we are impressed with you. Quite an extraordinary achievement ...an exciting sting operation." He closed his lips tight and nodded. "One criterion we're looking for is strong moral character. You pass that with high marks. My understanding is our Human Resource manager has outlined the duties of the support staff."

"Yes sir."

"I've read your application and believe you would fit in with our paralegal program. How do you feel about that?"

"Sounds important. That's wonderful." *Can I handle a technical thing like that?*

"The firm's pragmatic approach is for attorneys and staff to be team players ...and self-starters. Besides three partners, there are eight associate attorneys."

"Thank you, sir. I appreciate the offer and look forward to a position with your firm."

"Excellent. By the way, I hope your black eye was not too painful," he said with a playful grin.

"As they say, sir, you should see the other guy."

He laughed.

I believed I had found the proper niche for a long-term career. My father always said to find a pursuit that made me feel I'd made a contribution, even in a small way. I was confident that a paralegal position provided that opportunity.

The first few weeks at Dickson, Dickson and Pennington were predictably hard on me. While the professional staff was mostly supportive, I was slow to pick up on some basic clerical procedures. Still, I did my best to maintain an upbeat disposition and superficial air of confidence.

Although I didn't realize it at the time, I made one blunder that resulted in a reprimand from Michael Metcalf, an associate and the firm's top litigator. He required several files for a consultation with an important client and his attorney. Later he approached me, his deep-set eyes squinting and mouth closed tight, and dropped the files on my desk. His comment was, "These were not the damn files I requested. Next time, please follow my specific instructions!"

The best advice I received after this incident was from young Leonard Dickson who told me to "stick with it."

Angie was always quick to spot if my spirit was down or I appeared distracted. Despite her part-time job at the Point Pleasant City Hall, her interest in my career deserved an equivalent response to her needs. My love for her didn't always translate into putting her first.

"Why don't we go to a movie tonight?" she asked.

"No thanks. I'm too exhausted. Let's save it for the weekend."

"Drew, honey, you look so glum. Did anything go wrong at work today?" She pressed her hands together as if to pray. "Is there anything I can do?"

I thought for a second before shaking my head. "It was just things in general. I did mess up some files Mr. Metcalf expected."

Michael Metcalf had earned his reputation by brilliant

handling of court cases, preferring to litigate contract disputes rather than arranging negotiated settlements. His outward appearance was right out of Hollywood typecasting, from his handsome features at six-foot-three to his stylish attire. However, his curt demeanor outside the courtroom turned off his colleagues. Too quick to resentment and seemingly selfish, he played the role of the firm's prima donna with the apparent blessing of the senior partner. The façade didn't fool the staff at DD&P, although we respected his ability to attract a wealthy clientele. He performed at a fast pace, often juggling issues for several clients at the same time. Truth be told, I detected jealousy on the part of the other associates for Metcalf's lifestyle, his low handicap golf game, and his beauty queen wife. Rumor had it that young Dickson continued to fume over the fact his father had transferred all his cases to Metcalf before his pending retirement.

The less I have to do with Metcalf, the better.

"So what happened?" Angie pleaded. "Come on, tell me."

"Metcalf needed three files on a Shopping Mall project. I gave him a current one, but the other two, by mistake, related to the original version of the project where a worker fell off a scaffold to his death. That reminded the client and his attorney of a lawsuit—"

"That doesn't sound like such a big deal."

I mumbled, "It was to them." She followed right on my heels from the kitchen to the den.

"Do you think you're getting enough sleep? You've been turning over in bed a hundred times. Maybe you're not concentrating at work because you're tired." Arms folded, she awaited my answer.

"That might be it." I glanced at her anxious look and said, "Don't you worry though. Everyone's friendly and it'll work out. I'll work hard to get sponsored in the paralegal course that starts in a couple of months."

"Sure you will. I know what else that can begin then."

"What's that?"

"It's time we start our family."

The twinkle in her eye was irresistible. I put my arms around her neck and whispered in her ear, "I'm ready when you are."

I always marveled at her acceptance of children. If she had become pregnant before we were ready, so be it. Abortion was out of the question.

At Angie's urging, I attended St. Martha's Catholic Church in Point Pleasant with her each Sunday. It was comforting to see how devoted she was to her religion. One Sunday the choir sang the hymn, *Be Not Afraid*. Although the melody escaped me, its meaning was powerful. The same peacefulness that Angie felt became my expectation as well. It brought back memories of attending church with my parents in the Bronx. I was too shy to admit to her that reciting brief prayers had become natural for me. They were not predicated out of pity for myself, as were the many prayers on the sand dunes in total darkness.

One particular homily stuck with us. The priest had concluded, "Jesus was compelled to love us; by His life on earth; by healing the sick; and by His suffering and death on the cross."

Angie leaned over and whispered in my ear, "See that. You're not the only one with a compulsion."

As we drove home from church, the thought of my compulsion distracted me. Unlike the disorders Dr. Burkett had identified— gambling, drinking, etcetera— my condition was a cheerful one, providing it was not intrusive and ...

"Why are you smiling?" she asked.

"Oh nothing. Just happy to share church service with you."

Clearly, these services had been a missing link in my life. They offered a peace of mind that has been a positive stimulus on my mental health. Thank the Lord.

I had another tough day at work during the seventh week at DD&P. I forgot some procedures taught to me in the first weeks. Metcalf commented, "You better stay after work more often or study at home." His superior attitude reminded me of George Parker at my first job.

During the usual bi-weekly instructional session for the staff conducted by Leonard Dickson, a standard agenda item included pro bono assignments. Typically, Leonard referred to newspaper headlines to consider worthy causes. He had pointed to me concerning the case of a family devastated by the apparent suicide of their teenage son.

"I don't think I can handle that one, Mr. Dickson."

"Oh," he uttered, taken aback. "You're always the first one to volunteer, Drew. The divorced mother needs assistance with paperwork filing a counter-claim with their insurance carrier, who denied the claim. Basically, you're just holding her hand."

"I'm sorry, but the story is very disturbing and—"

"Watson & Watson are representing the family on the criminal charge and civil suit, so you can study a real interesting case."

"If you don't mind, I'll pass on this one." *Too many suicides with kids from broken homes. This case is too close to home to suit me.*

Rather than a cup of coffee that evening, I announced to Angie, "I have another headache, so I'm heading to bed now." The graphic photos of the violence and grieving mother at the scene remained with me.

"Okay, but take two Tylenol. Hope you feel better in the morning," she said, busing herself with cleaning the dining room table.

Angie was asleep when I woke up the next morning, still drowsy, and went to the kitchen to start the coffee maker. The fresh brew aroma roused her.

"Good morning, hon, how do you feel?"

"Much better, thanks," I answered unthinking.

She sipped her coffee and looked quizzically at me. "Who is Chuck Larsen?"

"Chuck Larsen?"

"Yes. You mentioned his name in your sleep several times."

I slouched back on the chair as drops of coffee spilled on the saucer. *Why would I think of him after all this time?*

"Earth to Drew. Can you tell me who he is?"

"Some guy I knew at Rutgers."

"Why in the world would you think of him at this time?"

I pushed away from the table and dumped the remaining coffee in the sink. With my back to Angie, I growled, "I'd rather not talk about it, so can we forget the whole thing?"

"Gee, okay, take it easy. Why the heck are you acting so strange?"

"Look, he was in my dorm in college. A weirdo. That's all there is to it." *Why is she making a big deal about this?*

"It only strikes me as curious his name would come up for the very first time. I figured you knew him in the military and—"

"Enough!" I said, harsher than I meant. "I have to get ready for work."

I stormed out of the kitchen to gather my thoughts. I'd dreamt that basketball game again last night and...*My God.*

Chuck was the one sitting next to me.

In the bathroom, I doused my face with water and stared in the mirror at myself. Simply because I was friendly to him, the poor slob hung around me all the time. I had agreed to go to the freaking basketball game with him rather than go see my sick mother. *When will I learn?*

The headache returned.

"Why did his name come up after all this time?" I asked myself. "Now I'm all bent out of shape and worrying Angie." *When is my life going to be normal*?

"Sorry for making a fuss," I said to Angie, who had waited at the kitchen table for my return.

"I know you are." She reached out and held my hand. "I want you to know I called Doctor Burkett while you were upstairs. Remember, he insisted I contact him if you show signs of unusual behavior. I told him the pressure of your new job was causing intense stress and sleep loss, so—"

"Okay," I interrupted. "I can understand why you called him, but I don't think it has anything to do with the law firm."

"Whatever the reason, he suggested we see him tomorrow morning. Okay?"

"Guess that's alright. Then we can do lunch and I'll go to work afterwards."

"Hope you don't mind, but I mentioned the name Chuck Larsen to him." She pressed her lips together, arching her eyebrows.

Why did she do that?

I had the blank stare of someone living in a different, far-away time—as a college student.

* * *

"I'm real sorry about your mother," Larsen said, barely above a whisper. "I picked up your class assignments. Let me know if there's anything else I can do for you."

This was my first chance meeting with Chuck Larsen since my mother's funeral. Frankly, I felt like telling him to go to hell. He was always bugging me to go with him to the cafeteria or movies or study hall. I wish I had never met the jerk. *Why did I attend the basketball game with him?*

"Naw, everything's cool. I need time alone for awhile, if you don't mind."

"Sure, Drew." He started to walk away, then turned back and said, "The drama club is putting on *The Odd Couple* next week. It's real funny. How about—"

"No thanks. I'll see ya." *Stupid misfit doesn't know when to give up. From now on, I'll avoid him like the plague.*

Two days later, he barged into my dorm room.

"Sorry to bother you, Drew, but the exam tomorrow on the Amendments to the Constitution has me stumped."

I jumped off my bunk ready to explode. *Control yourself.*

"Look, Chuck, I told you to give me some space. I can't continue to lead you by the hand on everything at school any more."

"I only thought—"

"Well don't think, and don't assume I'm here just to help you. I'm sorry I befriended you so much in the past. That's the way I am." I looked him in the eye and said, "Now let's go our own way and wish each other luck."

Oh brother, the guy looks devastated.

That was the last I saw of him.

* * *

I blinked at the sound of Angie's voice.

"Please sit down here, Drew," Angie ordered. "You're perspiring. Are you feeling okay?"

"Yeah, I was only daydreaming."

"Well, you're making me nervous. Let me get you a glass of water."

"I'm glad you made the appointment with Doctor Burkett."

After a sip of water, I put my arms around her and hugged her. "Maybe we can catch a movie tonight. I'll get home a few minutes earlier and we can get a quick bite to eat at McDonald's."

"That sounds like the right tonic for both of us." She sat down next to me, let out a deep breath and closed her eyes.

We returned from the movie at eleven. I was so focused on tomorrow's visit to Dr. Burkett that I couldn't even remember the title of the movie. Sleeping pills were a must for this night.

What ever happened to Chuck Larsen?

CHAPTER 26

In spite of a restful night's sleep, I felt uneasy entering the doctor's office, as if it were the first time. Fighting to control agitation at the subject matter of today's session, I fibbed about a mild toothache.

"Nice to see you both again," Burkett said. He pointed to the leather chair in front of his for me to face him. "I'm pleased you took the initiative and called me," he said to Angie, directing her to a chair in the corner of the room.

"Thank you for seeing us on such short notice," she replied.

"So, Drew, apparently there was more to the distressing effect of that basketball game that we discussed previously. Tell me all about Chuck Larsen."

Gee, he's getting right to it.

"There's not a lot to say about him," I answered feebly, looking first at the floor, then at the ceiling. "As freshmen the gag among classmates was he and I were joined at the hip. We were together on different things, like studying for tests in study hall and sitting next to each other in class. I encouraged him to socialize with others on weekends to no avail. We enjoyed a beer or two together, just hanging out, okay?"

"Not too unusual among new students establishing friendships," he said.

"After awhile, Larsen got on my nerves. I could never do enough for him. He began to stifle my life. Guys wouldn't call me because they figured that boring Larsen would tag along, so I had to—"

"Why do you think you spoke his name in your sleep?" Burkett interrupted me in a sharp tone. His eyes came at me like a laser beam.

"I dunno. I'll admit assignments at work have been challenging." I recalled to him and Angie the discussion at work of a family tragedy and my refusal to get involved. "Angie says my sleeping has been restless." My hands trembled as the vision of Chuck Larsen's face reappeared.

"I see. Perhaps that may have triggered your remembrance of him?" Burkett rubbed his chin. "And you've lost track of him. Is that correct?"

Burkett virtually got in my face to hear my answer. I felt like he backed me into a corner and stalked me.

"That's right, best I recall. After I finally set him straight, we didn't run into each other again. Not sure if he graduated, for that matter. I did feel sorry for the guy though, a sad sack type."

"But you don't know why he dropped out of sight?"

"He was out of my life, period. I never gave him a thought." Burkett's probing began to get under my skin.

Burkett stood. A stern look changed his appearance. He motioned to Angie to squeeze in next to me on the wide chair.

She held my hand. I could feel my heart flutter.

"Listen to me, Drew. I checked with school officials about Charles Larsen."

He paused, I guessed, to observe my reaction. His tone had moderated.

"Larsen committed suicide during his sophomore year."

The room began to swirl around. I felt faint. I stared at Angie and back to Burkett for an answer to my confusion. They looked at me with both apprehension and hope in their eyes, imploring me to explore my past.

Then I saw Chuck clearly in my mind.

The dorm bathroom. Razor blades. Dried blood on his hands and arms, and on his face and clothes.

I had a coughing fit and, once the fuzziness cleared, saw the concerned look on Angie's face. "What happened?" I asked.

"You passed out for more than a minute," she whispered, her voice quivering as emotional as a Judy Garland vocal.

Burkett, who had revived me with smelling salts, asked in a calm voice, "Drew, are you alright to talk about Chuck Larsen?"

"Yes, I'm okay." I took a deep breath. "The poor guy never had a chance in his life. It was tragic." I rubbed my eyes to expel the black spots appearing on and off like a neon sign. "His dysfunctional family had taken off to who knows where. He was all alone and I was his only real friend. I guess I should have anticipated his suicide once the two of us agreed to go our separate ways." I thought for a second. "Well, I mean I wanted to end our association."

"You've held these flashbacks inside you for too long, Drew. Now relax and let's step back and consider our sessions together." Burkett checked his notepad. "Although your decision to join the military after nine-eleven was a worthy motive, consistent with your need to help, it was also an escape from the traumas you had experienced." He motioned in Angie's direction and said to me, "If you wish, you may discuss the details of Larsen's suicide with Angie when you're back home. In my opinion, you have removed a big obstacle to the feeling of insecurity in your life."

"Thank, you, Doctor," she said, glancing sympathetically at me. "I want him to confide in me about everything."

"But how could I have erased his death from my mind, Doctor Burkett?"

"The basketball game you attended with Larsen became a focal point in your subconscious. The soccer ball shape in your nightmare was more likely a basketball. The stairs may have been the steep steps you climbed to rush out of the basketball arena to go to your mother."

"But I saw my father's face."

"I'm sure you did. It's possible he was looking down at you to absolve you of guilt in his death, your mother's death and the death of a friend. It may have symbolized his love and caring for you."

As a reflex action, I stood, then fell right back down in the cushioned chair. Speechless, I sat back in wonderment at Burkett's words. The pause allowed time for the meaning to seep into my brain and be absorbed.

"I guess it makes sense, but, my God, how complicated has my mental capacity been? It's a wonder I could function at all."

"I'm the professional and the complexities of the mind are mind-boggling, pardon the pun, even to me." Burkett raised his hands in wonderment.

The shock I had experienced so often from that wide-ranging nightmare was no longer a mystery. In that case, there was nothing more for me to fear.

I could tell from her startled look that Angie recognized my changed expression. She put her arm around my shoulder and patted my back. A reflective time to grasp the joy of a burden liberated from my mind and body. Years of grief faded out of my memory, as if lost in an early morning dense mist coming off the ocean.

"As I explained at our last session, Drew, your injury in Iraq caused shock which suppressed the memory of your inability to be there with your mother as well as guilt for your father's accident. Completely against your character. The basketball game also was the medium for parting ways with Chuck Larsen. Despite all the help you had given him, as a caretaker, it wasn't enough." He paused to wet his lips.

I sat wide-eyed, as Burkett became a storyteller.

"The short length of the timeline for these tragic events,

from age fourteen to sophomore year in college to Iraq after graduation, was too much for your mind to absorb. The fact you overcame post-traumatic stress is a significant attainment in your medical history."

Impulses flashed in my brain that connected all the adverse events in my life.

"Larsen should have received professional counseling in his freshman year," Burkett continued. "Your support, seemingly harmless meddling in his life, was not what he needed. However, it was his own mental disorder that resulted in his suicide, not anything you did or didn't do. Do you understand and accept that?"

After hesitating, I responded, "I think so. Yes, I concealed his death from reality to write off the fact my help was ineffective."

"There are medical terms to describe it, but basically, the dual debilitating effects associated with the basketball game induced your compulsive helping disorder to be overcome by guilt, insecurity, depression and periodic irrational behavior. Your one nightmare had multiple meanings, each of which competed with your compulsive disorder."

Burkett hesitated, then stood facing Angie and added, "As I've said before, he's had a remarkable life, despite everything."

"But Doctor, don't you see, that's what has attracted him to me," she said before looking my way. "Now I'm part of him as well. In good times and bad. In sickness and in health."

I felt reenergized and only nodded as I noted the tears forming in her eyes. I understood the ramification of my compulsion and its limitations. No more running away from it. Somehow, as an inane thought, my mind pictured a wildly happy Jimmy Stewart running through Main Street in Bedford Falls in the movie *It's a Wonderful Life.*

"Thank you so much, Doctor Burkett," Angie said as he opened the office door.

She wrapped her arm in mine, smiled broadly, and said in a loud voice, "Let's go home, Drew."

CHAPTER 27

After four months of employment, DD&P sponsored me to a three-nights-a-week, seventeen-week paralegal course. The program resulted in the most interesting learning period of my life. My dedication was stronger than the formative years at Rutgers. I looked forward to each new phase of legal services, actively participating in classroom discussions. While a broad range of legal topics was included, my primary focus related to CONTEMPORARY REAL ESTATE TRANSACTION THEORY, and BANKRUPTCY LAW.

With the full support of Angie, my ability to handle late evening classes, the homework and the tests flabbergasted me. Undoubtedly, the management of cases assisting the professional staff would be the most challenging in the real world. On the other hand, some legalese mystique was unraveled by the common use of boilerplate forms, wills, leases, contracts, questionnaires, etcetera. I felt prepared for my higher position and responsibilities.

Once I received the Paralegal Certificate, my confidence increased tenfold. I settled into the routine of support for the partners and associates, mostly on commercial real estate transactions. My performance was appraised on a par with the five other paralegals in the firm. I read the evaluation written by Leonard Dickson. The short commentary was positive and constructive except ...I mouthed the words, *although Mr. Baxter works diligently to meet agreed-upon schedules, his organizational skills and time management need improvement. Continuing education is encouraged.*

I handed the review back to Mr. Dickson and said, "Thank you, sir, for the review and constructive suggestions. I'm working hard at improving." I was pleased with the appraisal, but surprised he judged I failed to meet deadlines. I bit my lip to rein in an explanation, but it was no use.

"Sir, if you don't mind, the reference to meeting schedules is unfair."

"Oh."

"One assignment was delayed because I assisted another paralegal with a computer problem that lasted—"

"Stop right there! I've given you a candid appraisal of your job performance. Now accept it and deal with it. Don't become defensive!"

"Yes sir."

I wondered if Les Simmons, the senior paralegal, was out to screw me. He had asked me about new computer software, and then wasted my time bragging how important he was to the firm.

"Okay then," he added, "let me be honest with you, though. There was also a dissenting opinion on your overall performance."

Here it comes.

"I'm only telling you so you can be on your toes now that you'll be assigned more substantive matters."

"Thank you for the caution. I'm not taking this review for granted, and I do look forward to expanded duties."

"Good." He stood to signal the meeting was over, shook my hand and said, "You didn't ask, but the negative review came from Mr. Metcalf."

That big-headed Metcalf has been after my ass right from the beginning. "I'll be careful, Mr. Dickson."

I believe young Dickson has taken me under his wing. Unbelievable.

Leonard Dickson followed in the footsteps of his grandfather and father, but at his own pace. After high school, he was accepted at Harvard thanks to his philanthropic dad. His grades were average. Rather than continue the tradition in collegiate baseball, Leonard made the lacrosse team and became captain in senior year. His claim to fame was scoring the last two goals to beat Johns Hopkins in the Final Four National Championship game. Before moving on to Harvard Law, he spent two years in Appalachia in school construction and as a teacher to grade school children, both without pay. He admits to a more sober and studious approach in law school, and gained an unforeseen deference for the American judicial system. "I guess I was destined to be engrossed in all facets of jurisprudence," he acknowledged to friends and colleagues.

When it came to the practice of real estate legal issues, the family genes diverted. Leonard's disagreements with his father over the direction of DD&P were no secret. He felt there were more substantive societal matters in which to engage. He prepared a strategic plan, later available to the staff, which called for gradual expansion into local, state and federal constitutional law. His politics leaned to conservative and he was open to the possibility of seeking public office or accepting a judgeship. On several occasions, he asked me specific questions about the role of Cohen & Mahoney in Barnegat Junction.

Leonard's easygoing manner contrasted with his stern father. He was held in high esteem in the firm and among peers for his management style as well as fluent knowledge of the law and debating skill. With his wife, Elizabeth, he often entertained at their oceanfront home in Spring Lake. Angie and I were overjoyed with their friendship. Since he and I were about the same age, we were on a first name basis outside the office.

The aroma of fresh cut flowers delighted my senses as I opened the door to our home that night. My nostrils were treated further by Romano cheese, which led me straight to the kitchen. My mom's recipe for shrimp scampi had a similar effect.

"Surprise!" Angie announced. She had a colorful apron on over a light sweater and slacks. "I decided to have your favorite." She removed a small tray of meat lasagna from the oven to let it cool.

"Wow. I love it. What's the occasion?" *She hasn't hear about my performance review, has she?*

"Let's see. We never celebrated your paralegal certificate achievement." She paused and asked, "Is there any other reason to rejoice?"

"You're fantastic." I gave her a hug and kiss followed by a smooch, which made her laugh. I held off mentioning my review.

"Stop, you're tickling me." She took the apron off and motioned for us to take a seat. "Don't you remember I had a doctor's appointment today?"

Oh Jeez, I forgot. "So what did she say?"

"To get right to the point, I'm two months pregnant."

What did she say?

"That's wonderful," I screamed. Then I jumped up and held her in my arms. "Great news!" The idea finally hit me as a thrilling addition in our life. "Are you doing alright? I'll take care of everything. Don't you worry about a thing! Let me—"

She gently placed her hand over my mouth. "Hush! Of course you'll be a big help, Drew."

The next day, a Saturday, we were still in awe of what was to come in a matter of months. We gulped down our cereal as fast countless thoughts maneuvered through our heads.

"I'm on cloud nine," she said in a giddy tone.

"Me too."

"Tell you what, hon. You've never been to Atlantic City so ...why don't we spend a couple of nights there as a last fling before I'm unable to travel?"

Her exuberance was catching.

"If you can handle it, that's a fabulous suggestion." I nodded emphatically and said, "Let's do it! I'm finishing up a project with Mr. Pennington on Monday morning. Since the casinos are not as crowded on weekdays, I'll pick you up after lunch and we're off to Atlantic City. I'll handle the reservations."

"I knew you'd like the idea. But no blackjack, mister card shark." A wide grin crossed her face.

Even a subtle reminder of Las Vegas no longer saddened me. It was history, and I was over that chapter in my life.

Preparations for the trip made the time pass quickly. We checked into Trump Tower for two nights ready to relax, see a show, and gamble modestly.

After we snacked and caught a special performance by Tony Bennett, Angie was tired and went back to our room. I strolled around the casino and, like radar, ended up at a blackjack table. Fifty bucks was my max. Twenty minutes later, the money was gone. I'd picked the wrong time to double up when the Dealer pulled 21. On the fifth card no less.

As I meandered away, I glanced into the hi-limit room for blackjack players ...and did a double take. *Is that Michael Metcalf?* I moved on, but curiosity got to me. I reversed direction and strode close to the two steps leading to the large private room. A sign at the entrance read, *$100 Minimum*. Only the profile of the man was now clear in my line of vision. I watched for a second while a scantily-clad waitress served him and one other patron a drink.

"Do you wish to join us?" a host asked.

"Er, no thanks." I left to go to my room. Since Angie was sleeping, the news must wait until the morning.

I waited for Angie to get over morning sickness, chomping at the bit to tell her about Metcalf. She greeted me with a weak smile. Her reaction to the gossip was swift. "Drew, even if that were him, he's entitled to some fun, isn't he?" She took a bite of toast and added, "Don't make a big deal about it for godssake."

"Okay, I guess you're right. It was just a shock to see him there."

We relaxed during the day and, early that evening, caught the play, *Jersey Boys*. It was the highlight of the trip for Angie.

Except for my gambling and losing $50, the scene in the casino was repeated again the second night.

I had left our room about eleven, while Angie slept. Sure enough, Metcalf was in the same room, the same seat, and the same gentleman sat next to him, although two other men played at the table as well. After casually peering into the room, I wasn't absolutely sure it was him. *If I could only hear him speak.*

There was no way I'd hang around until he had enough gambling, so I went to my room in utter confusion. *I won't say anything to Angie this time.*

As we checked out the next morning, I looked about the lobby and observed people coming and going. Only strangers.

Even for only a short time out of the office, I faced a heavy backlog of work the morning I returned. It took three full days to put documentation together on several property sales and get caught up. Atlantic City was forgotten.

"Drew, I'd like you to check these time records of billable hours," Leonard Dickson said. "Campbell Development Corporation, one of my clients, has questioned their bill and the time for various assignments during last month."

"Sure thing. I'll get right to it."

"Oh, how did you enjoy your two days off in Atlantic City?"

"Just great." As an afterthought, I let slip out, "I'm not certain, but I believe I saw Mr. Metcalf there as well."

"You're kidding." He waved his arm up and said, "Yeah, well, he's always on the go."

I used a desk in the Accounting Department to spread out the timesheets and a computerized bill. About an hour later, I completed the review, discovering one job had been posted as ten hours instead of only one. *The client was right.*

Dickson instructed me to return the folder to the file cabinet in Accounting after informing the Chief Accountant of the error. As I searched under the letter C, the name Cal-Partners, Inc. attracted my attention. We all knew C-PI was the firm's largest, most diversified client, and Michael Metcalf handled the account. There was no restraining my inquisitiveness. Without removing the folder, I flipped pages until I found his time records.

Let me think. We were in A.C. on the 20th and 21st. I ran my finger down the columns from the two dates. I mouthed the slightest sound, "He charged five billable hours on the 20th and …eight on the 21st." I wondered how he spent time on the client's legal issues and got to the casino. Did he drive back and forth to Point Pleasant or the client's office in Metuchen? Was he on the telephone with the client all that time? The sequence of events didn't add up.

Maybe that wasn't Metcalf at all. Aw nuts, why should I give a damn?

A week later, Leonard Dickson called me into his office. I was taken aback to see Michael Metcalf sitting on the couch.

"Drew, I thought we should meet and clear the air on your statement to me that you saw Mr. Metcalf in Atlantic City, okay? He says he hasn't been there in over a year."

I felt unsteady and defenseless standing at Dickson's desk. I wished I could crawl into a crack in the wall or hide behind the portrait of Franklin Dickson. "Sir, it's entirely possible the man I saw only resembled Mr. Metcalf and—"

"That's a hell of a thing, Baxter," Metcalf cried out, bounding off the couch toward me. "You bring up my name at a gambling casino and you can't vouch it was me."

Man, I never said he was actually gambling.

"Did you want to embarrass me or what?"

I didn't look at Metcalf. "Mr. Dickson, it was only a casual remark. I had no ill intent."

Metcalf continued, "Then you're being naïve."

He's making a mountain out of a molehill. "Okay, I'm sorry," I responded to him as a firm retort.

It occurred to me, to paraphrase the Queen in Hamlet, *Metcalf doth protest too much.* I was proud of myself for not taking offense at being called naïve.

"Fine. I accept your apology."

Metcalf planted his hands on Dickson's desk and leaned forward saying, "Leonard, I'm willing to let this go as a slip of the tongue. So, to protect his career here, I don't think you should mention this to your father."

The arrogance of Metcalf had no bounds. However, I conceded to myself I hadn't learned my lesson from my demoralizing experience at Outsource Data Corp. to protect what's her name ...Carolyn.

Leonard Dickson simply shook his head and glared at me. His lower teeth bit into his upper lip.

About a week later, I attended the monthly luncheon of the firm's paralegals. Les Simmons was the oldest and most experienced paralegal, with DD&P since the firm's founding. A physical fitness nut, he still had the look of a middle linebacker from his college days. He had assisted Franklin Dickson for many years until the senior partner turned over his top clients to Michael Metcalf. As a diligent, no-nonsense worker, Simmons was a take-charge person who could stand up to Metcalf's abrasive manner. It was obvious Metcalf thought highly of his work, and liked him.

"Not too much gossip to bring up today," Simmons said. He held a spoonful of chocolate mousse at his lips. The group counted on him to know all the office scuttlebutt. "The good news is there's been an increase in the number of clients this year and billable hours are up, thanks mostly to Michael Metcalf. Keep your fingers crossed on the size of our bonus."

I piped up, "I understand Mr. Metcalf has been courting a large bank and—"

"We don't want to talk about that yet, Drew."

His tone made me wish I hadn't mentioned it in front of the group.

After lunch, Simmons pulled me aside and said, "Just between you, me and the lamppost, Metcalf has been wining and dining executives of a Newark bank. Even entertained them giving them a choice of Bermuda or Atlantic City."

"That's interesting!" I hoped Simmons didn't take notice of my startled expression.

"Enjoyed lunch with you, Drew. By the way, I've heard nice things about you from young Dickson."

I walked slowly back to my desk. That old sensation in the pit of my stomach was back gnawing away. Despite Metcalf's denial, I questioned if there was a connection between the bank entertainment and the dates I saw him, or think I did, in Atlantic City?

Later that day Simmons showed up unexpectedly at my work station. "I want to give you the scoop on that bank we talked about after lunch."

So why tell me?

"Looks like they'll be our newest client." He paused. "By the way, Metcalf did go to Bermuda with bank executives, but cut the trip short because he wasn't feeling well. He stayed at his home in Rumson for a couple of days while working on the Cal-Partners account."

"That's great news for the firm, Les," I acknowledged.

Did Metcalf put him up to this? I better watch my back with the two of them.

Once Simmons left I speculated on the information and his visit. I concluded that the story did make sense based on Metcalf's billable hours report, although I didn't know the exact dates of the trip to Bermuda. Even though a big issue had been made over my innocent comment to Leonard Dickson, I felt obliged to stick with my skepticism.

Several days passed.

I was assigned to research local variances in Ocean County for an out-of-state client. Leonard Dickson was anxious to receive the report for a scheduled conference call. When I had almost completed the assignment, Les Simmons and I noticed Metcalf enter and stride hurriedly into his office. A guest followed.

"Who's that?" I asked Simmons.

"That's Gregory Winburn who's the head of Cal-Partners real estate operations on the East Coast."

I strained my neck to watch the man. On the pretext of going to the bathroom, I passed the office and observed the two in an animated discussion.

I've seen that guy before.

I sat at my desk, scratching my head. No different than agonizing over the answer to a trivia question.

"Mr. Baxter, Mr. Dickson wants you to call him immediately," a secretary informed me.

I clenched my lips together. The report Dickson needed was no way near done. I reached for the telephone to ...

Hold on!

"I know that guy," I whispered. My mind raced back to

that private room in Atlantic City. I could see them toasting one another.

Metcalf's a freaking liar!

Leonard Dickson appeared at my workstation in a huff. "What's going on, Baxter? You know I have to call the client right away."

My hands trembled as I fumbled with the files on my desk. *I had no choice.* "Mr. Dickson, I'm sorry, but I was distracted—"

"What do you mean, distracted?"

"Please bear with me. The man in Mr. Metcalf's office is the same person I saw with him in Atlantic City."

"Atlantic City! Are you still carrying on about that? I think you're losing it, Drew. You better get your act together."

"This time I'm positive the two of them were in the special blackjack room. I don't know what it all means other than he lied to you and me." The stuttering in my voice had returned. "You've got to believe me."

He sat down mute and perplexed. After staring at me for an eternity, he said, "Let's go to my father's office."

I repeated the entire story to Franklin Dickson, who listened without a show of emotion. His only question was, "Do you understand that Michael Metcalf is an important member of this firm?"

"Yes sir, I do," I replied without hesitation.

Then his son excused me and advised me to go home for the day.

Am I going to be fired?

CHAPTER 28

The following afternoon the office was abuzz with hearsay, ranging from insinuations that DD&P had serious legal problems to a possible reduction in staff for budget reasons. The word leaked out that the president of Cal-Partners from California had arrived to attend a closed-door partners' meeting. The staff all left the office by 6:00 p.m. before there was any news out of the conference room.

My light-hearted banter at home that night did not go unnoticed by Angie.

"Must have been a great day at work," she said.

"You bet," I replied.

How I controlled the tense feeling gripping my body while we watched television was a wonderment. I don't think I slept more than an hour or so. I was in and out of the shower in the morning before Angie opened her eyes.

"I'll get breakfast at the office, Ang. Love you." I gave her a peck on the cheek as she changed her position in bed and said, "See you tonight."

The parking garage under the DD&P two-story office building was unexpectedly full. *Everyone's arrived early, as anxious about the situation as I am.*

The office atmosphere was like the gloom of a pending thunderstorm. Although I couldn't see Les Simmons in his office, his sobs were evident. Boxes and a large trash bin were outside the closed door of Metcalf's office. The usual hustle and bustle were missing. Whispers sounded like a beehive.

I felt awkward walking to my workstation as if my legs were prostheses. A strong cup of coffee might ease my discomfort.

"Please come into my office, Drew," Leonard Dickson ordered an hour later.

A rapid heartbeat delayed my response and arrival in his office.

After serving me a cup of coffee, which I readily accepted, he related the events of yesterday and the late-night meeting.

"The bottom line is Mr. Metcalf is no longer with the firm."

I was flabbergasted. A recollection of Dr. Burkett describing an addiction to power came to mind.

"The outside auditors worked through the night and uncovered erroneous billings with his accounts. In addition, based on your disclosure, we have corroborated that he was engaged in collusion and kickbacks with a client."

There was nothing for me to say. I listened intently, but could only feel sadness for Metcalf's family.

"Frankly, because of his litigation skills, we had allowed him to take unchecked liberties. Poor management policy for sure." He grasped his hands behind his neck, closing his eyes for an instant. The curl of his lip gave a hint of a repressed smile.

I sensed his satisfaction with the outcome.

"In any case, you should know that my father's respect for your integrity convinced him to pursue the matter to a proper conclusion. We owe you a debt of gratitude and extend our sincere thanks. "

If there were anything in the world more dramatic to raise my self-esteem, it was beyond my ability to articulate.

What more could any man want?

Angie would surely be astonished as well, while giving

all the credit to my instincts. Nevertheless, no one celebrated another's character defects.

Except for Les Simmons, who went home early feeling ill, each paralegal made phone calls to clients throughout the afternoon. "Better to get ahead of the rumor mill and announce his resignation," Leonard Dickson had said. I made my last call of the day when I noticed Simmons had returned.

"Terrible situation," I said to him.

"Yeah, shocking." While he was fully composed, his look was sullen, like he'd just lost his best friend.

In a brief meeting, Franklin Dickson was most gracious in his praise. "Once again, you have justified our decision to offer you employment. You exposed a corruption that might have resulted in the cessation of the firm."

I was last to leave the office for my car in the parking level. As I exited the elevator, I heard voices in the far corner of the garage. I squinted to identify two people facing each other between their automobiles.

"You're a no-good crook."

The shout was loud and clear throughout the garage. I recognized the voice of Les Simmons, but the circumstance mystified me.

"What's going on?" I mumbled to myself. "Who's that with …? I don't believe it. It's Michael Metcalf."

Should I bother getting drawn into their argument? I prefer to get home and tell Angie all the news.

My hesitation lasted a nanosecond. I didn't care if it were a personal rendezvous or disagreement; I had to find out why Metcalf was still on the premises.

As I walked purposeful toward them, Metcalf's voice became strident. I had been subjected to the same temper. He was fuming.

"Don't be so damn self-righteous, Les. You know what I've accomplished for this firm and how hard—"

"But, you ...I trusted you and—"

Metcalf cut Simmons short. His hollering now reflected controlled rage. "I took my share of what I earned for the firm so stop sounding so immature. You can thank me for your bonuses and the good life you lead." His tone became calmer. "If you stick by me, we can come out of this alright. Believe me!"

They abruptly turned toward me.

"You miniscule petty troublemaker," Metcalf screamed at me.

"Keep out of this, Baxter!" Simmons warned.

No way, or this will end badly.

"You think you're getting away with what you've done to me?" Metcalf took one step toward me, as furious as I have ever seen him

"Both of you stay right where you are!" Simmons ordered.

My eyes bulged at the gun Simmons pulled from his jacket inside pocket. A sneer appeared on his face as he glowered at his old boss. "Drew, get the hell outta here while you have a chance. This doesn't concern you."

"Listen to me, Les, please. This isn't right and you're distraught. Put the gun down! You're making matters worse by threatening—"

"This is no threat," he made clear. "He deceived me and my life is ruined."

"He betrayed all of us, not just you, Les. You and me, and our families, we'll all get through this if we just hang together." My knees wobbled, but adrenalin compelled me to prolong a dialogue.

If I could get to my cell phone, I'd ...Jesus, I left it on my desk.

"You have a wonderful reputation with the Dicksons and the entire staff for so many years of service. It's still intact, Les. Don't allow his corruption to destroy your good name."

"That's enough," Simmons moaned.

"If it wasn't for him, Les, we wouldn't be in this mess," Metcalf roared. "He couldn't keep his mouth shut. Our crisis is because of him and—"

"You conceited liar," I proclaimed. "You don't give a damn about Les, me, or anyone but yourself." I took two steps in his direction with my fists clenched.

Simmons looked confused as his eyes darted from me to Metcalf and back. Concentrating on me for a solution to his reckless plot, he failed to see Metcalf advance. With a sudden yell, Metcalf lunged at Simmons and wrestled him to the ground. Despite Simmons' strength, his subdued disposition gave Metcalf's surprise attack the upper hand. Metcalf quickly and easily extracted the weapon from Simmons' hand.

The speed of Metcalf's action momentarily mesmerized me. As he stood and gripped the gun, I jumped at him, shoving him against the car door. He pointed the gun at me and shouted, "Get down on the ground or I'll shoot!" He started to open his car door.

I knew that in his despondent and menacing state he meant it. Backing away as if to surrender, I pretended to go to my knees then charged him from a low crouch.

The gunshot smashed into the ceiling and reverberated in my ears.

Forcing his arm above his head, I secured his wrist and jabbed my fingers in his throat. He gagged and dropped the gun, which slid across the concrete floor. I kneed him in the groin and lashed out with my right fist to his jaw.

"Oooo," he cried out from the violent thud of his head hitting the car metal. The eerie wail echoed in the low ceiling garage.

I watched Metcalf slide down the car hood in slow motion and roll off onto his back. Blood streamed from his nose and skull.

Les Simmons was on his back, head raised, propping

himself up on his elbows, and gaped at me. He reached for my hand seemingly for assistance to stand.

Careful. Is he back to normal now or still upset with me?

As he stood, Les's bear hug conveyed his gratitude for my involvement and, at the same time, he cast a look of revulsion at the unconscious, beaten Michael Metcalf.

"What's a friend for?" I didn't know what else to say to him.

He reciprocated my big smile and shook my hand repeatedly. "Thanks for saving me from a big mistake."

We sat on the garage floor with our backs against his car. The police would turn up shortly, but, emotionally drained, we didn't care.

A scene of hand-to-hand combat in Fallujah crossed my mind for a split second.

Immediately thereafter, a wave of euphoria surged through me and gave me a sensation as potent as any narcotic.

"The good guys won one today, Les."

We gave each other high-fives.

CHAPTER 29

Four years later
    "I'm home."

I waited for Angie, as glamorous as ever, to come to the front door of our Point Pleasant home. Her normal routine was to enjoy the afternoon sun on the back porch. Her endearing dignity as a wife was even more evident as a mother. A few extra pounds here and there were like the finishing touches on an eye-catching portrait.

"Here's Daddy."

Little Danny came running to me as fast as his feet could move, as he did at 5:30 every weekday night. His giggle gave me goose bumps.

"How's my big boy? Whoopee." I picked him up above my head and jogged around the living room couch. His laugh was infectious and resounded throughout the house. I rubbed noses with him and whispered in his ear, "I love you, Danny boy."

"I love ya too, Daddy."

"He didn't have a nap today," Angie said, "so I fed him earlier. It's time I put him to bed." She cradled him in her arms and carried him upstairs. He waved at me all the way until he disappeared into his bedroom. It's hard to believe he expects to play pee-wee baseball next year.

* * *

With the generous support of Angie's parents, we had

purchased a home in Point Pleasant, not as close to the beach as Lavallette, but close enough. Best of all, I could walk to work on nice weather days.

As much as could be said about anyone's daily existence, our life was ordinary, somewhere between monotonous and ultra-active. That was a big deal for me to even admit, since my life had been anything but average. It's mind-boggling to see on TV or read about the violence which appears to surround us, thereby satisfying reporters' appetite for bad news. Sadly, places of filth and depravity are well known in the world. Despite that, what seems to keep many people happily engaged in their pattern of life is a basic faith, spiritual or otherwise, that recognizes that travails exist. Life is not perfect, and I can surely attest to that. Movies, which I thoroughly enjoy, cannot be the great escape from reality.

We had a scare when Angie was diagnosed with a cervical cyst. She consented to the necessity of a hysterectomy, mouthing the words, "Thy will be done."

It was uplifting to see the manner in which she accepted her fate and future consequences, come what may. Although the incident would have caused me to panic in the past, my composed support comforted Angie a great deal.

The ambition I had as a teenager to search out and achieve returned with vitality. Rather than a chore, going to work was a delight. The workplace at Dickson, Dickson & Pennington turned out to be a satisfying and rewarding experience, both physically and mentally.

Who would believe that employment as a paralegal is a calling! Then again, everyone needs a vocation.

At our last session months ago, Dr. Burkett had theorized that helping people served to prevent the reverse or opposite characteristics of my compulsive disorder, which led to abnormal behavior.

"You are one-of-a-kind," he had said. "Perhaps, I'll prepare a paper for publication in a medical journal and refer to your case as the Baxter Counter-Compulsion Symptom, and its application to other mental diseases. When one is unable to satisfy their compulsion or is detached from others' emotions, the result may be extreme or unpredictable behavioral patterns."

My reaction to his premise was, "How about that! You're going to make me famous. Given all the organizations that provide charity and the countries with severe poverty, perhaps a SUPER-compulsive helping disorder would be a good thing. That's my theory."

A spontaneous laugh howled from the good doctor.

A thoughtful Angie proposed, "Then if Drew's need to fulfill his compulsion was blocked in some way, the inner conflict in his mind became aggravated."

"Exactly," Burkett chimed in.

My relief was absolute. No more episodes like Las Vegas for me, thanks to my responsibilities at work ...as well as Angie's devotion.

Leonard Dickson had assumed the firm's leadership and implemented his plan to widen the scope of legal services at DD&P with the hiring of several attorneys and top law graduates with the required expertise. The range of client issues taxed the most knowledgeable of legal minds. As a paralegal, I played an active role with the clientele, mostly commercial real estate developers. My role in Metcalf's tragic downfall received high praise and advanced my influence among the paralegals.

Les Simmons opted for early retirement to be a football coach at the local high school. At a gala retirement party, his wife took me aside and asserted I had saved Les's life and their family by my intervention in his conflict with Metcalf. She thanked me and planted a big kiss on my cheek. I felt eight feet tall.

After two years, I had been promoted and received a generous pay raise. Financial affairs at home became manageable; a big relief. While Angie was elated, I sensed her concern that my responsibilities were too stressful for me to handle. She simply did not get it yet that this situation is what I had craved.

Isn't it astounding how things work out for everyone? Despite all I'd been through, my status with the job and my family couldn't be better. I guess I had to survive my personal purgatory on earth first. My old friends are doing great, too. Who could imagine Mario would end up as an engineer at NASA and Johnny was doing wonderful as a pediatrician. No surprise to me that Big Frank was recently promoted to detective on the NYPD. I feel real bad for Russ Williams. His young son drowned in the neighbor's pool. I deeply regretted disparaging Russ after we had been such close friends.

I don't believe we're predestined, but God surely has a hand in the ups, downs and coincidences in peoples' lives. I finally realized that my mom tolerated torment and sacrifices in her lifetime with quiet grace. Fate. How else can we explain that Thomas Jefferson and John Adams died within hours of each other on July 4th, fifty years after they signed the Declaration of Independence. Remarkable!

Angie and I are laying a foundation for Danny, but the rest is up to him. He'll know that we'll always be there for him, with the best guidance we can offer.

During the last four years, my visits to Dr. Burkett were infrequent. No more guilt, no more headaches, no more nightmares ...and no crying jags either. Even the painful time at Landstuhl Army Medical Center no longer seemed as grueling. Burkett marveled at my attitude, with minimal medication. The positive aspects of my compulsion were now evident in a more controlled environment as a paralegal. There had been one minor exception. I donated $100 on three occasions to an organization soliciting by phone to benefit the homeless. Subsequently, investigative reporters disclosed that numerous people were duped by the hoax and the money was never recovered.

A year ago we were saddened to read of the death of old Harold Trotter, a wonderful, feisty gentleman. His attorney had filed a civil suit against Jorgenson, Wilcox and the town, and Trotter was awarded fair compensation and punitive damages for his cranberry farm just months before he died.

* * *

"Is Dannyasleep yet?" I inquired, while I thumbed through the *Asbury Park Press*.

"He's out like a light already." Angie sat next to me on the couch and gently folded the newspaper closed. "But he behaved badly today. Very cranky, maybe something he ate or whatever." She shook her head in consternation.

It was the appropriate moment for my act. I hummed and sang, "Nobody knows the trouble I've seen." This old spiritual had become the standard buzzword for us to lighten the mood …and it worked.

"Okay, silly, enough. I was just having adult conversation."

"Yes dear. Sorry."

"So, tell me what went on today and how did the Ace Paper Manufacturing deal work out?" she asked, quickly changing the subject.

She maintained a keen interest in my assignments as a paralegal and often tutored me to verbalize specific cases of real estate procedure.

"All the closing documents I completed yesterday were reviewed by Leonard Dickson last night and this morning. He met with the parties this afternoon." I paused to look at the newspaper.

"Stop teasing! So what happened?"

"The contracts were signed, the client is satisfied, and Mr. Dickson gave me a thumbs-up. 'You did a great job,'" he said to me.

She threw her arms around my neck and kissed me. "I'm so proud of you. That's the biggest deal you've handled so far."

"Sure is; a sixteen million dollar project."

"So what's next? I hope you're not assigned any more pro bono work."

"You know I think those assignments are important," I responded firmly.

The fact of the matter was I often volunteered for projects for which the firm received no fee. The personal satisfaction was priceless. *Part of my nature, of course. Like father, like son.*

"Well, my hero, I want you to know I received two manuscripts today from the new advertisement of my typing and editing service. Furthermore, I was notified that City Hall will outsource projects to me in the future."

"Good for you. You're becoming a Fortune 500 company." I responded, tongue-in-cheek, which made her scoff at the ridiculous.

The turn of events in my life during this period was nothing short of miraculous. True love. Family. Contributing to society. It was as if I had assumed a new identity. I had no past. Yet, I questioned if normalcy and stability could go on. Are we in for a hitch from such auspicious circumstances?

Oh to be an optimist!

CHAPTER **30**

If it's not one thing, it's another.

Economic tough times that were prevalent in other parts of the country began to impact the New Jersey housing market. Experts predicted we were in for an elongated business down cycle. The one-two punch resulted in high unemployment and a decline in consumer confidence.

As we drank coffee after supper one evening, I informed Angie, "The office is swamped with residential foreclosures from Ocean and Monmouth counties, with a variety of legal issues. Leonard Dickson has reassigned staff to handle the workload, which he described as a major problem."

"You're still in the commercial department, right?"

"Well, ...I accepted a transfer to residential until the volume is reduced. Some overtime will be required."

"Oh, Drew, I hope you know what you're doing."

Later that night, I thought about my decision. I rationalized that, rather than drafting commercial leases or researching variances, residential work would be an interesting change of pace and expand my experience. Dickson said to me, "Thanks for helping us out of a bind for a month or so."

My mentor on residential legal matters was Samuel Pennington. The options to assist homeowners facing expected foreclosure varied based on individual situations. Pennington, an unemotional pro, started the process by suggesting negotiation with the mortgage company and skipping payments on low priority debts in order to make a mortgage payment. The facts in each case might warrant refinancing the home debt, but he advised to avoid balloon payments or turning over the deed to the creditor. He applauded my efforts in initial interviews with homeowners to gather relevant facts and review their goals. The option of last resort was bankruptcy.

Pennington's usual opening to ease his client's concern was, "I've reviewed your case. We can fight foreclosure."

It was all fascinating stuff to me. I visited clients with Mr. Pennington and, unlike the commercial side of the business, observed the stress experienced by many families caught up in a recessionary period. Some walked away from their mortgage obligation due to the decline in the value of the house and high property taxes.

I went home each night feeling incredible gratification for the opportunity to aid people in need. Too little compassion is a disservice to the client; too much compassion weakens the giver's overall performance.

I'd returned from lunch early, leaving Pennington with a client, when the receptionist said, "Mr. Baxter, there's a call for you on line two."

"Hello, Drew Baxter speaking."

"Hey Drew, this is Ronnie Smith. We met at the American Legion hall the other night. I'm an Iraqi vet like you, remember?"

I searched my memory. "Oh yeah, I remember."

Actually, I was introduced to so many guys that I wasn't exactly sure who Smith was. DD&P encouraged the entire staff to join local organizations; the firm would pick up dues. I considered joining the Point Pleasant Jaycees, but discovered they were too political and I was close to thirty-five retirement age for this young men's group, so it was a natural for me to associate with Legion members.

"What's up, Ronnie?"

"Listen, I heard someone at the bar say you're in the real estate business and work at a law firm."

"Right."

"I have a problem. The bank wants to foreclose on my house and I need some quick advice in order to—"

"Hold on! I'm just a paralegal, but I'll refer you to an attorney who can assist you more than I can."

"Actually, I just need to get some general information from a friend, that's all. I can't afford a fancy lawyer. It'll only take a few minutes ... less than an hour."

Who is he calling a friend?

"I'm not sure that I ...listen, you can get information from the local Legal Aid. They assist lots of people in the same boat as you."

"Please Drew, Mr. Baxter, I'm begging you. I'm in bad shape right now and only need some simple advice about a potential buyer. Frankly, I'm desperate."

I paused and looked around the office. Everyone was tied up with clients or out to lunch. This Smith guy sounded like he was going through hell.

"Where are you now?"

"I'm at the American Legion hall in Point Pleasant. My house is only ten minutes from here."

"Alright. I'm busy now, but I can be there at 4:15. I'll pick you up in the Legion hall parking lot." I figured that should be adequate time for me to assist Smith and arrive home at the regular time.

"I can't thank you enough, pal."

Before I left the office, I reviewed foreclosure options and hoped Smith had already checked out the buyer's financial credit. Pennington had informed me of scams perpetrated on unfortunate homeowners in financial difficulty, especially the elderly. Also, during the real estate price boom years, mortgage fraud had become rampant in several states.

"Never permit a client to send money in exchange for the keys to a summer rental," he had warned. "Too many unscrupulous characters pretend online they own the location to cheat a trusting buyer."

When I finally pulled into the parking lot, Smith was the only person waiting outside the building. "Good to see you again, Drew."

"Yeah, same here." I hardly recognized him sitting in the passenger seat wearing a fatigue cap. He smiled as we shook hands.

Driving west, we chatted about the Legion and our tours in the military. A divorce had worsened his situation. His unkempt appearance implied to me that the pressure from his financial problem was affecting his lifestyle.

Another few blocks and we're heading out toward Lakewood. I thought he said just ten minutes. The guy never stops talking.

"Turn down the next street," he said.

There were a half dozen Cape Cods on each side of the tree-lined street. The modest location, as Point Pleasant goes, had several foreclosure notices on the lawns. After passing two parked cars and a plumber's truck, we stopped in front of the last house on the right before the *cul du sac.*

"The bank has put up the foreclosure sign already?" That's odd, I thought.

He ignored my surprise and strolled up the two steps on the uneven brick walkway.

Following him closely, I didn't have a chance to observe the condition of the house, other than the poorly kept front lawn.

He opened the screen door. "Go right in," he said after using the lock box key. He pushed the door open for me to enter.

I stepped inside.

A blow to my head sent me sprawling amid covered furniture. I could see graffiti on the walls, which muddled my senses of time and place. The pain and shock made me woozy. I tried, but couldn't stand up.

"We meet again, smart ass."

I squinted up at the short frame incased in sunlight flooding through a bay window. I blinked several times to focus on the figure. Could my eyes be deceiving me in order to shield me from a dreadful delusion, or worse, danger?

Oh my God, it's Billy Wilcox.

CHAPTER **31**

Wilcox's right foot seemed to come out of nowhere as he kicked me in the stomach. I curled my lips closed tight together and desperately tried to breathe. His intermittent grunting and snickering sounded like a mad animal.

"How did a jerk like you end up with a bunch of sleazy rich attorneys," he snarled between his teeth.

I rolled over with my knees protecting my midsection and tried to clear my head. Even with a limited view from the floor, there was nowhere for me to hide. The throbbing became worse as blood smeared my forehead.

"You dirtbag. I spent three years in a suffocating cell because of you. But I knew my time would come." His glare was intimidating.

The guy's insane.

Smith, or whatever his name is, was watching and gloating with a perverse grin. I had a good look at his face for the first time. His long stringy hair, emaciated cheekbones and bug eyes gave him a ghoulish appearance. He lit a cigarette and blew smoke in my face. *Hell, that kind of harassment I can handle.*

"I planned different scenarios to get you, Baxter, and ran them over in my mind a thousand times," Wilcox growled. "Just be patient, I said to myself." He looked at Finley and said, "It's real sweet how we got him here, isn't it, Slim?" Satisfaction was written all over his face. "Same gullible idiot as he was before."

"Who knew he'd end up in the real estate business?" Finley chuckled. "Fell right into your lap, Billy."

I groaned and tried to get my bearings, without success. If I didn't move or talk, maybe they'd let me be.

Oh God. My cell phone's in the car.

Wilcox held me under the arms and pulled me up on a couch, while Finley grabbed a fistful of my hair. "Lousy snitch," Wilcox said, as he slapped my face twice and jammed his knee into my groin.

I screamed, then clamped my mouth shut in order to endure the agony. The matchless pain was worse than my injury in Iraq. When I opened my eyes, Wilcox's distorted face was staring at me. The thought hit me that he was uglier than I remembered.

What's he going to do to me?

Cold steel pressed against the back of my skull.

Finley has a gun.

Angie and Danny, I'm sorry. God protect them.

Snapshots of my parents, Chuck Larsen, Doc Burkett, and the old Yankee Stadium, all appeared before my eyes. *The room is spinning around.*

"I want him to suffer first," Wilcox ordered. "I had it made in Barnegat Junction with that big-shot mayor until this naive jerk stuck his nose in. Pitman and that bitch Angie are next on my list."

Not if I have anything to do with it.

"Okay Billy, but let's do this first and get the hell out of here, you hear!" Finley demanded. The pistol wobbled in his hand.

Finley was getting antsy, staring out the window every few seconds. If I kicked or knocked the cigarette out of his hand, maybe it would cause a fire and escape would be possible. I inched forward on the couch and bent over, faking I was about to upchuck. He stood close to me, holding the cigarette at his side.

"Oh-oh, the creep's gonna throw up," Finley said as he backed away.

It's my only chance.

"Get back there!" Wilcox slammed my shoulders to the back of the couch. "Buddy, you left all your brains in Iraq." He looked at Finley and laughed, "He was gonna pull a fast one on us. Didn't I tell you he was dumb? He reminds me of another Forrest Gump."

Wilcox yanked my chin up until it hurt. I gagged from the strain on my vocal chords. I felt like a POW must feel facing his captors.

"Get it over with, Slim!"

"Go to hell, both of you." I wasn't going to give them the satisfaction of seeing me beg for mercy.

Finley raised his arm and took aim at my forehead.

The gun barrel looming right before my eyes might as well have been a cannon. My heart stopped beating as the sad face of Angie stared at ...*No, is that my casket?*

Suddenly, the front and rear doors burst open. Shouts erupted from all directions. Chaos broke out all around me.

"FBI. Put your hands up!"

I had shielded my face, but easily recognized the thundering voice. *Agent Walsh.*

Finley redirected the pistol to the front door and at Walsh, who concentrated on his primary villain, Billy Wilcox.

He'll kill Walsh.

I leaped off the couch and threw my body at Finley's ribs just as he fired. The bullet whistled over Wash's head and lodged in the wall above the front door.

Instinctively, Finley hammered his elbow on my bad left ear, while still preoccupied with Walsh.

Fallujah again? But I'm on all fours on a plush beige rug.

Walsh reacted in an instant. His one and only shot ripped into Finley's neck. He grabbed his throat, staggered, and crumbled to the floor, rolling on his back next to me. Blood gushing from Finley's mouth and neck was followed by gurgling sounds, which lasted only seconds. Spasms stopped as fast as they had started.

Wilcox had knocked over a table and dashed to a side window.

"He's getting away," I roared.

Wilcox was halfway out the window when Walsh pulled him back in and slung him to the floor. He pressed his knee in Wilcox's back and handcuffed him.

"I've been waiting for this for a long time," Walsh stammered, breathing heavily. "Now you'll get what you deserve, you low-life. Here's a gift—Miranda rights just for you."

Once Wilcox was escorted outside, two agents walked me into the kitchen. They applied a wet towel to the gash on my head to stop the bleeding. Blood on my shirt and pants belonged to Finley. I felt exhausted, as if I had run five miles.

"Sorry you had to be in the middle again, Mr. Baxter," Walsh said. "We had no clue you would be their target until we saw you pick up Slim Finley today. The FBI has been trailing Wilcox ever since his release from prison. He's already pulled off two scams on foreclosed properties with his new partner, Finley. They gained access to this place, mounted a fake foreclosure sign, and used it as a kind of safe-house."

"You have a way of showing up at the last minute," I mumbled. "But I'm not complaining." I smiled and stood to shake his hand. "It's great to see you again." I hardly recognized him in dirty jeans and a denim work shirt covering an FBI jacket. *The plumber's truck parked on the street was their cover, I bet.*

"Baxter, I'm the one who should thank you."

After the FBI secured the area, Agent Walsh drove me to the emergency entrance of Toms River Hospital. The wound on my head required sixteen stitches before they finally discharged me. On the trip home, he filled me in on the surveillance of Wilcox, the stakeout on the foreclosed house, and today's climactic capture. His pride in the arrest was rightly justified.

"Wilcox will get a lengthy jail sentence this time. Jorgenson will be out long before he's even up for parole."

Nothing further was said until the car stopped in my driveway.

"If you don't mind me mentioning," Walsh said, "I found the closing summation of Jorgenson's attorney totally off-base. Their description of you as inexperienced and unsophisticated was a flawed attempt to confuse the jury in order to divert attention from the flagrant misconduct of Jorgenson. In my opinion, you're a real hero with enviable personal character standards ...respectful of others and the law."

A chill raised the hair on the back of my neck.

On behalf of the FBI, he apologized for my plight, thanked me once again and wished me luck. "Your effort and courage landed two bad apples today. Unfortunately, Barnegat Junction turned into double jeopardy for you."

"No need to apologize," I said. "Who would have ever guessed how it turned out? Besides, I have a wonderful wife and a great new life. Hey, that rhymes."

That's the absolute truth.

CHAPTER 32

It was 9:30 p.m. when Agent Walsh deposited me at my house.

"Angie, I'm here."

"Where have you ...oh my God, what happened?"

What else would a wife say seeing her husband with his head wrapped in a bandage. I purposely had asked the FBI not to call her to avoid creating anxiety. *Bad decision on my part.*

Her female instincts kicked in. Simultaneously, she cared for me and sympathetically led me to the living room couch, while berating my law office, the FBI and me for not calling.

"You could have at least let me know you were alright," she said, objecting to my explanation. "Now tell me what happened."

"First of all, I'm alright now, so don't worry." I hugged her and rubbed the nape of her neck. "You're not going to believe the story."

We sat on the couch while I recounted the details of the call from Finley, a.k.a. Smith, and Billy Wilcox's assault on me and his arrest. I didn't dare admit to my close brush with death.

"What an awful man," she said, her words accompanied by a sigh of disbelief. "They better keep him as well as Jorgenson locked up for a long time."

"It's an incredible story for sure. We can be thankful the FBI stayed on the case. Walsh had great intuition about Wilcox and kept a trail on him after his freedom from prison. But he never anticipated Wilcox would resort to violence."

"You just had to listen to that Finley character's phony tale of woe, didn't you?" Her whisper was loud enough for me to appreciate her anguish.

We sat silently reflecting on what might have been. For the first time since the threat on my life, fear hit me, causing my lips to tremble. I thought of the scoundrels that society had to contend with the likes of--the Parkers, the Jorgensons, the Wilcoxs, the Metcalfs; I did and I'm a survivor.

"Does it hurt? Are you hungry?" She peered at me longingly.

"No on both counts. I am sleepy though from whatever I was given in the hospital." I closed my eyes for a second.

I straightened up in a jiffy. "How's Danny?"

"He was asking for you. I had to rock him to sleep."

Angie was on the verge of tears.

"Everything's okay now, hon. Please don't cry."

"I can't help it," she moaned. "I want to be strong for you, but how much more can I take? I was just thinking of how Danny, I mean, *we* missed you and ..."

"Hold on." I kissed her cheek to lessen her distress. "I have all next week off, so we'll have quality time together. Maybe we can take Danny on the kiddie rides in Seaside Heights." I needed them as much as they needed me, probably more so.

"Leonard Dickson showed up at the hospital and said if there's anything we need, let him know."

We sat holding hands for several moments in silence. Thanks to her, I am finally comfortable being alone, without the misery of loneliness.

"Should I give Doctor Burkett a call about my slip-up today?"

In the past, my first inclination was to see the psychiatrist about a behavior problem or thoughtless act. Burkett had become my mental crutch.

"No way," she exclaimed, wiping away a tear. "From now

on I'm in charge. Your only concern is this family. No extra duty at work, no special projects that I'm not aware of. I love you too much to let your compulsion and noble intentions get you in trouble all the time. That's the way it's going to be!"

She had laid down the gauntlet.

"Yes dear," I said, as if responding to a master sergeant's command.

Her expression changed to a broad beam.

I thought of our happiness together and how much we try to be worthy parents for Danny. I craved to cherish this chapter of his life. Human frailties cruelly cause us to forget the everyday togetherness with young ones. I'm not going to interfere in his adult decisions, either. *This is the definitive helping hand to live for and mark my life.*

Look how beautiful she looks staring at me! This memory will stick with me into our fifties ...when we have grandchildren, I hope.

"Like the song goes, Angie, I love you. I honestly love you."

She started to giggle, but couldn't control a slight quiver in her lips.

Her healing touch on my head was magical. Tender loving care from her heart extended through me to Danny like electric currents.

A picture of sunset on the lonely Lavallette beach flashed before my eyes.

My prayers had been answered.